Thomas Edgar Pemberton

The Life and Writings of T.W. Robertson

Thomas Edgar Pemberton

The Life and Writings of T.W. Robertson

ISBN/EAN: 9783337056179

Printed in Europe, USA, Canada, Australia, Japan

Cover: Foto ©Raphael Reischuk / pixelio.de

More available books at **www.hansebooks.com**

LONDON   RICHARD BENTLEY & SON   1892

THE
LIFE AND WRITINGS

OF

T. W. ROBERTSON

BY

T. EDGAR PEMBERTON

AUTHOR OF
'A MEMOIR OF E. A. SOTHERN,' ETC.

LONDON
RICHARD BENTLEY AND SON
Publishers in Ordinary to Her Majesty the Queen
1893

PREFACE

ALTHOUGH my name appears as the writer of this book, I desire to state that it could not have been produced without the cordial co-operation of my friend, the present T. W. Robertson, who, in collecting facts connected with his father's life, did, in fact, a large share of the work. Having exhausted every possible source of information, he generously left the entire matter in my hands, and this volume would be incomplete without the record of his labours, and the expression of my appreciation of his confidence.

In view of my somewhat voluminous quotations, I think it not unlikely that I may be accused of "book-making." It has been my aim to deal not only with the life, but with the early and forgotten writings of the author of "Caste"; and if I succeed in gaining for these appreciative readers, it is a charge to which I shall willingly plead guilty.

T. EDGAR PEMBERTON.

August 11*th*, 1892.

CONTENTS

LIST OF ILLUSTRATIONS.

THE

LIFE AND WRITINGS OF T. W. ROBERTSON

———◆———

CHAPTER I.

THE LINCOLN CIRCUIT.

THE honourable connection of the Robertson family with the English stage dates back far more than a century ; for the following obituary notice appeared, in the latter part of 1795, in the *European Magazine and London Review :*

"At York, aged 82, Mr. James Robertson, formerly the Shuter or Edwin * at the York theatre, from which he retired in 1779, after forty years' service. He possessed the estimable qualities of private life in a high degree, and was the author of many pieces of merit, and particularly a volume of poems by ' Nobody,' as the title-page announced."

---

* Shuter and Edwin were celebrated comedians in their day, and those who took their parts were inevitably associated with their names.

1

This James Robertson, who originally came from Perth, was the great-grandfather of the subject of this memoir, and was, as this little notice points out, himself an actor and an author. He married a Miss Fowler, an heiress, and became the father of three sons—Thomas, James, and George. Following in their father's footsteps (it seemed as natural for the Robertsons to take to the stage as ducklings do to water), Thomas and James became actors. The former assumed the management of the Lincoln circuit, and the latter achieved the then important position of principal comedian in the York Company. Referring to the elder James, Tate Wilkinson, in his "Memoirs," speaks of visiting York as a "star," and says that he was not very well received in a certain part, because the audience "preferred their favourite Robertson, and deservedly, as he was a comedian of true merit." The younger James Robertson ran away with and married a Miss Robinson, the eldest daughter, by a former husband, of Mrs. Wrench, the wife of Wrench, the celebrated Corinthian Tom in "Tom and Jerry."

At this time James Robertson was a member of Mrs. Wrench's Company, and Miss Robinson, who was only sixteen years of age, was at a boarding-school at York. They were married on a Saturday, and it is on record that he sent an invitation to his mother-in-law, who was very averse to the match, to dine with them on the following Monday, the inducement held out being " roast goose."

The young couple had seven children—Georgina, Henry, William, Fanny, Caroline, Maria, and Eliza.

This second James Robertson (the grandfather of T. W. Robertson) had his inevitable share of domestic worry, and drifted into the anxieties of theatrical management, as is shown by the following extracts from two characteristic letters addressed by him to his friend Mr. Craven, " Opposite Saddler's Wells Toll-bar, Islington ":

" Chesterfield, September 19, 1813.

" DEAR CRAVEN,

" It is a long time since I have written to you, as I conceived writing to Henry was the same ; but I fancy I have been mistaken, for I think he has *sunk* some part of my letters. His have been merely a recapitulation of his poverty and requesting assistance, and every time was to be the ' last.' I have always sent him what he asked for till the last time, when he sent for a loan of two pounds. It was not convenient to send *two*, therefore I sent *one* as a present. By Mr. Miller's letter to me, he seems to accuse me of sending him nothing. What has become of Henry's independence of spirit, which he has ever professed, when he sinks into supineness, neglects his business, and wishes to deprive his younger sisters of having as good an education as himself, by applying for repeated loans, when I expected he was independent of me two years ago?   I wrote him my mind in my last. However, to keep him from going to the devil head-long a little sooner (for it must happen when laziness comes in the way), I will send him two or three pounds upon receiving an answer from you signifying I am right in so doing.   It is the disposition of every child I have (as well as my wife) to have no 'middle' in their disposition.   They are always in the cellar or garret.   I want them to find a dining-room—neither to be too much depressed by common occurrences, nor too elevated at trifling success. *Apropos*, at the back of the song which Henry sent me a year ago (now lying on the table) are the following words : 'Dear Father, your last has most sensibly affected me, and I shall not be entirely easy from apprehension for some time ; but, come American war or European famine—and if credit or money were both spent—whilst a morsel is to be had you and I shall share it.'   When he wrote that, I sincerely believe he meant what he said; still, it is what I call being 'in the garret,' for he forgot, should I have wanted, he had not the means to give it to me, no more than I have always the means to give him what he wants, or *thinks* he wants.

"I am not one that grumbles much about ' times.' If I can make all ends meet at the year's end I think I have done well—which, thank God, I have this year, and cleared a little by management, for the first time these two years. But that has gone to my daughter Georgina. You would perhaps hardly credit that. Well as she says she is doing, she is continually writing to me for money. I sent her last week £20, which makes £70 she has had of me since she has settled, which is only a year and a quarter. This is *one* draw. William,* at Derby— I give Mary half a guinea per week to board him and wash him. I paid that up, and left twelve guineas in hand to keep him till Christmas. Caroline's last half-year's boarding school was £20, and Maria's £13, which, together with my travelling expenses, and £50 worth of different articles in my house at Nottingham, can't have left me a deal *in hand.* However, I don't owe *one guinea.*

" The reason that I have cleared a little by manage-

* William Robertson, the father of T. W. Robertson was articled to Mr. Whitson, a lawyer in Derby, but (being a Robertson) he left the study of the law to become an actor, and ultimately found a home in his uncle Tom's Lincoln Company, of which he afterwards became manager.

ment this year is that I have put my wife to be a check-taker, and the receipts are so much better—visible to every eye, except Mr. M——'s, who, many people do not scruple to say, has had a finger in the pie. Information of *that* nature made me place Mrs. Robertson to take checks, and he could not refuse it, as it was (as I observed) to save his pocket and my own. I assure you, Nottingham races before the last, the houses were robbed as much as £10 per night, and in proportion through the year. I might well be *minus!* However, my eyes are opened, though we have had a grand blow up, and a fight in consequence, wherein I had the *honour* of being *victorious,* if there is any *honour* in such blackguard work. M—— has tried to sicken Mrs. Robertson of check-taking after the first fortnight, by placing obstacles, and finding fault to tire her ; but he forgot woman's disposition. Opposition only adds fuel to the fire, and has made her double her exertions for my interest. . . .

" Your son is a fine boy, a pretty boy, and a sharp boy. I doubt he is a little bit spoiled ; but that is your concern and none of mine, for I never interfere in a parent's system of education. Mrs. Cowley observes in ' The Wonder,' ' When parents have but one child, they generally make him either a madman or a fool.' Now, it is impossible to make your boy a fool, and I think you will take care that he shan't be a madman. . . . We have had Mr. Betty with us, and answered very well. He opens Sheffield Theatre with us the second week in October."

The second letter, which is dated from Nottingham, November 26, 1822, shows, among other things, how the grandfather of T. W. Robertson added the art of scene-painting to his other theatrical occupations. " I anticipated," he says, " your having a cold ride ; but am glad to hear you have not got a cold from it. I continue in the old Gobbo and Launcelot way, and I suppose I shall do till spring. However, I never cough in bed, and sleep like a hound, which is heaven in comparison to my brother Thomas, who writes me word that he has rest neither night nor day for his cough. . . . Your uncle yesterday sent me his new 'Framed Chamber,' to paint on both sides, and a rare lumber-headed thing it is ; also a grove scene. These (as the days are short) will take me till near Christmas. . . . If I return with your father to London, I think I shall give my wife the slip for three weeks or a month, and say I am going to Boston to paint the theatre, as that will be about the time I should have gone ; but I believe my brother means to put it off till next year, when I am

to go over and do it thoroughly. . . . Do you know
(from opposition) we can buy fine oysters at Nottingham at eightpence per score ? . . . My brother sent
me word 'Tom and Jerry' brought them £20 the first
night at Newark, when they would not have had £2
with anything else. It was lucky I persuaded him
to get it up. M—— is going on very badly indeed.
I doubt he must either sell his concern or do worse
in a few months. I hate writing to him, but I must,
as he owes me £26 of my last half-year's income,
due last September. I know I shall receive a croaking
letter ; but I must have my bond—as Shylock says
—indeed, I can't do without it."

James Robertson used the author's pen as well as
the artist's brush, and there is in existence a little
volume, dated 1804, the title-page of which runs as
follows : " A Collection of Comic Songs, Written,
Compil'd, Etch'd, and Engrav'd, by J. Robertson,
and sung by him at the theatres at Nottingham,
Derby, Stamford, Halifax, Chesterfield, and Redford."
It was published at Peterborough, and " printed and
sold by G. Robertson."[*] These comic songs were,
according to the custom of those days, sung by the
low comedian of the company between the plays that
formed the dramatic entertainment of the evening,
and something of their nature may be gathered from

---

[*] His younger brother.

THE BEGGARS.
By J: Robertson.

TUNE.

SKETCH FROM AN OLD SONG BOOK.

THE HUMOURS OF THE TURF

written & sung by J. Robertson.

TUNE

SKETCH FROM AN OLD SONG BOOK.

their titles—such as "The Humours of the Turf," "The Drunken Bucks," "The Medley of Lovers," "The Contented Tar," "What's a Buck without a Tail?" "John Bumpkin upon Drill," "Dr. Last, Sole and Body Mender," "Tommy Strawyard's Dance at the Wake," "The Pig-selling Jew," and so forth.

Here is the opening verse of one entitled "The Beggar's Imitations":

> "There's a difference between a beggar and a queen,
>   And I'll tell you the reason why;
> A queen cannot swagger, nor get drunk as a beggar,
>   Nor be half so happy as I.

"*Speaking.*—To be sure, they are obliged to support a dignified character. Now, I can change my character as often as I please, though, I believe, I am generally a solicitor; for I practise at the court of requests; and as to honesty—why, honesty is—

"Toll de roll—toll de roll." (*Once through for chorus.*)

These choruses are exceedingly varied, and quaintly characteristic of their period. For example, a racing song has for its refrain:

> "Fillaloo, Smalliloo, Ditheroo, whack,
>   If you're young on the turf, I'd have you go back,
> Or the knowing and deep ones will pocket your pelf,
>   That you may go to the devil and shake yourself."

A drinking song winds up with:

> "Tipsy, dizzy, muzzy, fuzzy, groggy drinking port,
> We bucks are always muzzy—Oh, damme, that's your sort!"

—and one in which an impossible stage Frenchman is held up to ridicule has for its chorus :

> " With my dauça, la, la, dança long merry ton,
> Dança long merry ton, dança, la, la."

The etched, and in some instances coloured, illustrations to these songs are exceedingly droll and clever, reminding one of the best work of Rowlandson and Cruikshank. An old play-bill, dated Nottingham, 1806, where this most industrious of men took a benefit, shows how, in addition to acting (among other things he played clown), and singing between the acts, he painted the scenery, and had a hand in writing the pieces. It also has the odd announcement that "admittance behind the scenes" is rated at "half a guinea," and it concludes as follows :

" Mr. Robertson respectfully informs those ladies and gentlemen that did him the favour of subscribing to the PRINT OF NOTTINGHAM MARKET-PLACE that he has coloured several in varnish colours. A specimen may be seen at Messrs. Burbage and Stretton's, and may be had of Mr. Robertson, at his lodgings in Woolpack Lane ; price half a guinea."

William Robertson, as we have seen, left the profession that his versatile father had chosen for him to join his uncle Thomas on the Lincoln circuit. In his dramatic company he met Miss Marinus, a charming young actress, to whom he was married in 1828. They had a very large family, of whom Thomas William Robertson (born at Newark-upon-Trent, Nottinghamshire, on January 9, 1829) was the eldest, and Madge Robertson (Mrs. Kendal, born at Great Grimsby twenty years later) the youngest. It would appear that at the time that William Robertson joined him, his uncle's health had begun to fail, and that, probably, is why he soon became the manager of the company. But the conditions of the circuit at that period, and the difficulties under which those who worked it laboured, will be best described by some extracts taken from the carefully kept diary of Mrs. Thomas Robertson. In these will be found the first mention of "little Thomas," who was subsequently adopted and educated by this kindly and noble-hearted lady.

" *Boston, April,* 1830. — The season is over. What a world of anticipated evils have passed away with seven weeks! Take everything into consideration, and I have been tolerably happy, my lodgings good, my friends pleased to see me—kind in inviting me, and attentive in showing me every possible politeness —the public favourable, and but for the private misfortunes, deaths, and other contingencies which affected the box audience, we should have had an average season ; but I am thankful it is even as it is. The journey to Wisbech has been for the last few years anything but pleasant. Rain ! rain ! rain ! together

with high winds and bad roads, has made it a matter
of unpleasant anticipation ; but, like other anticipated evils, it was more in apprehension than reality.
I arrived safe and into a pleasant lodging. What a
train of thoughts crowded on my memory ! It is
nearly thirty years since I lodged in these same
rooms. As I sat alone I thought of the past. What
a change ! I asked myself this question : ' Could the
same hours return, with the feelings you now have,
would they give you happiness ?' No. I would
not be as I then was, to be restored to the same
state of youth. If I had had the advantages of the
improvement of mind which time and reflection and
study have since given me, what a different creature
I should have been ! but I am most grateful being
as I am, for in comparing my present state with
the past I am happier, having a thousand ways of
pleasing myself innocently, and thus increasing my
real felicity. Anticipated pleasure is a source of
comfort to the heart ; it gives a tranquillity to the
mind. How I anticipated seeing pretty little Thomas,
with his golden curls, on my arrival ! how I reckoned
on his little feet pattering about my large room,
and his fine eyes looking up to me for approval,
assistance, or joy! Alas! he was ill, very ill, all the
time we were laying plans how we were first to see
him, and wondering if he would recognise us. No !

What a change did reality produce in the mind, to see the sweet child in one short week of absence so reduced, his eyes heavy and clouded, fretful at being out of his mother's arms a moment, and hiding his head from our sight. But he is better—thank God! he is better, and I pray humbly that he may be spared, for I truly love him. . . .

"*Sunday, April* 25, 1830.—The first day of anything like spring. Friday was a dreadful night. I have just heard that two vessels were lost in Boston Deep. I hope it is not true. I could not sleep for thinking of our goods. All that we have is on the water in a little barge. Once all was in great danger, for they were driven on shore; but they fortunately got off free from damage."

* * * * * *

In little ways Mr. Robertson seemed often to annoy his wife; for she goes on to say: "The weather beautiful. I have had three very pleasant rides. I took out the child" (this was, of course, our friend Tom); "he is better, but sadly still. I often wonder how I still go on sacrificing my own particular comforts for the sake of others, seeing how frequently the wish to give pleasure has turned out the reverse. This morning, in proposing and arranging how to please both parties—for Mr. Robertson has taken a great fancy to riding, and he and little Tom cannot go out at the same time—I only fatigued myself and gave displeasure to others. I wish I could be more selfish. I really think I should be happier.

"May has commenced—loveliest May! I am happy in being able to say that nothing has occurred to destroy or disturb the ease and tranquillity of my mind. Little Thomas has recovered, and comes every day.

*   *   *   *   *   *

"What a lovely country ! If the weather would suffer me to enjoy it; but alas ! rain, rain, rain! One would be apt to say, 'The heavens do lower upon us for some ill.' Took a drive to Furming Wood, the seat of the Ladies Fitzpatrick. They give their name, and take £2 in tickets. Well, that's worth asking for, and it is too far to expect their personal attendance as they are ' well stricken in years.'

"The theatre has been open four nights, and the business bad. I fear I shall again lose a heavy sum, and if so, I think I shall sing, ' Oundle, farewell !'

"Have had little Thomas to visit me. God bless the child ! I fear he has all his father's horrid temper ! Like him—only please him constantly, and you may pass a day tolerably ; but only thwart his will, and the devil appears in all his majesty! Still, I think with *care* it may be corrected ; but it must be by more judgment, poor boy ! than I fear will fall to his lot to receive. I took a long walk yesterday to a garden. Strange how frequently in this place I have met with people who knew me long since. The gardener said, when I asked him if he would indulge me with a few flowers, that though it was not his custom to gather them, he should feel a pleasure in obliging me, for he had gathered many for me twenty years before. Here was another *old new* acquaintance! He was very civil, and gave me some beautiful flowers, and I gave him an order for the play. The gardener also gave me the chrysalis of a tiger moth, so in August I must watch its awakening.

*   *   *   *   *   *

" *Huntingdon, Tuesday, September* 6, 1831.—What a train of eventful occurrences have followed each other since I opened this book! Now, indeed, I have cause for serious reflection, active exertion, and an humble reliance on that God who alone can deliver and protect me, and on whose mercies and long-suffering and eternal goodness I rely for my future hope and comfort. My suffering husband departed this life at seven o'clock exactly on Wednesday, the last day of August, 1831, without one struggle or even a sigh. May it please the Disposer of all good that my end may be as tranquil, as easy! It seems as if a particular providence was over me, directing all the great events of my life, for my comforts are much more than any free judgment of my own could direct. Mr. and Mrs. Harper's kindness can never be forgotten. Mr. Harper directed all things for the funeral, which but for his judicious arrangements must have cost twice the sum at least had I been anywhere else, and to have appeared in the same style of respectability. All is over ! I have administered to his will, and no one can molest me. I have paid the funeral expenses, and am engaged in arranging the rest. I have written to Mr. Pavy, Dr. Stanton, Mr. Lawrence, Mr. Swanborough, Mr. Freeman, Mr. R. Turner, and Mr. R. Mason of Lincoln, the latter to solicit his advice relative to a circular addressed to the different corporations.

" *Wednesday, September* 7.—Left Huntingdon at eight in the morning, the weather heavenly, and arrived at Norman at half-past ten, and set off again. I observed that the roads were bad, and that a great deal of rain must recently have fallen. Within two miles of Peterborough I was overtaken by a heavy storm of rain (heavy then, I thought), but I still proceeded on to Deeping. Left Deeping about four o'clock, and after going about three miles was over-taken with one of the most violent storms of rain, hail, and thunder I ever was out in. It lasted *in torrents* for nearly half an hour, and then, as if to cheer me, one of the finest rainbows appeared directly before me, showing the way I was going. This may appear a childish idea, but I could not help thinking it an emblem of my state. I have had enough of storms and tempests. God grant that the rainbow of peace and hope may show the horizon of my future days! Arrived safe, though greatly fatigued, at Spalding, the same day, about half-past six. William met me about a mile from the town *very kindly*, and seems solicitous for my welfare. Dear little Tom came to see me. He looks rather thin and pale. The little girl also came in the morning. She grows less like me, and more like Tom.

" *Thursday, September* 8.—Awoke, refreshed, at six. Very comfortable at my old lodgings. Rain, rain, rain! What a day for a coronation! William *dines out* with the gentlemen. *All necessary.* Dear little Tom in very neat mourning for his uncle. I think it a pretty attention, which I am much pleased with. I have spoken to William relative to the sale of my pony. All things considered, it will be *better* not to have even *the appearance* of any unnecessary expense.

*   *   *   *   *   *

" I am better. The great excitement of the week is over, and within a few pounds of last year. Bad enough, 'tis true; but I am grateful even as it is. Discharged Mr. G—— and Mr. Hodgson. I think I have done what I ought in both instances. I have sent £20 to Boston, £20 to Newark, and £5 to Wisbeach, so that there is £45 of debt met. God give me the means, through His mercy, *to pay every one*, and I will *ask no more*.

*   *   *   *   *   *

" *Louth, Sunday, February* 12, 1832.—It is four months since I wrote my thoughts and acts, and what a four months I have passed ! No matter ; it *is* past, and all comment useless. Harass of mind, disappointment, loss, and suffering have closed the year 1831. Never, never to be forgotten are those figures ! 1832 opened on me with brighter hopes. Grantham was comparatively good business. I had a delightful lodging, and my old friends were pleased to see me. I have paid upwards of £100 of my husband's debts, and Hope pointed to the future with cheerfulness. Alas ! Louth is again a place of ruin. What I am to do God only knows. I begin to be ' aweary of the sun.' Constant claims, and no proceeds to meet them. I hope and hope till thought sickens on the delusive shadow. Well, let the worst come, I can safely say that everything that human prudence could do to prevent the ruin was done. I am miserable."

" *Boston, April,* 1832.—Recovered my health and spirits much. Alas ! good as the season was, the expenses exceeded. My own living, too, was more than I expected, and I was obliged to lend money.

" *November* 11, 1832.—What a gap in my journal ! April to November ! But better not record such a summer as I have passed. God deliver me from such another. What suffering, what anguish, and loss ! Whittlesea ! Shall I ever have the idea of entering that place again ? The cholera there raged in all its fury. I was numbered amongst its victims, and, false or true, was certainly dreadfully ill. All Peterborough was in a languishing state. Mr. Walker, the surgeon, behaved most kindly, and never charged me a shilling."*

There is surely something very touching in the picture of this courageous and high-principled woman, driving in her pony-chaise along the bad roads, of which she had reminiscences extending over thirty years, deploring the perpetual " Rain ! rain ! rain !" that she knew must keep the people out of the theatre at the journey's end, and bewailing the Money ! the Money ! that was at all times so slow to come in. Very tenderly expressed, too, are her love for " little

* " Let me correct this error. The year after he sent me in a bill of £5 14s. 6d. !!"

Thomas " and her apprehensions with regard to his temper. Her little economies, her simple pleasures, her love of flowers and books, her trust in Omnipotence, the little episode of the " tiger moth," are all pleasant things to note ; and no one will deny that her determination to struggle on with a fast-dwindling business, in order that she might pay off the liabilities of her dead husband, was absolutely heroic.

The Louth disaster receives confirmation from Macready, who on November 29, 1834, joined the Robertson Company as a star, and who in his journal writes :

" When I was ready to go on the stage " (he was to open in ' Virginius '), " Mr. Robertson appeared with a face full of dismay ; he began to apologize, and I guessed the remainder. ' Bad house ?' ' Bad, sir ! there's no one !' ' What ! nobody at all ?' ' Not a soul, sir, except the Warden's party in the boxes.' ' What the devil ! not one person in the pit or gallery ?' ' Oh yes ; there are one or two.' ' Are there five ?' ' Oh yes ; five.' ' Then go on ; we have no right to give ourselves airs if the people do not choose to come and see us ; go on at once !' Mr. Robertson was astonished at what he thought my philosophy, being accustomed, as he said, to be ' blown up ' by his *stars* when the houses were bad."

In connection with Louth, Mr. John Coleman tells

a story* of another famous actor, Samuel Phelps, which, as it shows what had to be endured by those engaged to perform on the old Lincoln circuit, may be appropriately reproduced here. Mr. Coleman, by the way, makes Phelps tell his own story of his memorable walk from Gainsborough to the unappreciative town, in the following words :

" As soon as the clock struck five in the morning I leaped out of bed. It was as dark as pitch, but I slipped into my clothes, and made a start. It had been snowing over-night, and, unfortunately, the snow had given place to a black frost.

" Getting over the ground as well as I could, I reached the half-way house before eleven, had a mouth full of bread-and-cheese, a glass of mulled ale, and a pipe. Then off I went again. What with the frost and the sharp wind, I thought the weather was almost as bad as it could be. I was mistaken, however, for about two a dense fog sprang up—so dense and so dark that I could not see a hand's turn before me.

" Although we were to open that night with 'Virginius' and 'The Young Widow,' could I have

* " Players and Playwrights I have known," by John Coleman. This, and subsequent anecdotes, will convey to the reader of to-day some idea of the difficulties under which the actors of the past laboured.

been sure of making my way back in safety to the half-way house, I most certainly would have chanced it, whether we opened or shut ; but hours before I had passed the junction of the four roads, so that if actually I succeeded in retracing my steps as far back, I could not be sure of taking the right turning. To keep straight on was the wisest and safest thing to do, so I plodded mile after mile through the fog and the darkness, without hearing a single sound of life, and without encountering a solitary sign of light, or human habitation, or landmark of any description whatever. That I had lost my way was now quite certain, and every step I took might lead me into one of the bogs or quagmires of the terrible fen country, and then, remembering Burbage's significant epitaph in the Abbey, I arrived at the conclusion that no epitaph would ever be written over my nameless grave.

" The weather now began to change. The fog, without lifting or losing its density, became damp and drizzling, and the frost beneath my feet began to melt into sludge of the consistency of pudding. It was as much as I could do to drag my feet through it.

" Presently I was drenched to the skin, and stricken as with an ague. My teeth began to chatter, my limbs to tremble beneath me. At last I could scarce keep my feet. Yet either to stand still or to give up the struggle meant death—death imminent and inevitable.

" The thought of the poor wife I had left behind nerved my heart, and gave me strength and courage to struggle on for another half-hour, which seemed half a century.

" At last, having done all that man could do, I gave it up as a bad job. A few steps more and it would all be over, and then, ' Exit Samuel Phelps !'

" ' God help her, and take care of her, anyhow !' I gasped, as I fell forward, prone and helpless, to the ground.

" Even as I did so, at that very moment, loud and clear, and high above my head in the immediate vicinity, a silvery peal of bells rang out the chimes. A quarter, half-hour, three-quarters, four—then silence.

" Would it never strike ?

" At last ! One, two, three, four, five, six—seven !

" It was seven o'clock, and I had fallen at the very gate of Louth churchyard !

" The next instant I was on my feet. I knew my way well enough now. A few moments more and I was in the playhouse. The boys stripped my wet things off me, rubbed me from head to foot, and made me swallow two or three glasses of boiling-hot whisky-and-water. Old Abbott himself brought me, not one, but two mutton-chops, broiled to a turn, and a dish of tea; and with the aid of this strange, incongruous, but potent mixture, at eight o'clock I was on the stage ladling out Appius Claudius as became a noble Roman. Nay, more; after the play I kicked up my heels and danced about like a parched pea, in the humours of Mandeville in 'The Young Widow,' to the delight of a crowded audience, who yelled at my eccentric vagaries. I don't think that I ever played to a better audience in my life."

Here is another interesting, albeit sad, glimpse of the Lincoln circuit from the pen of Mr. Coleman, who, in alluding to Mrs. Cuthbert (Phœbe Carey), the disowned sister of Edmund Kean, says:

"During a short engagement at Stamford, my brother came to me and said: 'There is a show in the fair, and those poor Cuthberts are acting there.' It was a terrible winter, and the snow lay deep upon the ground. It appeared simply awful to contemplate the idea of these unfortunates being exposed to the inclemency of the weather at their time of life. Without hesitation, I went down to the fair, found and interviewed them. Poor souls! they had drifted down to the lowest ebb."

Chiefly through the influence of Mr. Coleman, Edmund Kean's unlucky sister and her poor old husband became inmates of the Dramatic College, where, he says, " they made a good end on't."

From the same book we may perhaps be permitted to quote Mr. John Ryder, who says : " I was engaged for walking gentlemen and ' utility ' at a guinea a week, commencing at Hull" (Hull, by the way, is perhaps hardly in the Lincoln circuit, but it is certainly not far off it), "in January, 1838. Having seen all the great people in town, I thought I knew all about it, and I flattered myself that I was going to astonish the wretched country actors; but, by Jove ! they astonished me. In the first place, there was the magnificent theatre in Humber Street, with its two tiers of boxes, a grand entrance, and a lobby round which you might drive a carriage and pair, two galleries, a pit like Her Majesty's, two green-rooms, lots of dressing-rooms, and a company of forty or fifty first-rate people—in fact, a much better company than you can find in any West-End theatre just now.

" On the night of my arrival the play was ' Macbeth.' Creswick was Macbeth ; James Chute, Macduff ; Compton, the First Witch ; Downe, Duncan ; and Mrs. Morton Brookes, Lady Macbeth. The rest of the company was equally strong. The piece was capitally mounted, and the music admirable. When I saw this specimen of country acting, I felt that there was not much chance of my setting the Humber on fire.

" Next night I opened as Frederick in ' The Wonder,' and I immediately got dismissed, which I suppose served me right for having the conceit to think that such a green gosling as myself could pass muster amongst such a crowd. Downe was (except William Farren and Murray) about the best old man on the stage, but the three C's (Creswick, Compton and Chute) were the ' great guns ' of the concern. The first, full of life and go and enthusiasm, was our leading man ; the second was our low comedian ; the third, a most versatile and accomplished actor, and a very handsome man to boot, was our light comedian."

Little Thomas—or, as we shall from this point call him, Robertson—was no doubt much indebted for his literary and artistic inclinations to the fostering care of his great-aunt, who wrote charming poetry, was an excellent actress, and in every way a lady of culture and refinement. That he was not long allowed to remain idle the following play-bill will show :

THEATRE, WISBECH.

FOR THE BENEFIT OF

MR. SHIELD AND MRS. DANBY.

On FRIDAY EVENING, June 13, 1834,

Will be performed the Musical Drama (taken from the celebrated novel of the same name) called

ROB ROY ;

OR, AULD LANG SYNE.

Rob Roy Macgregor Campbell	MR. FLORINGTON.
Sir Frederick Vernon	MR. HOWELL.
Rashleigh Osbaldiston	MR. CHILDE.
Francis Osbaldiston	MR. HOUGHTON.
Captain Thornton	MR. BATTIE.
MacStuart	MR. WILSON.
Major Galbraith	MR. W. ROBERTSON.
Hamish (*Rob Roy's Son*)	MASTER T. ROBERTSON.
Dougal	MR. SHIELD.
Andrew	MR. SNAPE.
Baillie Nicol Jarvie	MR. COMPTON.
Helen Macgregor	MRS. W. ROBERTSON.
Mattie	MISS WEBB.
Martha	MISS SPRAY.
Jean M'Alpine	MRS. DANBY.
Diana Vernon	MRS. HOWELL.

A Variety of Songs, Duets, etc., incidental to the Piece.

A COMIC SONG BY MR. COMPTON.
A FAVOURITE SONG BY MR. HOUGHTON.

To conclude with the favourite Farce of

THE BEEHIVE ;

OR, INDUSTRY MUST PROSPER.

Mingle	MR. COMPTON.
Captain Merton	MR. CHILDE.
Rattan	MR. SHIELD.
Joey	MR. HOWELL.
Mrs. Mingle	MRS. DANBY.
Cicely	MISS WEBB.
Emily (*with a Song*)	MRS. HOWELL.

Doors opened at six, to begin at seven.   Boxes, 3s. 6d. ;
Pit, 2s. ; Gallery, 1s.

Tickets to be had of Mr. Shield, at Mr. Copeman's, near the Baths ; of Mrs. Danby, at Mr. Ellis's, Market Place ; at the Printing Office, and the usual places.

On MONDAY, the 16th, Performances for the Benefit of Mr. and Mrs. HOWELL.

On TUESDAY, the 17th, for the Benefit of Messrs. COMPTON and HOUGHTON, the Comedy of "The Poor Gentleman," with "The Illustrious Stranger," by desire of the Wisbech Independent Lodge of Odd Fellows.

Thus at the early age of five years Robertson made his first appearance on the stage, and until he was sent to school he was the young Roscius of the Lincoln circuit.   In connection with this first appearance it is interesting to note that thirty-five years later Compton, who was the Baillie Nicol Jarvie of the occasion, played at the Haymarket the eccentric comedy part of Captain Mountraffe, in

" Home," the now well-known comedy, in three acts, by this same " Master T. Robertson."

Of the days when she and her brother Tom used to play children's parts on the circuit, Miss Fanny Robertson says : " The towns visited were Lincoln, Boston, Grantham, Newark, Stamford, Wisbech, Peterborough, Whittlesea, Huntingdon, and others. We stayed for three or four weeks in each town, returning for any special occasion, such as a fair or a race-week. In the summer the journeys were very pleasant, and we youngsters greatly enjoyed them. At many a wayside inn, where we used to stay to refresh on ham and eggs, and bread and cheese (delicious fare when one is really hungry), our coming used to be eagerly anticipated, and I have often heard a landlord say : ' I thought you would be here soon ; I have been expecting you. We were always welcomed with a smile, and we children were allowed to gather flowers and fruit. In the winter it was not so agreeable. We had to rise in the dark, and very often had to get out of our convey-ance to walk up the hills in the snow. I remember once going up a hill close by Grantham ; we were ' stuck fast,' and all had to alight, the gentlemen of the company literally ' putting their shoulders to the wheel.' "

Of Robertson's juvenile efforts as an actor, his

sister says: " My brother Tom as a little boy played Cora's child in ' Pizarro,' the Count's child in ' The Stranger,' and other parts of a similar nature, until, when he was about seven years old, he was sent to school by his great-aunt, Mrs. T. Robertson.   My first remembrance of him on the stage was when he played the young King Charles in ' Faint Heart never won Fair Lady,' on the occasion of his aunt's benefit at Boston.   He was then home for his holidays. Young as he was, he showed his ready wit and aptitude for the stage; for being unable to open a door where his exit should have been made, he turned to Ruy Gomez, and said with the utmost coolness, ' The door is locked; follow me to the corridor !' and, amid the applause and laughter of the audience, strolled off on the opposite side.   He was then between eleven and twelve years of age.

" He also played François in ' Richelieu ' with Macready.   This was at Stamford, on the occasion of one of the celebrated tragedian's visits to my father's circuit.   He was then about fourteen, and in the act where Richelieu says, ' Never say fail again !' he quite upset the great actor's equilibrium.   Macready's business was to recall François just as he was quitting the stage ; but not knowing this, Tom remained on the same spot.   On seeing this, Macready, who was always irritable at rehearsal, turned angrily upon him, and said, 'Well, sir, what are you doing here?' Tom looked rather foolish, but instantly replied, 'Waiting for you to speak.' 'I told you to go,' shouted Macready. 'Turn and leave the stage at once, sir! If *I* do not recall you in time it will be *my* fault!' Macready rehearsed this exit of Tom's several times, each time, in order to catch him off his guard or to see that he understood him, doing it differently. At one moment he would recall him, at others he would let him get quite off the stage; and the result was that at night Tom, bewildered and annoyed at these tediously repeated rehearsals, left the stage so rapidly on being told to 'go,' that before Macready could recall him he was down the stairs and in his dressing-room, and the famous words, 'Never say fail again!' had to be spoken to empty space. Macready was very angry with Tom, and after the act sent for him to his dressing-room, but François refused to be lectured by Richelieu, and declined to go."

But these were "holiday tasks," and it is to Robertson's school-days that we must now refer.

He was about seven years of age when he was sent to the Spalding Academy, of which Mr. Henry Young was the head-master, and during the four or five years that he remained there he was exceedingly popular, both with the masters and his schoolfellows.

Often some quaint and *apropos* quotation from a part
that he had played in his childhood would " set the
schoolroom in a roar." It was, indeed, owing to his
early connection with the stage that the boys of the
Spalding Academy accustomed themselves to give
amateur performances in the old Spalding theatre.

" He was," writes one of his old schoolfellows,
" one of the wits of the school, and if he were at the
blackboard ('slates' they were then called) of one
division, and another boy named Adderley Howard
at the other, the school, to the consternation of the
good old dominie, was sure to be convulsed with
laughter. We used to have public 'speakings' in the
old theatre in Broad Street, and at these Robertson
was, of course, a star. I recollect that at one of them
he represented a tailor in a farce, while I was cast for
the part of the Prince of Wales in a scene from
' Richard III.' A worthy gentleman (I think he was
a Wesleyan minister) asked Robertson, after the performance was over, if he would not rather have been
' the little boy who sat in the great chair ?' This was,
by the way, the Worshipful Master's chair from the
Freemasons' Lodge. 'No,' promptly responded
Robertson ; 'I'd rather be a real tailor than such a
tailor of a prince as that.' A little later on we had an
usher of poor abilities, who was very unpopular in the
school. On November 5 Robertson managed, while

Mr. Young was out of the room, to light a cracker under this gentleman's chair, the consequence being that the unfortunate and timid teacher was nearly driven out of his wits. Terrible things were threatened, but Robertson's popularity was so great that, although every boy in the school knew who had done the deed, no one would betray him."

" I saw him," says the writer of this letter, "a very short time prior to his death, when he was passing through Spalding, and called upon me. We had a long chat together ; but he seemed depressed in spirits, and in his appearance was so altered that at first I did not recognise him."

From the Spalding Academy Robertson was sent to a school at Whittlesea, and there he remained until business in the Lincoln circuit became so bad that economy compelled, rather than suggested, his return to the stage.

He was then about fifteen years of age ; and as other little Robertsons had in the meantime grown up to play mere children's parts (it used to be said in those days that the much-tried William Robertson and the good Margherita Elisabetta, *née* Marinus, his wife, always had a juvenile stock company available for any emergency ready to hand), Robertson and his elder sister, whose reminiscences have already been of service to us, figured in the play-bills under the imposing names of " Mr. Williams" and " Miss Frances."

Of this period Miss Fanny Robertson writes : " At Malton, Burlington Quay, Darlington, Stockton,* and the other towns that I have mentioned, my brother played every description of part. At Malton lived the father of Charles Dickens, with his son Alfred, and they came constantly to the theatre. From Alfred Dickens my brother received much praise for his performance of John Peerybingle in a stage version of ' The Cricket on the Hearth,' and he came several times to see the piece, which was chiefly played by the members of our family. My brother was especially clever in eccentric comedy, and in what are technically known on the English stage as ' French' parts. The well-known Monsieur Jacques was a very favourite part of his. He was also very popular as Dr. Pangloss, Jeremy Diddler, Young Marlow, Charles Surface, and a host of other parts too numerous to mention. Be-tween the pieces he and I, as Charity Boy and Girl, used to sing a comic duet, called ' One Day while Working at the Plough,' finishing with a dance. I remember on one occasion, at Burlington Quay, during the race-week, my brother wrote a song in which it was advertised he would tell the winner of the next

* Efforts had evidently been made to extend the moribund Lincoln circuit.

day's race. I need scarcely say that this was 'The Horse that came in First.'"

At this time Robertson wrote a great number of the then popular low comedian's *entr'acte* songs, and even in this poor form of dramatic art (we have in this connection already quoted his grandfather) he attempted reforms.

" Tom," says Miss Fanny Robertson, " was always clever with his pen, and as soon as he could write, he was at work at plays for us to act as children. Later on he wrote for the company. As soon as the book was published (he was then seventeen years of age) he dramatized Charles Dickens's story, ' The Battle of Life,' and two years later he produced a stage version of ' The Haunted Man.' I remember our waiting very anxiously to get the earliest possible copies of these Christmas books, and how we at once went with them to the theatre, I acting as amanuensis, and he walking about with the story in his hand and dictating to me. When the manuscript was finished it was taken home to be altered or approved by our father. Both plays were produced at Boston."

For a considerable time Robertson continued to write, act, manage, prompt, paint, and perform every conceivable duty, in the theatres on the Lincoln circuit, and it can be gathered that, as far as he was concerned, his famous remark of being nursed on

" rose-pink and cradled in properties " had abundant foundation. But from a business point of view things were going from bad to worse ; and restless and ambitious, and wishing to see something of the world, he determined to make a new departure on his own account. During all these hard-working days he had not for one moment relaxed his studies. From his father he received abundant assistance, and he had especially perfected himself in the French language, which from that time forth he spoke as if to the manner born. His desire to read and write and add to his education was insatiable, and it was this that induced him, in 1848, to apply for the position of English-speaking usher in a school at Utrecht, in Holland. His application was successful, but his experiences were bitterly disappointing. Arriving, after great difficulties, at Utrecht, he found himself in a small academy of limited means and a still more limited number of pupils, who immediately took as strong a liking for him as they had hatred for a red-haired native-born usher, who was a harsh, cruel, and in every respect objectionable man. The consequence of this was that relations between the two masters became hopelessly uncomfortable, and, added to this, the salary was paltry and the food bad, being served up in a way which Robertson subsequently described as " sowing the first seeds of biliousness " in his delicate constitution. Meat, vegetables, and pudding were piled on one plate, with a hunch of horrible-looking black bread on the top, " gazing down with a scowl and an ' eat-me-if-you-dare ' look on its sable surface." Thoroughly sickened of this wretched existence, he pined for home ; but his slender means had been absorbed in his outfit and outward journey, and without money or friends he could not reach it. In his perplexity he called on the British Consul, and through his kindly aid was enabled, after a very brief absence, to rejoin his family at his own birthplace—Newark.

In later years Robertson would keep his children amused for hours with stories of his treatment of the boys when he was a schoolmaster, and of how he used to encourage them to plague the " native " usher, who subsequently had the unenviable honour of figuring as the cleverly drawn but unamiable character of Krux in the comedy called " School."

This attempt at a new life having failed, Robertson resignedly settled down to his old work, and played everything, from Hamlet down to the low comedy parts in such farces as " Did you ever send your wife to Camberwell ?" but most particularly distinguishing himself in broken English and French parts.

Hard and conscientious work, however, could do nothing for the numbered days of the Lincoln circuit.

Every season became worse. Lincoln, Boston, Grantham, Peterborough, Newark, Spalding, Wisbech, and the other at-one-time faithful towns, no longer supported the time-honoured and industrious little company. Railways had sprung up and destroyed the comparative isolation of the small from the larger towns, and local interests became absorbed in the now accessible wonders to be seen in the great world outside the little circle to which they had been accustomed. The end soon came, and the pecuniary obligations which had been contracted in the fond hope of a turn in the tide of affairs led to such embarrassments that William Robertson was compelled to disband his company, and the familiar and historical Lincoln circuit became a thing of the past.

It was a sad breaking-up. The anxieties and troubles were not so hard to bear as the severance of family ties—for the Robertsons had been a noble example of self-sacrifice to each other's interests ; but it had to be, and, amongst the rest, " Tom " was for the first time in his life face to face with the world.

It is pleasant to note that William Robertson, who, in spite of his anxious and troubled early life, achieved a ripe old age, lived to see his eldest son the most cultured and prosperous dramatist of his day, and his youngest daughter one of the most brilliant actresses that have graced the English stage. The second James Robertson died in 1828, and was buried in the same grave as his partner M——, with whom he once fought! The record of this is to be found at St. Mary's Church, "opposite Barrow's Yard," Nottingham. Mrs. Thomas Robertson, from whose diary quotations have been freely taken, died December 19, 1855, aged eighty-seven. William Robertson died in 1872; in four years his devoted wife followed him; and they lie together in Highgate Cemetery.

Left to his own resources, "Tom" Robertson—then about twenty years of age—naturally sought the great world of London, and, to use his own words, "ceased to live and began to exist."

CHAPTER II.

It is painful to write of Robertson's early days in London. Able and anxious to work with his pen, he was wholly unable to meet with encouragement or remunerative employment, and, in order "to keep body and soul together," the poor fellow was compelled to hover about the theatres in order to secure such paltry acting engagements as chance placed in his way. These sometimes took him into the country, sometimes kept him in London; but they were always of the briefest duration, and were generally under the management of a gentleman who "had been occasionally known to pay half-salaries, but full ones never." That Robertson was anything but a bad actor will soon be shown; but he was at this time little more than a boy, and the wonder is that he obtained a sufficient number of these precarious engagements to enable him to live.

But never for one moment losing dignity or self-possession, he contrived to rub on ; and that, even in those sad struggling days, his heart was in his pen is proved by the fact that in his leisure hours he contrived to write an original two-act comic drama, entitled " A Night's Adventure; or, Highways and Byeways." This was in due course submitted to Mr. William Farren, the then manager of the Olympic Theatre, and, to the unbounded delight of Robertson, accepted. It is easy to picture the joy of the eager and persevering young dramatist. An original play from his pen was about to be produced (by a first-class company) at a West-End theatre ! Fame and Fortune henceforth lay at his feet. One can fancy the enthusiastic messages that were despatched to his hard-working and anxious father, and his old friends of the Lincoln circuit, and how they would congratulate " Tom " on the successful result of his hard work, and (for you always have to add the saving clause) his " slice of luck." Poor Tom ! It was a slice so unsatisfactory that it served neither to whet nor stay the appetite.

" A Night's Adventure " was produced at the Olympic on August 25, 1851 ; and in the cast were Mr. H. Farren, Mr. Diddear, Mr. G. Cooke, Mr. Kinloch, Mr. Norton, Mr. Clifton, Mr. Shelders, Mrs. Adams, and Miss Louisa Howard. It was preceded by " Hearts are Trumps," with Mr. William

Farren, Mr. Compton, and Mrs. Stirling in the leading characters; and the evening's performance termi-
nated with the representation of Robert Soutar's farce
entitled " The Fast Coach."

As " A Night's Adventure " was the first play of
importance produced under the name of T. W.
Robertson, a brief account of its plot and purpose
may be excused.

The story turned on one of those supposititious
intrigues carried on (on the stage) for the restoration
of the Pretender, Charles Edward Stuart, in the
reign of George II. Claude Du Val, " the ladies'
highwayman," in the exercise of his vocation stops
on a lonely road the carriage of Lord Chief Justice
Pleadon, and in the politest manner possible robs his
lordship and his daughter Clorinda—taking from
them not only rings, watches, money, and other
" portable properties," but a box of important
Government documents. By some means the adven-
turous Claude obtains possession of a letter of
introduction (with which the Comte de Chambord, a
secret agent of the Pretender, had been entrusted) to
a certain Justice Jolterhead, who plays a double game
of politics by being openly a magistrate in the
commission of the peace under the Hanoverian King,
and secretly a partisan of the Stuart dynasty. By
means of this letter the highwayman introduces

himself and two of his gang as the Comte de Chambord and his servants into the house of the muddle-pated double-faced justice, where he meets with two genuine agents of the Pretender—the one a Scotch major, and the other an Irish captain—who entrust to the pseudo-Count a large sum of money for the support of the cause, and a valuable miniature of Charles Edward set in emeralds. The justice himself places £1,000 in the " Count's " hands as the bribe for an earldom which he hopes to get when the Jacobite King comes into "his own"; and Dolly, the cherry-cheeked and comely daughter of the justice, falling desperately in love with the supposed gallant foreigner, unhesitatingly agrees to run away with him, and give him her hand, heart, and fortune. In the midst of the highwayman's successes the Lord Chief Justice and his daughter arrive at Justice Jolterhead's. It is the morning after the robbery, but, notwithstanding the manifest suspicions of his victims, Claude determines to brazen things out, and does so with such convincing assurance that Clorinda entrusts him with the care of a valuable diamond necklace intended for a friend in Paris. Meanwhile a large party of the Stuart adherents arrive, and one among them, who is personally acquainted with the real Comte de Chambord, denounces Claude as an impostor. The Chief Justice is also recognised, and

the Jacobites are about to secure their own safety by
running both through the body, when Claude blows
his whistle, his armed followers rush in, and the scale
is turned in favour of the Hanoverians. Between the
two parties a compromise is now effected. As a
reward for the service just rendered him, the Chief
Justice willingly pardons Claude. On laying down
their arms the conspirators are permitted to escape ;
Dolly has her jewels and settlements restored to her ;
and Claude, keeping for himself the £1,000, the
miniature of the Pretender, and the papers of the
Comte de Chambord, returns to the Chief Justice
and his daughter the things of which he robbed
them.

When " A Night's Adventure " was produced at
the Olympic, the counter-attractions at the other
leading London theatres were : Italian opera at Her
Majesty's and Covent Garden ; an American and
French equestrian troupe at the historic Drury Lane ;
" Good for Nothing," " Queen of a Day," and other
light pieces at the Haymarket, then under the
management of Benjamin Webster ; "The Gamester "
and the inevitable supplementary farce at the
Princess's. At the Lyceum Madame Vestris offered
her patrons a bill of fare that included " Court
Beauties," " King Charming," and " Box and Cox."
At the St. James's the clever Bateman children were

to be seen in " Richard III." and " The Young Couple "; Phelps in " Hamlet " was the attraction at Sadler's Wells; " Punch's Playhouse " (now the Strand) offered, under the direction of Mr. W. R. Copeland, a varied programme which wound up with a burlesque on the well-worn theme of " Lady Godiva "; and at the Adelphi the 319th night of " The Green Bushes " was proudly announced, from which it will be seen that " long runs " were not unknown in 1851.

" A Night's Adventure " was advertised as " a great success " by the management ; but it was condemned by the critics, and had a brief and inglorious run.

Poor Robertson's disappointment cut him to the heart, and when Farren, chagrined by the loss and vexation consequent upon failure, angrily declared that it was " a d——d bad play," he unwisely sealed his fate at the Olympic by hotly retorting (Robertson was ever ready with a retort) that it was " not so bad as the acting."

So far from being a bad play, " A Night's Adventure " was, according to the taste of the times in which it was produced, an exceedingly good one— full of action and picturesque situation, but, like many other well-conceived and well-written plays, it lacked what Robertson's gifted sister, Mrs. Kendal, has not very long ago summed up as " the indefinable *something* "—and failed to attract audiences.

What this meant to Robertson, and how he suffered under the disaster, no tongue can tell. He was but twenty-two years of age, and after two years of friendless struggle in London he had managed by dint of incessant hard work and indomitable perseverance to float in the longed-for harbour of the unacted dramatist. A play of his had been accepted at a recognised West-End theatre. Fancy, if it had succeeded, what this would have meant for him! For his quickly conceived and rapidly written plays there would have been a ready market, and in a modest way reputation and a regular income would have been his ; but " A Night's Adventure" was damned, and with the terrible hall-mark of " failure " stamped boldly upon him, its luckless author had to fall back into the unknown crowd and, smarting under defeat, to earn his living as best he might among those who do duty in the rank and file of stageland.

That " A Night's Adventure," its failure notwithstanding, was a play of considerable merit is proved by the fact that it was (albeit the work of an unknown dramatist) accepted and produced by the astute William Farren ; but it was condemned by the press and public, and, as a matter of consequence, did its struggling author far more harm than good.

He had once more to resort to his acting, and having been lucky enough to obtain an engagement under the management of Mr. Phelps at Sadler's Wells, he appeared as Cleomenes in " Winter's Tale," Ross in " Macbeth," Osric in " Hamlet," De Beringhen in " Richelieu," Gaspard in " The Lady of Lyons," Lord Glossmore in " Money," and other characters of a kindred type.

At a summer season at this theatre, under the temporary management of Mr. Davenport, he made a notable hit as Captain Crosstree in Douglas Jerrold's well-known play, the Black-eyed Susan of the cast being Miss Fanny Vining.

It was just at this time that Henry Irving, then a mere boy, had at Sadler's Wells his first taste of the theatre. Phelps played Hamlet, and Irving— destined to be the finest Hamlet of the day—has often told the friends of his later life of the profound impression that the play and the acting made upon his mind. There is hardly any doubt that the Osric of that memorable evening was Robertson.

A little later on he became a member of the company at the Theatre Royal, Richmond, then under the management of Messrs. S. and M. Dias, and here he played all sorts of parts in the popular dramas and farces of those days, repeating, among other things, his successful impersonation of Captain Crosstree. It is curious to note that this time the Susan was an actress bearing the unusual name of Feist — the maiden name of Robertson's second wife.

It was during this epoch that Robertson first became acquainted with H. J. Byron, and the close friendship commenced which lasted in a brotherly fashion all their lives. They acted together in provincial stock companies, and many were the schemes that they formed for giving their talents free play, and escaping the irksome drudgery of their existences.

Once, during a long period when no engagements of any sort were to be obtained, they were in London together, and decided that the time to assert themselves had arrived. In the country they had carefully written an " entertainment," which had in due course been produced, and although their acting in it had so far done little towards making their fortunes, they had sufficient faith in its drawing powers and in themselves to resolve to try its effect on London audiences. Accordingly, a room in the Gallery of Illustration was engaged, and no effort was spared to make the venture a success. The entertainment was so ingeniously constructed that, while Byron was facing the auditorium in its first part, Robertson acted as money-taker ; and when Robertson made his appearance on the miniature stage, and prior to their

appearance in a duologue, which was the last item on
the programme, Byron took his turn in the pay-box,
a proceeding which he subsequently declared to have
been " wholly unnecessary."

It was not without the assistance of a kind friend,
who paid the first week's rent in advance, and helped
with the printing, advertisements, and other inevitable
preliminary expenses, that the enterprise was floated,
and when the fateful opening night arrived the poor
" entertainers" had not a farthing between them.
Robertson was sanguine, and hoped that the experiment might result in a permanent success, but Byron
was less hopeful, and listened to his friend's predictions with a sickly smile and a sinking heart.

The performance was advertised to commence at
eight, but the clock stood at a good ten minutes past
that hour before anyone troubled the anxious Robertson in his little box-office. At last a gentleman
tendered a sovereign, and asked if " there were any
front seats left." " Oh yes," replied Robertson
pleasantly, " both right and left. I will bring you
your change " (poor fellow ! he had none of his own)
" in a minute, sir." The gentleman entered the
empty room. Robertson rushed out to get change,
returned eighteen shillings to his patron, and expended fourpence out of the remaining two shillings
on stout for the dejected Byron, who, in an agony of

nervousness, was peeping through the curtain.   In his own hands Robertson bore to his partner the pewter containing the invigorating draught.

" Have the critics arrived ?" asked Byron in an anxious voice.

" No," replied Robertson ; " but, then, they are always late."

" Are they ?" asked Byron dubiously.

" Of course they are," was the answer. " Come, you had better commence and get it over."

" Tom," said Byron, with the spirit of prophecy upon him, " I think this is going to be a failure."

To this Robertson deigned no reply, and returned to his pay-box.

The pianist (of course there was a pianist) rattled through an overture; the curtain rose; and Byron, attired in the evening-dress that Robertson was to wear later on, commenced " the entertainment." The first part of the programme was entitled " The Origin of Man "; and looking fixedly at the solitary occupant of " the house," the unfortunate entertainer commenced as follows :

" In the beginning there was only one man——"

" Yes," interrupted " the house" ; " and I'm the d——d fool ;" and hurrying out to Robertson, this inconsiderate gentleman demanded his money back, and said he had come to see " The Chinese."

Depressed, but not disconcerted, Robertson assured the malcontent that Byron was a Chinaman; but the money had to be returned. Here a little difficulty occurred. "The house" had received its change for its sovereign; fourpence out of its two shillings had been expended on Byron's stout; and this the "pay-box" was in no position to refund. Robertson, however, dejected though he must have been, was equal to the emergency; and returning one shilling and eightpence, said calmly that "on such occasions they only charged fourpence."

It appears that, in another room in the Gallery of Illustration, some ingenious Chinese jugglers were giving a performance, and that a stray lamb had wandered into the wrong fold. It is easy to smile at all this now, but the experience at the time must have been truly painful to the two clever but impecunious men, who throughout their lives remained stanch friends.

Byron was the first to make a substantial success, and, as will presently be seen, he was more than ready to give his old comrade and partner a sorely needed helping hand. And so it came about that the friends, who together had gone through bitter disappointment and privation, lived to see each other popular and prosperous.

Up to the year 1854 there is no further record of

the production of an original play from Robertson's pen, although he was continually writing and translating; and the following receipt tells its own sad little tale :

"City Theatre.

"I hereby assign all rights of my drama, entitled 'Castles in the Air,' to Messrs. Johnson and Nelson Lee, making it their sole property for town or country, on consideration of receiving the sum of £3.

"Signed, Thomas W. Robertson."

"March 29, 1854."

The City Theatre, it should be noted, was then a prosperous little house in Bishopsgate ; the managers were well-respected and clever men ; and no doubt poor Robertson was very grateful to them when he received his three pounds for his three-act play. "Castles in the Air" was produced on April 29, 1854, and was quickly forgotten. That its author set some store by it is proved by the fact that, in more prosperous times, he repurchased the play, the receipt being found with the manuscript after his death.

Among the adaptations made by Robertson during his years of toil and struggle were "Noémie," a drama in two acts, from the French of MM. Dennery and Clement ; "The Star of the North," which was

of course a version of " L'Etoile du Nord "; " Birds
of Prey; or, A Duel in the Dark "; " Peace at any
Price "; " The Half-Caste "; " Jocrisse the Juggler ";
" The Ladies' Battle," from the French of MM. Scribe
and Legouvé — an admirably written adaptation,
which still holds the stage ; the popular one-act
farce, " The Clockmaker's Hat"; " The Duke's
Daughter ; or, The Hunchback of Paris," which was
one of the many versions of the famous " Le Bossu "
—best known on the English stage as " The Duke's
Motto "; " Faust and Marguerite," told in three well-
arranged and vigorously written acts ; " My Wife's
Diary," a farce from the French of MM. Dennery
and Clairville ; " Ruy Blas," written in scholarly
blank verse ; " The Sea of Ice ; or, The Prayer of
the Wrecked," and " The Gold-seeker of Mexico "
(fancy the monosyllabic author of " Society," "Ours,"
and " Caste " being compelled to give this chapter of
titles to a play !), from the French of MM. Dennery
and Dugue; " The Chevalier de St. George"; " A
Glass of Water," from Scribe's admirable " Verre
d'Eau "; and many others.

Most of these plays were disposed of to Thomas
Hailes Lacy, the well-known theatrical bookseller and
publisher, and are now on the list of his successor,
Mr. Samuel French.

It was during the year 1854 that Robertson became

prompter at the Olympic—then under the management of Charles Mathews and Madame Vestris—at a salary of £3 a week ; and it is easy to conjure up the picture of the eager, ambitious, and constantly disappointed young dramatist as, prompt-book in hand, his eyes fell upon the stage that had witnessed the production of his ill-fated " A Night's Adventure "; but though the engagement was not a lucrative one, it no doubt did good service.

In speaking of his connection with the Olympic, Charles ·Mathews in his autobiography wrote : " The lighter phase of comedy, representing the more natural and less laboured school of modern life, and holding the mirror up to nature without regard to the conventionalities of the theatre, was the aim I had in view. The Olympic was then the only house where this could be achieved, and to the Olympic I at once attached myself. There was introduced for the first time in England that reform in all theatrical matters which has since been adopted in every theatre in the kingdom. Drawing-rooms were fitted up like drawing-rooms, and furnished with care and taste. Two chairs no longer indicated that two persons were to be seated, the two chairs being removed indicating that the two persons were not to be seated. A claret-coloured coat, salmon-coloured trousers with a broad black stripe, a sky-blue neckcloth with a large paste brooch, and a cut-steel eyeglass with a pink ribbon, no longer marked the light comedy gentleman, and the public at once recognised and appreciated the change." That these reforms were not lost upon the observant " prompter " is a matter of certainty ; and we all know that when, after years of hard work and weary waiting, his own turn came, he produced plays with an attention to artistic detail undreamt of even by Charles Mathews in halcyon Olympic days.

With characteristic foresight Mathews always believed in the future of Robertson, and was one of the few then in power who extended to him (in the charming Bohemian manner of equality for which he was famous with the younger members of his pro-fession in whom he recognised talent) the hand of good-fellowship ; and no one was more delighted than he when, after his hard and well-fought fight, the quondam prompter won his victory and was hailed as the most brilliant dramatist of his day. Before he went to India Mathews wrote as follows :

" Greenock, December 3, 1869.

" MY DEAR ROBERTSON,

" On Tuesday morning, January 3, I expect the pleasure of a few friends on the stage of Covent Garden to say good-bye if so inclined, or if not, to *wish* it, and shake hands. May I hope to see you among my ' distinguished visitors '?

> " Yours faithfully,
>
> " CHARLES MATHEWS."

After the termination of his engagement at the Olympic, Robertson encountered nothing but disappointment and vicissitude. One-act farces, then in vogue, were the safest and apparently the easiest of stepping-stones to the stage, and these, one after the other, he wrote and wrote, but to no purpose. One of them, entitled " Photographs and Ices," is in its way exceedingly good, the character of a Cockney shoe-black boy being especially well drawn. This young gentleman has a proclivity for reciting doggerel parodies of Shakespeare shaped to advertise his vocation—for example :

" All the world's a shoe,
   And all the men and women merely leather ;
   And each man in his time wears many sorts,
   Their shapes being seven sizes.
   First the Infant's, mooing and kicking in a worsted sock ;
   And then the waddling School-boy with his blucher
   Shining, tightly laced, studded with nails
   (Not studying in school) ;
   And then the Lover in tight French things varnished,
   With woful bunion, made by his too tight high-lows.
   And the Policeman, broad at the toes,
   Contract made—strong and hard—
   Heavy on pavement—crushing in sand or gravel

Seeking the cooks in situations, ever with open mouth.
And then the Justice, in good round Wellington with hair-
    socks lined—soles flat and square,
Of an old-fashioned cut—full of soft corns
That make him wince a bit: his toe his tend'rest part.
And next he sinks into the very slippered spoon
With fleecy worsted hose.   Boots thrown aside—
His youthful shoes, thrice soled, sizes too small
For his swollen feet, and his big manly tread
Turning again to childish toddle trips and tumbles on the
    ground.
Last sort of all is second childish—wear
Nothing but stockings on,
Sans calf, sans kid, sans buff,
Sans any description of boot or shoe,
Town or Northampton made."

Later on there is a line that is decidedly Robertsonian.   The precocious boot-black has maintained
that he is "an artist," and on this being pooh-poohed,
he falls to work on a pair of boots, saying : "Ain't I,
though ? You see me put a polish on! Make'm
look like a looking-glass gone into mourning for the
loss of the quicksilver."

All the characters in the little piece are well drawn,
and it affords excellent acting opportunities; but no
manager would entertain its production, and a similar
fate befell a charming one-act comedy entitled "Over
the Way," and farces called " My Wife's Diary" and
"A Row in the House,"* which, together with many

* It is interesting to record that some thirty years later " A
Row in the House " was very successfully produced by his son at

others, he sold to Lacy when his worldly affairs were *in extremis.*

Weary at heart, and sickened with constant disappointment, both he and H. J. Byron, who were then "keeping body and soul together" by writing for two or three small newspapers, and obtaining such poor theatrical engagements as fell in their way, determined to enlist, and for that purpose presented themselves at the Horse Guards. For a reason unexplained at the time—but which was no doubt the organic disease of the heart that subsequently hastened his end—Robertson failed to pass the medical examiner ; and, stoutly declining to accept the shilling without his friend for a comrade, Byron abandoned his intention, and the two went back to fight their weary war against editors and theatrical managers.

The rebuffs he was in the daily habit of receiving at this period, and the manner in which he chafed under them, were, in more prosperous times, described by Robertson in a satirical speech put into the mouth of Rudolph Harfthal, a character in his comedy entitled " Dreams." Harfthal, who is a gifted young composer, thus speaks of the trials and troubles ex-

Toole's Theatre—then under his temporary management. In the cast were Mr. Albert Chevalier, Mr. J. H. Darnley, and Robertson's daughter—Miss Maud Robertson.

perienced by the novice anxious to obtain a hearing in London: " In England," he says bitterly, " yesterday is always considered so much better than to-day; last week is superior to this; and this week so superior to the week after next; thirty years ago is much more brilliant an era than the present; the moon that shone over the earth in the last century so much brighter and more grand than the paltry planet that lit up the night last past! I shall explain myself better if I give my own personal reasons for making a crusade against age. In this country I find age so respected, so run after, so courted, so worshipped, that it becomes intolerable. I compose music; I wish to sell it. I go to a purchaser, and tell him so; he looks at me, and says, ' You look so young,' in the same tone that he would say, ' You look like an impostor or a pickpocket.' I apologize as humbly as I can for not having been born fifty years earlier; and the publisher, struck by my contrition, thinks to himself, ' Poor young man! after all, he cannot help being so young;' and, addressing me as if I were a baby, says, ' My dear sir, very likely your compositions may have merit—I do not dispute it—but, you see, Mr. So-and-so, aged sixty, and Mr. Such-an-one, aged seventy, and Mr. T'other, aged eighty, and Mr. Somebody-else, aged ninety, write for us; and the public are accustomed to their productions; and we make it a rule never to give the world anything written by a man under fifty-five years old. Go away now; keep to your work for the next thirty years: during that time exert yourself to grow older—you will succeed if you try hard—turn gray, be bald; it's not a bad substitute—lose your teeth, your health, your vigour, your fire, your freshness, your genius—in one short word, your terrible, abominable youth; and some day or other, if you don't die in the interim, you may get the chance of being a great man !"

The attempt to become a soldier having failed, he was compelled to return to the old life of drudgery, selling his plays and adaptations to Lacy (always regarded by him as a good friend), and acting in minor theatres. Of this period of his uphill career he preserved no record; and though in the days of his brilliant successes he would sometimes laugh as he recalled some comical incident connected with it, he would more often sigh when he briefly spoke of what he called his "starring, not to say starving, engagements."

In later years an old friend of his—Mr. Edward Draper—came across a partly printed document which ran somewhat as follows : " Whereby the signatory, T. W. Robertson, agrees to pay an agency fee to George Fisher of one half-week's salary, within four weeks, on an engagement with Mr. A. W. Young to play at the Theatre Royal, Woolwich, at a salary of one guinea per week." Before handing this document over to the mercies of the autograph-collector, Mr. Draper submitted it to Robertson, who said : "Pray do as you like with it. I had so many engagements at a guinea a week—or less—and was so glad to get them, that I cannot mind anyone having records of them now."

With the year 1855 there seemed to come the promise of better things. At this time Robertson's father, in partnership with Mr. W. J. Wallack, was managing the Marylebone Theatre (a house which more than once threatened to become a north-western rival to Sadler's Wells in the north-east), and our struggling actor-author was engaged to play the parts technically embodied under the term of "juvenile lead." The latter-day history of the luckless Marylebone Theatre has been such a sorry one that it might be stated here that its aims under the Wallack-Robertson régime were of the highest, and in proof of this contention we may quote the *Sunday Times* when it said : " On a former occasion we stated that the residents of the neighbourhood of the Marylebone Road ought to consider themselves fortunate in the proximity of a dramatic establishment conducted with so much taste and propriety. We repeat the

statement, because, although the merits of Mr. Wallack
as an actor, as a manager, and as a liberal encourager
of the high-class drama have been expatiated upon
with unqualified praise by the whole of the London
press, we fear that the house is not sufficiently
appreciated in the region where a proper estimate of
its merits would be productive of the most solid
benefit. . . .   That we may do our utmost to remove
a foolish and unjust prejudice that exists nowhere but
in Marylebone itself, we assert without reserve that
there is not a more respectably managed theatre in
London than the Marylebone Theatre under the
present management, that at few theatres in London
can pieces comprising a greater number of characters
be more adequately represented, and that the in-
habitants of St. John's Wood, who travel elsewhere
for an evening's amusement, may possibly ' go further,
and fare worse.' "

By the way, it was on these boards, and under
this management, that Madge Robertson (our Mrs.
Kendal of to-day) acted her first part, and the
incident has been thus recorded by that indefatigable
stage historian, Mr. William Archer :

" Little Madge was only four years old when she
made her first appearance on the stage.   One evening
' The Stranger ' was put in the bills, and the manager's
little daughter was dressed in her Sunday frock to

run on the stage and soften the heart of Kotzebue's gloomy nobleman. Like many an older *débutante*, she was far more concerned about the adornments of her person than about the artistic merits of her performance ; and catching sight of her nurse in the front row of the pit (in those days stalls were unknown, at least in Marylebone), she astonished the actors and enraptured the audience by calling out : ' Oh, nursey, look at my new shoes !' Mrs. Kendal may thus be said to have begun life characteristically by introducing an irresistible touch of nature among the overstrung and conventional emotions of the quasi-legitimate drama. Of this event she naturally has no recollection ; but the play-bill of the performance was given to her some years ago by the late Mr. E. F. Edgar, who was at the time a member of the company. It was not until February 26, 1855, that, at the same theatre, she played the Blind Child in ' The Seven Poor Travellers,' which is usually stated to have been her first part."*

It was at this time that poor Craven Robertson, who subsequently became an excellent actor, doing admirable service in his brother's successful comedies,

* During his Marylebone engagement Robertson appeared in a stage version (probably from his own pen) of Charles Dickens's " Hard Times." Concerning this the critic of the *Sunday Times* said : " The Tom Gradgrind of Mr. Robertson junior was a very capital piece of acting."

and whose premature death was a source of sorrow to all who knew him, made his first appearance on the stage. At the conclusion of the Marylebone season Robertson joined a company which, with the object of giving a series of English plays in Paris, was recruited by a M. Ruin de Fée. It included Mr. and Mrs. J. W. Wallack, Miss Cleveland (Mrs. Arthur Stirling), Mr. and Mrs. William Robertson, Mr. Charles Sennett, Mr. and Mrs. Henry Marston, Mr. George Honey, Mr. George Bennett, Hoskins (of Sadler's Wells, who officiated as stage-manager), the brothers Marshall, Miss Polly Marshall, Mr. George Cooke, Miss Rosina Wright, and Mr. Edward Righton. There was also an efficient English corps de ballet with the well-known sisters Miss Lizzie and Miss Nellie Purvis, specially engaged for the then popular " Pas de Fascination." Robertson's position was that of general acting manager and interpreter. The venture was in every form, shape and way an ill-judged and a disastrous one, the deluded company playing for only three weeks, and receiving for their services one week's salary. Speaking of it in later years, Miss Lizzie Purvis (Mrs. Edward Fletcher) said : " I had sent home twenty francs out of our first week's money, but as there was no ' treasury ' after the first week, we found ourselves stranded in a strange land without means. A meeting of the company was held in the green-room, and at all hazards it was resolved to send the corps de ballet home to London. It was Mr. Robertson who collected the money, and under the care of Mr. George Cooke we arrived there safely."

By this time Robertson, being the only member of the company who could really speak French, had not only been elected stage-manager, but had to grapple with all the difficulties and troubles of a foolish undertaking for which he was not in any way responsible. The demands made upon him by his anxious comrades may be easily imagined, and he always declared that these melancholy Parisian experiences nearly " worried him to death."

Mr. Edward Righton, who was then a careless lad of twelve, was probably the least apprehensive member of the company, and he only remembers the engagement inasmuch as it enabled him to make his first pun. When M. Ruin de Fée declared his inability to pay Miss Purvis and the other ladies of the ballet, Righton suggested that he might appropriately be called M. Ruin de Cory*phée!*

It was in the year 1855 that Robertson, playing for a benefit in the " Dusthole," as the old Queen's Theatre in Tottenham Street was then contemptuously, but not undeservedly, named, met the lady who soon afterwards became his loving and devoted wife. It is very curious to note that this happy meeting took place within the walls of the theatre which was destined to become (thanks in no small measure to his genius) the most popular and fashionable place of entertainment of London, and the scene of his brilliant triumphs.

Few London theatres have experienced greater changes of fortune. Before it became known as the Queen's (and the Dusthole) it had been called the Regency, the Dilettanti, the Tottenham Street and the Fitzroy; it was destined as the Prince of Wales's to win transient but ever-memorable glory under the management of the Bancrofts; it made a fortune for their successor, and it is now one of the strongholds of the Salvation Army. It may claim, however, to be the parent of the modernized and greatly improved Haymarket and the handsome new Prince of Wales's.

In the days of 1855 it was under the management of Mr. C. J. James. In the company, playing the " walking ladies' " parts was Miss Elizabeth Burton, a beautiful young girl of nineteen. Robertson fell in love with her—she returned his affection ; and while the foundation-stone for years of happy wedded life was well and truly laid, the joys and the anxieties of a troubled and so far disappointed existence were doubled.

INTERIOR OF THE REGENCY THEATRE, AFTERWARDS PRINCE OF WALES'S THEATRE.

Built on the Site of the King's Concert Rooms.

EXTERIOR OF THE REGENCY THEATRE.

Miss Burton's father was the son of a stalwart Yorkshire farmer, who, meeting with early reverses, made his way to London, joined the Life Guards, served through the Spanish campaign with Sir John Moore, and subsequently became a member of the body-guard of Louis Philippe when he reascended the throne of France. His history was in many respects a peculiar and romantic one, and Robertson, always on the alert for material, embodied it in a Christmas contribution to one of the many magazines for which he wrote, under the title of " The Soldier's Story." His name was John Mountain Taylor, that of Burton having been assumed by the young lady of the Queen's Theatre for stage purposes.

Her entrance to the ranks of the theatrical profession was brought about under somewhat peculiar circumstances. When quite a young girl she attended a school in South Molton Street in which a well-known lady of title took a friendly interest. Visiting the school one day, this lady heard Miss Burton (or, more properly speaking, Miss Taylor) recite some passages from Shakespeare, and was so delighted with her grace and intelligence that she invited her to her house in Grosvenor Square to read before a critical audience. Having successfully passed through this ordeal, her ambition was naturally fired, and she determined to try her fortune on the stage.

Her first public appearance was in a small part in
a benefit performance given at the Queen's, and so
pleased was Mr. James with the manner in which the
young actress acquitted herself, that he at once offered
her an engagement in his company. It is true that
the opening salary (twelve shillings a week for three
years) was a small one, but Miss Burton recognised
the value of work and experience, and very wisely
accepted it. Her reward soon came, for in the course
of three weeks she had done so well that the management voluntarily increased the amount to twenty-
one shillings a week. Soon after this, while playing
a short engagement at the City of London Theatre,
she was so highly spoken of by the critics that Mr.
and Mrs. Charles Kean were attracted, and asked her
to call upon them, with a view to an engagement at
the Princess's.

Accompanied by her mother, Miss Burton presented herself before the eminent actor-manager and
his accomplished wife, and was at once asked to go
through the part of Lady Macbeth. This she did so
satisfactorily that an engagement was immediately
offered and accepted. The necessary papers had even
been drawn out, when, just as she was about to sign,
the ambitious and independent young actress noticed
that the parts that she would be required to play
were not specified. In reply to her question on this

point, Kean gravely said that she would probably have to commence by merely walking on the stage with other beginners, and that her progress must be left entirely to the discretion of himself and Mrs. Kean. Whereupon she resolutely declared that she would allow neither the one nor the other to select parts for her; and, declining to put her signature to the document that she felt would tie her hands, and interfere with the bright career that she had mapped out for herself, she serenely bade them good-day.

Miss Burton had been some three years at the Queen's Theatre when Robertson met and fell in love with her, and on August 27, 1856—when he was twenty-seven and she but twenty years of age, and their combined salaries made up a pitiful income—they were at Marylebone Church, and with the full consent of their parents, right happily married.

One of the first engagements that the young couple obtained was at the Theatre Royal, Dublin, where she appeared as "leading lady," and he took character-parts, and performed the duties of assistant stage - manager. This was succeeded by appearances at Dundalk and Belfast, and they did not return to England until twelve months had come and gone.

Of Robertson as an actor, and of this period of

his career, Mr. J. F. Warden (whose name has been so long and so honourably associated with the fortunes of the Theatre Royal, Belfast) has some interesting things to say.

It was while fulfilling an engagement at North Shields that Mr. Warden first met Robertson. In those days the theatre of that town was under the management of Sam Roxby (the brother of William Beverley, the celebrated scenic artist, and of Robert Roxby, long and favourably known as the stage-manager of the Haymarket and Drury Lane Theatres); and in the company was Frederick Younge, the original D'Alroy of "Caste." For Younge's benefit H. J. Byron, then a very young actor, promised to appear, and Robertson accompanied his friend. Byron undertook to play the well-known part of Jim Baggs in the then popular farce, "The Wandering Minstrel," and in this Mr. Warden, who was the "juvenile singing walking gentleman" of the company, sang an old ballad so much to the satisfaction of his audience that he was rewarded by a hearty encore. Upon this Robertson, who had been applauding frantically at the wings, said: "Why, you're quite a Reeves!" To which the (even in those early and troubled days) incorrigible Byron added: "So it *Sims!*"

Some time after this Mr. Warden met Robertson

on the old Norwich circuit, and they became stock actors in the same company. In view of the facts that Robertson was wont to speak lightly, and even slightingly, of his own histrionic powers and achievements, and so soon as he was able abandoned the boards and devoted himself to his desk, it is interesting to note that his fellow-player—a keen critic, and an undoubted judge of good acting—regarded him as one of the best character actors of his day. Among other things, Mr. Warden recalls that Robertson played the part of Sir Arthur Lascelles in "All that Glitters is not Gold" in a cool and natural manner that, judged by the light of later events, was exactly what might have been expected from one who was destined to do so much for the natural school of acting, but which in those days was so unorthodox as to be almost startling. So good and so impressive was the performance, that at his final exit in the last act his manager (Charles Gill), who was playing the low-comedy part of Toby Twinkle, quite forgot that he had a line which, if spoken, would have checked the applause that flew out to Robertson, and, in theatrical parlance, "dried up." Again, in the part of Gratiano in "The Merchant of Venice" Robertson was delightful. In fact, wherever a natural and unstilted manner was required, he was admirable. With the artificial school of acting then in vogue he had no patience, and in it he resolutely (and probably to his immediate pecuniary disadvantage) declined to take honours.

During the Dublin engagement to which we have referred, the sometime famous Sir William Don, Bart., " starred " at the Theatre Royal, and Robertson and his sweet young wife played with him in comedy, farce, and drama; Robertson especially distinguishing himself as Charles Fenton in " Toodles," Sir Arthur in " All that Glitters is not Gold," Major Murray in " The Jacobite," Frank Brown in " Mrs. White," and other kindred parts. Later on in the season he made a great impression by the excellence of his acting in the character of Rashleigh Osbaldistone in a revival of " Rob Roy," and (supporting Mr. and Mrs. Barney Williams) in one of those Anglo-French parts in which he always revelled and had no rivals, in a drama entitled " Ireland as it Was; or, The Agent." But, as we have seen, Robertson not only acted during this engagement, but was assistant stage-manager—an important post in the then bright days of a busy Dublin season, when all sorts and conditions of operatic companies dovetailed their productions between those of the regular stock companies and the occasional stars. At this time nearly all the leading operatic artistes—Mario, Grisi, Piccolomini, and their brilliant contemporaries—

appeared at the Dublin Theatre Royal, and many and various were the differences of opinion concerning the mounting of historic productions that occurred between Mr. Stage-Manager Granby (an excellent actor of the old school) and his revolutionary young ally, who wanted to make all sorts of alterations and innovations in "stage business" that had (and surely, from the Granby point of view, this was enough) stood the test of time. Indeed, there seems little reason to doubt that Robertson's "new-fangled notions," yoked to his characteristic persistency, ultimately cost him his engagement. Robertson then wrote an "entertainment" (subsequently most humorously described by him in a Christmas number of *London Society*), with which the young couple endeavoured to make money in the smaller Irish towns. The venture was not a successful one : they were looked upon as something between banshees and bushrangers, and made the best of their way back to England.

A short engagement at the Surrey was followed by a reappearance at the Marylebone, where Mrs. Robertson made a marked success as Black-eyed Susan, and her husband worked, acted, wrote, and stage-managed in his usual untiring fashion. At this time the industrious pair were living in Lisson Grove; and here, on December 2, 1857, "a son and heir"—or, as Robertson playfully put it, " a very little son and still less *hair* "—was born to them.

In the following Christmas season they were engaged by J. R. Newcombe, of pleasant memory and sporting proclivities, as members of his stock company at the Theatre Royal, Plymouth. There they appeared in pantomime, farce, comedy, and drama, and after some ten months' absence returned to London. On the birth of a little daughter Robertson accepted another short engagement at the Theatre Royal, Woolwich; and later on husband and wife were to be seen at the Theatres Royal, Rochester and Windsor. At this time the last-named playhouse was under the management of Mr. C. A. Clarke, a kindly man of literary inclinations. He and Robertson soon became great friends; but, unhappily, a pleasant engagement, during which H.R.H. the Prince Consort and other members of the Royal Family patronized the theatre and signified their appreciation of the entertainment there provided, was, to the intense grief of Robertson, who was passionately fond of his children, saddened by the death of the baby girl.

It was at about the time that this little creature was laid to rest in Slough Churchyard that Robertson made up his mind to give up acting, and devote himself to literature. No doubt it was not without many misgivings that he "burnt his boats," for he was becoming very popular on the stage, and the loss of a steady, if small, income must have been a matter of serious moment to him; but he loved his pen, had faith in himself as a writer, and was compelled to recognise the fact that his restless, roving life gave him little or no chance of securing literary renown. His temperament was essentially nervous, and, to say nothing of the time that had to be devoted to rehearsals and acting, he could not settle down to his desk while subjected to perpetual change. An amusing story, which he used to tell of himself in later days, will show how little he was suited to the life of a travelling actor. Seeing "Apartments to let" written up in the windows of a house situated in a town in which he was to play for a week or so, he knocked at the door, and was taken in hand by an eager landlady. Against the more than comfortable rooms he could say nothing; but the price asked for them was far more than he could afford to pay. In his sensitive nervousness the poor fellow wondered how he could best make a graceful retreat. He walked round the rooms, admired the furniture, praised the outlook from the windows; and the good landlady no doubt thought that he was about to conclude a bargain, when he said, " Yes, I like it all immensely; this is just the place I want; but—you must excuse the question—how about the coach-house?"   "The coach-house ?—we haven't got a coach-house!" was the reply.   "Dear me! then I am extremely sorry," said Robertson.   "As far as the rooms are concerned, they would have suited me admirably; but I always find a coach-house indispensable."   The landlady expressed her regret; her promising tenant offered his thanks and apologies, bowed himself out of the house, and once more breathed freely.

With him the actor's life, as it had then to be lived by those who were not the prime favourites of the hour, was "all against the grain."   Speaking in later years of the days of stock companies, so often described by actors with weak and forgiving memories as "palmy days," he said : "Those were the days when I had one meal a day, and three parts a night to play; now I have three meals a day, and no part to play; and for this relief Providence has my heartfelt thanks."

But the step that, after due consultation with his affectionate wife, he resolved to take was an important and hazardous one, and probably it would not have been ventured had not Mrs. Robertson declared that she would contribute her share to their modest housekeeping expenses by continuing to act as often as suitable opportunities presented themselves.

Once more Robertson wrote and adapted plays for Mr. Thomas Hailes Lacey, and in addition to this he soon became associated with a number of journals and magazines, to which he sent contributions on all sorts of subjects. He was a wonderfully rapid writer, and kept a large stock of sketches and short stories by him ; so that he became noted for his ability to " execute orders " at the " smallest possible notice."

But original work for the stage was the aim and end of his ambition, and by dint of perseverance he managed to obtain a hearing for his one-act farce entitled " The Cantab," which was accepted and produced at the Strand Theatre (then under the well-remembered management of Mrs. Swanborough) on February 14, 1861. In the cast were Mr. W. H. Swanborough, Mr. James Bland, Mr. James Danvers, Miss Kate Carson, and Miss Lavine, and in its small way the piece was very successful.

Miss Marie Wilton, whose name was subsequently associated with Robertson's greatest triumphs, was then a member of the Strand company, playing " burlesque boys' " parts in a fashion that excited the warm admiration of that keenest of dramatic critics, Charles Dickens.

That Robertson was anxious to write a burlesque character for this talented actress is evidenced by the fact that there is in existence a travesty from his pen on the old-fashioned drama " Raymond and Agnes," with the proposed cast pencilled in in his own hand-writing as follows :

RAYMOND AND AGNES;

OR,

IN LOVE AND INN-GRATITUDE.

Don Felix	MR. POYNTER.
Don Raymond	MISS MARIA SIMPSON.
Theodora (*his Servant*)	MR. JAMES ROGERS.
Baptista (*a Bandit Host*)	MR. JAMES BLAND.
Robert } (*his Sons*)	MISS CHARLOTTE SAUNDERS.
Jaques }	MISS MARIE WILTON.
Agnes	MISS M. OLIVER.
Cunegonda	MR. J. CLARKE.

" Raymond and Agnes" as burlesqued by Robertson was never produced ; and little did the disappointed author dream, as he went home with his rejected manuscript in his pocket, that he would in a few years be the means of establishing Miss Marie Wilton and Mr. John Clarke as ranking amongst the best comedians, in the highest sense of the actor's calling, of their day.

That the piece was written up to burlesque standard may be shown by the following amusing parody (put into the mouth of Don Raymond) on Claude Melnotte's famous speech in " The Lady of Lyons":

" RAYMOND, *speaking to* AGNES.

I'll order dinner.   Could I paint the feast,
Could love fulfil its prayers, I'd give thee—list—
A damask cloth whose whiteness snow surpasses,
Laid with decanters, knives, forks, finger-glasses,
With a bride-cake, and bon-bons fringed with gold,
And cast in Gunter's costliest, tastiest mould
A pudding filled with fruits of burning summer,
Rasp, gooseb, and strawberry and swan's egg plum a,
With barley-sugar wall and pillars rising
From silver dishes with such nice hot pies in,
Musical with birds of heaviest *expense*,
Who when the pies ope warble songs of sixpence.
At noon, our arms enlaced in lock sublime,
We'd sit both wishing for the dinner time,
And wonder how Earth was unhappy, sweet,
While Heaven still left us youth and lots to eat :
We'd have no friends that were not hungry—nay,
No ambition but t' eat more than they.
We'd read no books that were not gastronomical,
Mrs. Glasse, Rundle, Soyer's Economical,
That we might smile at those digestive powers
That hate the pastry of such tarts as ours ;
And when night came in twilight's deep'ning gray,
We'd sit and think on what we'd have next day.
Dost like the picture? (*ecstatically*).
AGNES.   'Tis a vision bright
     Of happy hours and happy *happy-tite*.
RAYMOND. A *happy-tie-to* us will marriage be."

And so on, *ad lib.*

This travesty could only have been written in the
vain hope that its production would bring in welcome

grist to a scantily supplied mill.   Pure and original comedy was Robertson's goal, and that he was ever, and with untiring perseverance, aiming at it is proved by the manuscripts of his unproduced plays.   One of these, bearing (in his own handwriting) the date of 1857, and entitled " Down in Our Village," is in many respects as dainty in conception and as graceful in execution as any of the subsequent comedies from his prolific pen.   But his day had not yet come.

His brief connection with the Strand Theatre brought him into close companionship with his old friend H. J. Byron and a certain lady manageress noted for occasionally perpetrating what is known as a " malapropism."   To the two inveterate jokers the opportunity that here presented itself was irresistible, and the subsequent wonderful stories set afloat of this good lady's extraordinary sayings were really the fruit of their fertile imaginations.   Attributing them all to their unconscious victim, they vied with each other in the invention of the most outrageous and humorous word-blunders ; and to such a pitch did this arrive that, if they happened to meet in the streets, each primed with " Have you heard the latest ?" they would burst into peals of laughter, and rapidly go opposite ways, the onlookers taking them for madmen.

Among other work in these days he wrote—sometimes under his own name, and at others under the pseudonym of " Hugo Vamp "—many descriptive songs and comic sketches. Some of these became very popular, particularly a burlesque one on " The Corsican Brothers." He also supplied entertainments for Mr. W. S. Woodin, of " Carpet Bag " fame ; for Mr. and Mrs. Howard Paul (in their hands an explanatory skit on the French Exhibition, entitled " Our Lively Neighbours," became a notable attraction); and for two ladies who were very favourably known to provincial audiences as " Sophia and Annie."

" Sophia and Annie " were related to Robertson, and they have handed down an anecdote of the days that preceded his marriage which is worth recording. It clearly proves that with him the often-quoted maxim, " Duty first and pleasure afterwards," was not only preached, but practised.

The two ladies were giving their entertainment in a country town where Robertson happened to be fulfilling a theatrical engagement. As a matter of course he called upon them, and, being young and susceptible, he soon asked one of them to accompany him on walks to the neighbouring places of interest, and in many ways showed her marked attention. Gossips' tongues were wagging freely, and " the other of them " was anxiously awaiting an explanation of the young gentleman's " intentions," when suddenly his visits ceased and he was seen no more. Years afterwards they met again, and he then explained why he had behaved so strangely. It appears that during the period of this " calf-love " he had received a letter from his mother telling him of distress at home, and begging of him to send her anything he could spare to " keep things going." His meagre salary barely sufficed for his own small wants, but he could not bear to think of his family lacking (as, in good truth, they sometimes nearly did) the necessaries of life ; and without another thought he sold all his little valuables, together with his presentable clothes, sent the proceeds to his troubled parents, and left himself with one poor worn suit, wholly (in his estimation) unfit for association with his Sophia (or Annie). Long, long afterwards Annie (or Sophia) heard this little story from his own confessing lips.

Returning to our own story, we find that Robertson, having always valiantly done his duty by his father, mother, and all those near and dear to him, had at this time to put his willing shoulder to the wheel in order to " keep things going " for his young wife and baby boy ; and as London managers were not yet eager to secure his plays, he gladly turned his pen into the groove of more immediately though less remunerative journalism.

The little success gained by " The Cantab " at the Strand Theatre fortunately brought him into contact with many of the leading journalists and humorists of the day, and he not only soon became an indefatigable contributor to many important newspapers and magazines, but created life-long and invaluable friendships.

He also tried his hand at novel-writing. The manuscript of a drama " prepared for the stage " by J. B. Johnstone, from T. W. Robertson's novel of " Stephen Caldrick," points to the existence of a work not to be found amongst his own manuscripts, which include two hundred pages of an unnamed novel ; chapters six and seven (ending the first volume) of another entitled " Vauxhall"; together with " A History of Old Vauxhall," which is complete ; many small items evidently written in scraps for subsequent use ; and another novel, " Dazzled, not Blinded." The manuscript of this is perfect with the exception of the first forty-nine pages, which are missing. The moral of the story may be deduced from the last paragraph. " So, dear readers, as you pass through life tried by failure, or tried still more by success, may your bright prospects, like a blossom-ripening summer, ever dazzle, not blind you !"

As time went on he became a contributor to quite a host of newspapers and periodicals now more or less defunct. To *Fun,* under the genial editorship of the younger Tom Hood, he was, with Mr. W. S. Gilbert, an original contributor. It will be remembered that it was in the pages of this popular paper that Mr. Gilbert's immortal " Bab Ballads " first appeared. He and Robertson were then "literary humorists " and dramatic critics, and were in the habit of attending " first nights " together.

Amongst other publications to which Robertson became an indefatigable contributor were *The Welcome Guest,* edited by G. A. Sala and R. B. Brough ; *The Liverpool Porcupine; The Comic News,* edited by H. J. Byron ; *The Glowworm,* a short-lived evening paper published in London, and edited by his intimate friend, Thomas Archer ; *Beeton's Dictionary* and *Beeton's Englishwoman's Domestic Magazine ; The Boy's Own Magazine,* to which he contributed the charades ; *Colman's Magazine ;* a weekly paper called *Saturday Night ; The Wag,* another comic paper edited by H. J. Byron ; " Christmas numbers " of all sorts and sizes, including *London Society ;* and the then very popular weekly journal *The Illustrated Times.* On the staff of this paper were from time to time George Augustus Sala, Geoffrey Prowse, Edmund Yates, W. B. Rands (known in literature as Matthew Brown, Harry Holbeach, and half a dozen other aliases), Sutherland Edwards, Deffet Francis,

Augustus Mayhew, Godfrey Turner, the Brothers Brough, James Hannay, Thomas Archer, Clement Scott and Edward Draper. The artists were Julian Portch (who sent sketches to the papers from before Sebastopol during the Crimean War), Thomas Nicholson (the modeller of the D'Orsay statuette), the comic artists being William McConnell and Charles. In short, Robertson was a welcome sojourner in the very capital of the pleasant land of the Bohemia of happy memory—a capital of which poor Prowse wrote :

> "The longitude's rather uncertain,
> The latitude's equally vague ;
> But that person I pity who knows not the city,
> The beautiful city of Prague."

In those days he was to be seen at the Savage, Reunion, and Arundel Clubs, and was, says his old friend and brother-Savage, Charles Millward, "delightful company," ever ready with a smart and pungent rejoinder to a merry remark or witty sally directed at him by one of his fellow-members. Indeed, if the impromptu witticisms, brilliant sayings, and smart repartees of Robertson could be collected and published, they would fill volumes.

But the Arundel was Robertson's favourite club. There he met Leicester Buckingham, Belford, Hepworth Dixon, Blanchard, Sothern, Arthur

Sketchley, Joseph Knight, W. S. Gilbert, Clement Scott, and all the best of the young literary lions.

In speaking of these days, and the outcome of them, Mr. Clement Scott in his delightful and (happily) published lecture, "Thirty Years at the Play," says: "For my own part, I am inclined to think that full credit for his share in the dramatic revival was never given to my old friend and faithful comrade, Tom Hood, a poet, and the son of a poet dear to every Englishman. He was a desperately hard-worked man at the time, quill-driving at the War Office all day, and burning the midnight-oil at night—not a dramatic critic by profession, and yet passionately fond of the play—but Tom Hood had an influence among the younger writers and artists of his day that cannot be overrated. He was the most unselfish and least jealous of men. He loved to get his friends around him to talk shop, and to encourage one another in their various callings. Every Friday night of his life, though not particularly blessed with this world's riches, he gave a cheery Bohemian supper-party, to which the best fellows in the world were invited. Who that was privileged to attend them can have forgotten Tom Hood's 'Friday nights' in South Street, Brompton, where after a pipe and music, conversation and poetry readings, we sat down to a homely meal of cold joint and roast potatoes, and discussed all the wonderful things that we youngsters intended to do in the future ?   Was it a wonder that we were true and loyal to our old comrade, Tom Robertson, who was the brightest of the conversationalists present, and the best of company ?"

In succession to Edmund Yates, Robertson became the dramatic critic ("The Theatrical Lounger," as he was styled) of *The Illustrated Times*, and to its columns he contributed a series of articles entitled "Theatrical Types," which are in their way inimitable. Since those days many changes have taken place in stageland, and we think that the following extracts from his exhaustive series of now forgotten articles will prove interesting.   They will show the state of things theatrical in those byegone times, and how they appeared to one whose knowledge of them was almost painfully complete.

Of "Leading Ladies" he says :

"The love of acting spreads over so wide a surface of society that Leading Ladies are recruited from all classes.   Daughters of wealthy men who have bent their knees imploring to *soi-disant* Siddonses ; daughters of ruined gentlemen forced to seek their bread, and insufficiently accomplished for the dreadful trade of 'governessing'; daughters of actors born and reared to it; and daughters of publicans who keep theatrical taverns where the portraits of popular

actors and actresses are framed, glazed, and enriched
with autographs—all these are raw material which
time, tact, patience, and the horse labour of a rising
barrister, manufacture into dramatic heroines.   While
speaking of portraits, it is impossible not to remark
on the blessing of photography to small celebrities
seeking popularity.

" The Leading Actress in the country will rise at
nine, and, after laving her hot forehead and pale face
with water, and snatching a cup of turbid, provincially
prepared coffee, rush to the theatre for the 'call' for
rehearsal at ten.   The drama of ' Susan Hopley,' in
which she sustains the character of that pattern
of domestic young ladies in service, occupies her till
past twelve.   She then waits till two — for the
eminent tragedian Mr. Lara Thunderstone, who is to
'star' as Macbeth that night, does not rise early,
and always keeps rehearsals waiting.   The 'eminent'
having at last arrived, bilious of stomach and
fastidious of taste, protracts the rehearsal, and at
half-past four, faint, sick, and tired, the sinking
actress reaches her lodgings.   Her dinner has been
waiting two hours ; it is half cold and wholly
clammy.   She is past appetite, and orders tea, which
is prepared as detestably as was the morning's coffee.
Dresses have then to be looked out, unpacked, altered,
trimmings changed, and gold lace ripped off and

' run on.' The basket, that wondrous mystery, is packed, and the actress follows it to the dressing-room, where she is installed by six. For five hours and a half she acts, and acts, and acts, speaks, and speaks, and speaks, changes her dress, changes her dress, and changes her dress, and all the time she never sits down for a moment. Home by midnight, she eats and enjoys her supper, the only meal hard fate permits her. ' She sleeps well after that,' might say an unbelieving reader. Sleep ! she sits up till day-light studying Evadne in Sheil's play, for the eminent tragedian Mr. Lara Thunderstone, of the Theatre Royal everywhere, has chosen to play ' Colonna ' on the following evening. Ladies at the head of establish-ments, schoolmistresses, governesses, shop-girls, milliners, cooks, housemaids, laundresses, and char-women, what is your work to this ?

" The power that sustains the actress through her enormous daily and nightly task is the artiste's nervous irritability, love of applause, and hope of future fame—that hope so delusive that in green-room diction it is called ' The Phantom.'

" Those who know but little of theatres and their belongings often regret that actresses in private life so little resemble the heroines they portray. If they could look on them not by the false medium of bat-wing burners, but by domestic daylight or economical composites, they would regret that heroines did not oftener idealize the real virtues of actresses—virtues intensified and polished by the cultivation of the most emotional of arts. Though all leading dramatic heroines do not become the wives of baronets, the practice of their calling so refines and educates their sentiments that they are always ladies.

*   *   *   *   *   *

" There are as many varieties of Tragedian as there are of fancy pigeon, paletot, or armchair. They are generally grave men with deep voices and manners of solemn, not to say sepulchral, politeness. Some of them carry this peculiarity so far as to resemble animated statues rather than living men, and many a good-natured but ghastly actor has sat upon the spirits of the guests at a jolly supper-party by conducting himself like the equestrian spectre of Don Guzman by trying to adapt himself to circumstances, or the shade of the blood-boltered Banquo endeavouring to spend a pleasant evening *chez* Macbeth. The habit of addressing distant galleries gives a fearful distinctness to their utterance. They are terribly impartial to each letter of every word they utter, and ask with such syllabic emphasis for ‘ mashed potatoes ’ as to make ‘ mashed ’ sound like sarcasm, and ‘ potatoes ’ like denunciation.

" It is a common error to suppose that all this

arises from affectation — from a desire to appear singular, and to ' pose ' melodramatically. The constant use of the voice renders its tones deep, rich, and mellow ; the close-shaven cheeks make the face look pale and hollow ; and the practice of assuming different costumes, and of ' suiting the action to the word, and the word to the action,' brings the hands out of the familiar region of the trousers-pockets to aid in illustrating their owner's speech. So artifical an act as acting naturally begets artificial manners ; but though artificial, they are entirely apart from affectation. The gravity of a judge, the upright carriage of a soldier, or the swing of a sailor, are habits, not affectations. So is the actor's hand in his vest, so are his knuckles on his hip, so are his folded arms—though we should all be glad to see those favourite stock attitudes banished from the stage, with the footman in top-boots, and the chambermaids in white muslins and pink ribbons.

" Tragedians spring from all grades of society— from the Oxford man who has taken honours, to the journeyman carpenter endowed with dark eyes and a loud voice. In private life Tragedians are simple and single-minded ; they know little of the real world around them ; they draw their views of historical personages entirely from plays, and in politics side with that party which is the most picturesque of costume and flowery of speech. They are invariably married, and as invariably fathers of large families, on whom they dote, and with whom they play. *Les extrêmes se touchent.* Ignorant of realities, unconscious of everything save through a gaudy-tinted medium, the father-actor and his child meet upon a level ground of fairy fiction and poetic fancy.

*　　*　　*　　*　　*　　*

"The Light Comedian is the actor who represents the characters of young patricians, volatile lovers, voluble swindlers, well-dressed captains, swells in and out of luck, and the upper classes generally on this side of forty years of age. He is purely and entirely the creation of the dramatist; for neither in nature nor in society was the like of this bustling, talkative creature ever seen, for which let nature and society be thankful: for, not excepting neuralgia, snakes, or earnest men with missions, the presence of a high-spirited, high-voiced, highly-dressed hero of comedy is the most intolerable nuisance.

"Conceive a boisterous, blatant fellow in a green coat and brass buttons, buckskin breeches and boots, or in a blue frock, white waistcoat, and straw-coloured continuations, always talking at the top of his voice, slapping you heavily on the back, laughing for five minutes consecutively, jumping over the chairs and tables, haranguing a mob from your

drawing-room window, going down upon his knees
to your daughter or your wife, or both, kissing your
servant-maid, borrowing your loose cash, and introducing a sheriff's officer to your family as an old
college friend, and you form some idea of the type
of animal the dramatic writers of the last century
forced upon the public as the beau-ideal of a gentleman, a blood, and ' A fine fellow, sir, by Gad !'

" The Light Comedian—when not born of theatrical
parents, and fixed in the light-comedy groove, and
told to rattle on as rapidly as ardent hopes and a thin
tongue will permit—may have been a clerk, or an
army captain, or the son of a poor gentleman, or of
a widow lady ; but, whatever his rank, s'ation, or
degree, he belongs to the numerous category of young
men of good appearance.

" He has usually fine hair and teeth. He is
' dressy,' and particular about his ' back parting,'
his hat, and his boots ; has a self-conscious sort of
walk—half swagger, half skip—and is keenly sensitive as to the tie of his cravat and the fall of his
trousers over the instep. He is a well-brushed young
man, and at the age of eighteen addicted to perfumes.
It is his pride and glory to have a white handkerchief
peeping from either his coat-tail or his breast-pocket,
and he takes it out with a flourish. When he carries
a cane it is a light one, and has a pretty gold head,

and he either swings it jauntily or taps his trousers with it militarily. It must be admitted, frankly, it is vanity that brings him on the stage : the desire to dazzle and delight, to wear becoming costumes, carry a sword, bully bailiffs, carry off heiresses, hoax papas, and pink rivals. ' Woman, lovely woman,' is the toast he is always proposing to himself and always doing honour to, though it must be confessed that he is less in love with the sex than with the honour of being loved by them. It is not the battle that he cares for, but the medals.

" Having once achieved a London reputation, the Light Comedian's life is one sheen of silk stocking and sparkle of champagne. If he has the good sense to eschew low company, society opens its portals to him, and he may leave the drawing-room for the dressing-room, and the dressing-room for the ball.

" Come, then, the costumier, the wig-maker, and the tailor to take his measure for costumes, wigs, and clothes ; and after them—at the respectful distance becoming his inferior calling—the author to take his measure for a part. Is he an Irishman, the scene shall be laid in the county of Galway ; if he dance well, the principal incident shall happen in a ball-room ; does he speak French, he shall assume the accent of the Gaul ; has he a small hand, it shall be frequently alluded to ; has he white teeth, he shall laugh continually. Give your orders, gentlemen; the author is in the room. . . . Debt, difficulties, sickness, and trouble are the lot of Light Comedians, as of all; and when the limber-tongued, rattling actor cheerily asks his kind friends in front to forgive the follies he has committed in his ' Uncle's Villa,' or during his ' Day in Dunstable,' or in his ' First Fit of Love,' or whatever the title of the farce may be, how can his applauding auditors know what is waiting for him at the curtain's fall?

*   *   *   *   *   *

" The actor on whom devolves the delineation of stage Old Men must be an artist of considerable versatility. The leading parts in tragedy all bear some resemblance to each other — or, at least, tragedians play them in exactly the same manner, which is much the same thing. Light comedy characters have all the same dash, banter, laugh, swagger, swindle, and assurance. A low comedian must always be industriously funny; but there are Serious Old Men and Comic Old Men, and there are different sorts of both.

" One description of a Serious Old Man is very happily termed by the French a ' noble father '; and the word ' noble ' must be understood to apply to exalted sentiment and incorruptible integrity, and high-mindedness and virtue, not to social rank. He is frequently a patrician of the loftiest nobility; and, in that phase, his consciousness of the purity of his blood, of the baseness of any mean fellow below the degree of a duke, and his horror of a *mésalliance*, would shame a real French marquis of the year 1770. He is equally ready to disinherit as to curse degenerate offspring, and, in his antipathy to grown-up children having any voice in such small matters as the choice of a profession or a partner for life, is as selfish and obstinate as any real father in real life, which is a somewhat round assertion.

"The *père noble* is frequently plebeian by birth, though patrician by nature; and when he is, his virtues are so intolerably virtuous that self-examining spectators almost wish to see him fall into the depths of sin, he is so annoyingly good, so exasperatingly beneficent. There is nothing more provoking to mere frail flesh and blood than a virtuous old peasant in a long fleecy, silvery-white wig. When the disguised prince, wrapped in a huge cloak and belated in the storm, knocks at the cottage of the V. O. P. (Virtuous Old Peasant) and asks for shelter, the V. O. P. improves the occasion in the irritating manner peculiar to him by saying:

" ' Enter, Sir Stranger; my roof is humble, but it is honest, and never did my door refuse to ope its rusty hinges to the weary or the wayworn. Enter, sir, and welcome, though my poor house boasts nought to offer to your Excellency but brown bread and integrity.'

"All the time this well-spoken and aggravating rustic has kept the wayworn traveller in the rain, hail, wind, snow, thunder and lightning. The auditor with mere average good qualities endures much at the hands, or rather mouth, of the V. O. P., and feels a certain sense of gratified spite when the V. O. P.'s only daughter listens too eagerly to the too flattering tale of the prince or count, and elopes from a paternal roof whose virtue was only exceeded by its dulness. No wonder the poor girl runs away!

"The child once fled from the paternal roof to the arms of a villain, the V. O. P. feels that he has not lived in vain. He takes down his hat and staff, and turns his full flood of metaphor upon his unfortunate wife, or 'dame,' who replies only by wiping the wettest of eyes on the whitest possible of aprons. Pocket-handkerchiefs are the attributes of a corrupt and vicious aristocracy; the feminine apron or the manly sleeve is the proper resource of the afflicted lowly. The contempt of the V. O. P. for money, considered as a styptic to a bleeding heart, is only equalled by the length of the silver hair to which he so frequently makes allusion. It is a portion of the aggravation of the plebeian *père noble* that, when he

discovers that his child has been married to the man
of her heart in the correctest way possible, family
reasons having for a time compelled the contracting
parties to keep their union secret, it only affords him
another opportunity for tears. Tears are the V. O. P.'s
speciality, and he turns them out with a facility un-
surpassed by the immortal Job Trotter in immortal
' Pickwick.' ' Bless you, my children ! bless you !'
sobs the emotional father, who then retires with his
dame to the unrestricted use of apron and sleeve for
the remainder of a well-spent and lachrymose existence.

" In his choice between patrician and plebeian
parents the actor of Old Men is guided by his nose
and his stomach. If his nose be of the Julius Cæsar,
Wellington, or Napier pattern, or if his figure be
thin, he at once decides for the noble fathers; if the
most prominent feature of his face be represented by
two nostrils and no bridge to speak of, or if his
stomach be of globular formation, he goes over to the
hearty vulgarians. No audience would believe in a
patrician with a small nose ; no audience would
tolerate a rich old citizen without plenty of protuber-
ance. The British public is exacting, and refuses
credence alike to thin aldermen or to fat dukes.

" The actor of Old Men, in adopting his line of
business, exhibits an artistic feeling and self-abnega-

tion of which the Tragedian, Light Comedian, and Low Comedian are incapable. The Tragedian loves to be posed as a *grand homme incompris*—a Manfred, Conrad, or Timon; it is his delight to be a hero, and to hear himself utter the poetry written by others as if it were his own immediate inspiration. The Light Comedian loves to dazzle; is fond of the admiration of the opposite sex, whether in box, pit, or gallery, and of taking by storm hearts that the author has arranged to capitulate in the last act. The Low Comedian is a pure egotist, and would run after an imaginary butterfly and hit his nose against a buttress, while Constance was bewailing her dead son, for the sake of half a chuckle from a wide-mouthed little boy. Not so the Old Man: he dresses in unbecoming clothes, sinks his juvenility, assumes dotage, is made the scoff of the audience, is befooled by his own niece, ward, or daughter, bamboozled by impecunious captains on no pay, ridiculed by the low comedy footman and smart *soubrette*, bullied by his wife, and treated as a butt by the whole *dramatis personæ*.

*   *   *   *   *   *

"No matter who or what the auditors—short-haired swell, brilliant belle, smart clerk, blasé critic, or ardent mechanic shouting in his shirt-sleeves in the gallery—the Low Comedian is a general favourite.

"It is a strange vocation to come into the world

for the sole purpose of making people laugh ; yet such would seem to be the destiny of the genuine Low Comedian—the Low Comedian *de naissance ;* not the heavy-browed, lantern-jawed, rigid-cheeked misanthrope who adopts low comedy as a calling, but your light-haired, snub-nosed, wide-mouthed variety of the *genus homo,* to whom you would assign no place in the world but the theatre, and no post in the theatre but that of funny man. . . . He is usually a queer, cock-eyed sort of baby, who makes his mother laugh, and his father laugh, and his nurse, and his nurse's friends, and even the grave doctor. He is always content, and always happy. If pap be too long in preparation, he will allay the pangs of hunger with the knob of the kitchen-poker; if sweetmeats be unattainable, a lump of coal or a well-done cinder will satisfy him for hours. He is one of those miraculous children who have the measles favourably, and makes an attack of the mumps a credit to his parents. When he falls down four pairs of stairs he does not hurt himself; he feels refreshed by the exercise, and is rewarded for his exertion by the scrap of orange-peel, three weeks old, which he finds beneath the mat.

" As a boy he is the funny fellow of the school, who makes faces behind his slate and gets other boys caned for laughing at him. He is a pet with the master, and the ushers, and the maids, and everybody.

He has the gift of popularity; his very mistakes are jests, his faults pleasantries, and his ugliness—for he is ugly—a sort of exaggerated and comic comeliness.

" He sees the humorous side of everything, and is a wonderful mimic. He imitates his father's voice and cough so perfectly as to deceive the practised ears and instinctive affection of his mother. He calls out to the servant in his mother's tones, and laughs at her surprise. Though not a dullard, he is slow at learning, and his anxious parents bind him 'prentice to a chemist and druggist, in the hope that the odour of drugs and the constant contemplation of gilt labels on shop-drawers may make him scholarly and serious.

" But nor poppy, nor mandragora, nor all the drowsy syrups of the pharmacopœia can kill his love of fun. He nearly ruins his master's business by imitating his customers to their faces. So quick and varied are his powers of facial contortion that he is not as one boy behind the counter, but twenty. Then dawns on him the cheap comic song-book, and the half-price to the theatre. What, then, to him is balsam of tolu to the ' Tooral-lal-looral-lalooral-li-day ' of the popular vocalist, or to his ecstasies as he sees his favourite actor -- the one with the short trousers too large for him at the back—tumble into the cucumber-frame. Hence assafœtida and all thy vain delights! The playhouse and the public-house are from that time his love, his future, and his glory.

"Finally, he is completely un-chemisted and de-druggistized by the Private Amateur Theatre, where his first appearance is hailed with uproarious delight; and even the leader of the orchestra—who is a real professional and can read music at sight, and has a minim of baldness on the back of his head, and green spectacles, and other orchestral peculiarities—says he is the funniest man he has seen—'Since Liston, since Liston!' In vain does his irate master inform his father; in vain his father storm, his mother sob. Fate cries out. He cancels his indentures by running away from them. and by means of a theatrical agent, or luck, or perseverance, obtains employment in a small provincial theatre. . . . and in seven years he is an accepted London favourite.

"The Low Comedian is always an especial and privileged person. For him is a latitude of speech and action permitted to none other. Practical jokes, sufficient for an action at law or for a personal encounter, are in him considered only things of custom, strokes of humour, sallies of sly wit. 'Tis his vocation.

*   *   *   *   *   *

"The Managers of London theatres are a peculiar race. There are but about twenty theatres in London;

it follows then, as a matter of course, that there can
be but twenty London Managers, and as the popula-
tion of these isles amounts to some millions, it also
follows that twenty men among those millions following one particular calling must have a natural
sympathy with each other as Managers, for in no
other respect does the least sympathy exist between
them.

" As we intend these sketches to be types of
character and not photographic portraits, we shall go
as far back as the beginning of the present century
for the subject of our photographs. In the course of
the last fifteen years the whole aspect of theatrical
affairs has so changed that the man of forty summers
may consider himself a sort of connecting link
between what was the stage and what it is—between
the buckskin breeches, top-boots and white hats of the
comedies of Colman junior and the gibus, patent
leathers, floppy trousers and frizzy beard of modern
melodrama as it talks, and stalks, bows, banters,
fights duels and feigns indifference. . . . The Actor
Manager of thirty years ago was a man of totally
different type to his successor of the present day. He
was an intensely clever, bustling, wrong-headed,
highly appreciative fellow, fond of his authors, his
company, his orchestra, his scene-shifters, his supernumeraries and all that belonged to the little world he

ruled. During the rehearsal of a new piece he would swear horribly and stamp on the stage till the soles of his feet tingled again. On the night of its production, attired in his character dress, he would be here, there and everywhere—assisting the actors in the adjustment of their wigs, finding fault with the coiffure of a soubrette, discharging the prompter, imprecating every portion of the anatomy of his stage-manager, helping a carpenter in the ' setting ' of a rock-piece, challenging his leading tragedian to mortal combat on the morrow, making speeches to the audience to appease them for the long delays between the acts, and conducting himself generally like a lunatic in fancy costume; but, the piece over, he would raise the prompter's salary, ask his stage-manager to join him in a bottle of champagne, treat the carpenters to beer, invite his leading tragedian to dine with him on Sunday, and thank his generous and liberal public for once more cr-r-r-owning his humble efforts with their kind approval. The first to recognise merit in an aspirant, he was the last to listen to the grumbling of a fastidious author or a tyrannical stage-manager. Beloved by all tragedians, comedians, carpenters, call-boys, scene-shifters, and supernumeraries, his funeral presented a long procession of grateful and weeping mourners, who dated all the events of their lives from his death, and who said constantly, 'When poor Yorick was living he would never,' etc. 'Alas! poor Yorick!' Hie over the last five-and-twenty years to the present caterers for the public! The change is great, and, like many other changes, the reverse of an improvement. There are so many varieties of the species that our limits will only permit us to touch upon a few. . . . The Commercial Manager is a very common type, and is willing to turn to good account opera, ballet, equestrianism and Shakespeare in this present practical theatrical age. He takes an entirely commercial view of all things — Ramo - Samee - Indiarubber Peruvians, real water, the legitimate drama, speaking pantomine, or pantomimic tragedy—so that it brings in the ready sixpence. He prides himself greatly upon his practical common-sense, distrusts manuscripts, fears authors, but places great reliance upon his costumier and property man. His conversation is not choice, except as regards oaths, which are of a raciness and full flavour that would do credit to an irate cabman. Although be professes a high respect for dramatic literature, he judges of the merit of a drama like a butterman — by its weight in paper. He is a great man for bargains, and will buy a quantity of damaged velvets for a fabulously small sum, after which he will search for an author to write him a piece for the velvets. 'Lovely velvets—

make any piece popular them velvets would,' says the Commercial Manager. The drama found, if it fail he despairs of the prospects of the theatre. Public are so fickle nowadays. 'Who would have thought that with them velvets any piece could fail?' The Commercial Manager is a great financial genius, and cuts down salaries and expenses to the very lowest scale. He is also fertile in expedients for stopping a night's salary from his employés, and was the original inventor and introducer of that wonderful piece of economical meanness, a Complimentary Benefit, which means a benefit for the manager, on which occasion the actors, actresses, scene-shifters, supernumeraries and all give their services gratuitously. . . . Lastly, the Commercial Manager is very litigious, and always involved in lawsuits ; in fact, an attorney is laid on to his establishment like gas, and picks out holes in engagements and flaws in arrangements for his clever client's interest. The Actor-Manager is a good second or third rate sort of artist, who forces himself into a prominent position by taking a theatre, and, by carefully stewing down the abilities of the authors and actors he employs, and mixing with his own their mental and artistic porridge, makes his weak water-gruel talents thick and savoury. Just now the stage is terribly plagued by various sorts of these self-sufficient entrepreneurs. There is your

Tragedian Manager, who kindly puts Shakespeare right and explains what that erring author really meant; and there is your High Comedy Manager, who knows three lords to speak to, and once met a countess at a ball, and is in consequence a great authority on fashionable life, and, like Goldsmith's bear-leader, can't abide anything that is low. These two varieties are very fond of teaching young actors how to act, and so successful is their tuition, that very often a promising young comedian from the provinces has in six difficult lessons been tamed and tortured into the ineffective and passionless delivery which forms so valuable a setting to managerial mediocrity. Another of these peculiarities is remarkable. They seldom, if ever, engage an actor or actress taller than themselves. An engagement at their theatre depends more on inches than genius. No mere actor should be taller than his manager. Banquo should always be smaller than Macbeth, and the *jeune premier* rôle shorter than the *grand premier* rôle. Height, like individual talent, must be kept down to one regulation standard. In regard to their well-disguised servility to the gentlemen who notice the theatres in the daily and weekly papers, Actor-Managers are by no means more open to ani-madversion than either the commercial or the in-visible ones. . . . There are many other varieties of

Managers, too many for us to give a full and particular account of ; many well-meaning, kind-hearted and honourable gentlemen—the sort of men who require no detailed description, for the good of all classes are alike.

*   *   *   *   *   *

" During the last seven years burlesques and extravaganzas have taken so strong a hold on public favour that their authorship has become a distinct and separate form of dramatic writing. More than this ; it has become a lucrative one, and is therefore much followed. That very large majority of persons who are not burlesque writers, burlesque actors, theatrical managers, and amateurs, would be astonished if they knew what serious importance is attached to the production of these rhymed travesties, what crowds they attract, and what large receipts they bring.

" About the end of August, when London streams to the seaside, and Londoners do not stream into the theatres; when managers have acted their favourite characters to undiscriminating audiences who have graciously accepted free admissions, they begin to think seriously of Christmas, and invite their pantomime or burlesque writer to a solemn conference. Then follows a long and earnest discussion on 'subjects.' Fairy lore, the Countess d'Aulnois, Walter

Scott, everything has been *done*.   Wanted, something new.   Required, where to find it.   The burlesque writer says he will look over his memoranda, and write.

"As it has never been made the subject of a burlesque, and therefore cannot be invidious or personal, we will suppose that Lord Byron's poem of 'Lara' is the theme hit upon by the author, and approved of by the manager.

"The exigences of modern taste and the requirements of playbills immediately suggest as a striking Christmas comic chorus sort of title, 'Right-fal-LARA-whack!'

"The original poem is, as the reader knows, a sequel to 'The Corsair,' and but a misty and imperfect one.   If anyone would read the story in its entirety, they will find it in George Sand's Venetian novel, 'L'Uscoque.'

"There being little plot and less incident in 'Lara,' the burlesque writer invents a thrilling and dramatic story, which he tells by means of contrastive and impossible characters, and in so doing exhibits a power of construction which is the nobler portion of his art.   Lara is a misanthropic hero of the true Byronic model, who holds self-communion in the picture-gallery of his lonely castle, attended by a mysterious and faithful page, known in the travesty

as Buttoni, which is, of course, burlesque Italian for
'Buttons.'   The poem runs :

> " ' In trembling pairs (alone they dared not) crawl
> The astonished slaves, and shun the fated hall ;
> The waving banner and the clapping door,
> The rustling tapestry and the echoing floor,
> The long dim shadows of surrounding trees,
> The flapping bat, the night song of the breeze ;
> Aught they behold or hear their thought appals,
> As evening saddens o'er the dark gray walls.'

" This is rendered into a troop of timid servants,
with pale cheeks and agitated knees, to whom Gatesauce, the fat cook, rushes on pale and trembling,
with white cheeks and an exaggerated nightcap :

DISHUPPA (*the scullion*). Cook, what's the matter ?
GALLOPPA (*the courier*).   Tell us, is there danger ?
SWINDELLO (*the steward*). Thy looks are blank !
JOUSCOTTA (*the groom*).   Ay, blanker than *blank*-manger !
GALLOPPA.   Stand up.   [GATESAUCE *falls on the stage.*
SWINDELLO.   He's down.
JOUSCOTTA (*assisting him to rise*). How with his weight I'm
burdened !
DISHUPPA. He can't be *down*, 'cos he's a *upper* servant !
GATESAUCE (*recovering*). Oh la !   [*Faints again.*
DISHUPPA.   Tell more.
JOUSCOTTA.   Encore.

GATESAUCE (*recovering*). You bore !   *Eau d'or !*   (*They bring
him liqueur.   He drinks and recovers.*)   My friends (*they gather round
him*), I can't !   I'll sing you what I saw.

" And a song follows, to the air of the Phantom

Chorus in 'La Sonnambula' or 'Pretty Polly Perkins of Paddington Green.'

" Buttoni is, of course, a lady, who, though she has followed Lara, disguised as an errand-boy and general servant, will not, though she love him, listen to his suit, even though he proffer marriage. As she says, she is :

" ' In form a tiger, and at heart a tigress.'

" Lara, otherwise O'Leary, reminds her of past delights :

" Remember, love, our cottage by the sea,
   Where we were happy as could mortals be,
   With toast and tarts, and shrimps and whelks for tea.
      [*Trying to put his arm round her waist. She repulses him.*

KALED. You'll take no whelks, or liberty, with me.

" At the festival in Otho's Hall there is a grand ballet, after which St. Ezzelino, the stranger, makes his first appearance, and defies Lara to mortal combat, which affords an opportunity for some smart allusions to the recent tourney between King and Heenan, much approved of by the gallery, and still more by the carefully-combed male occupants of the stalls.

" In the battle at the end of the piece, Kaled, the page, fights and conquers the entire opposing force; but, despite his or her prowess, Lara is wounded mortally. Here we must again quote from the original :

> " ' Beneath a lime, remoter from the scene,
>   Where but for him that strife had never been,
>   A breathing but devoted warrior lay :
>   'Twas Lara, bleeding fast from life away.
>   His follower once, and now his only guide,
>   Kneels Kaled, watchful o'er his welling side.
>
>   *   *   *   *   *   *
>
>   He clasps the hand that pang which would assuage,
>   And sadly smiles his thanks to that dark page,
>   Who nothing fears, nor feels, nor heeds, nor sees,
>   Save that damp brow which rests upon his knees,
>   Save that pale aspect, where the eye, though dim,
>   Held all the light that shone on earth for him.'

" This is changed to—

LARA. Kaled, I'm licked !

KALED.   And yet I threw his lunge up.

LARA (*falling*). I cannot come to time, so throw the sponge up.

KALED. Strive, sir, to rise. I'll bear thee hence.

LARA (*faintly*).   No, no !

His *strong arms* dealt me a really *Armstrong* blow.

KALED. Let me assist thee.

LARA.   Dearest ! 'tis too late ;

Like Heenan, I am now *heenan*-imate.

Enter OTHO, EZZELINO, *and all the opposing party.* KALED *again
protects* LARA. *Kills half a dozen assailants, but is at length
overpowered by numbers, and is ordered for immediate execution.*

" The poet sings :

> " ' Oh ! never yet beneath
>   The breast of man such trusty love may breathe !
>   That trying moment hath at once revealed
>   The secret long, and yet but half concealed ;
>   In baring to revive that lifeless breast,
>   Its grief seemed ended, but the sex confessed,

And life returned, and Kaled felt no shame—
What now to her was Womanhood or Fame ?'

" The burlesque author chants :

EZZELINO. The page boy lies at death. The headsman summon.
KALED (*her foot on her prostrate antagonists*). Pity the weakness
of my sex !
OMNES (*astonished*).   A woman !

" The disguised page is pardoned, Lara recovers,
every marriageable person plights his or her troth to
another, and a *finale* is sung to a popular air :

EZZELINO. Our little piece is ended,
OTHO. Your kindness, friends, we lack ;
KALED. Naught but a jest's intended,
            By Right-fal-Lara-whack !
CHORUS (*dancing and clapping their hands together on the last
syllable*). By Right-fal-Lara-whack !
LARA. And ere we drop the curtain,
KALED. Oh, say you'll all come back,
LARA. And so ensure the fortune
KALED. Of Right-fal-Lara-whack !
CHORUS. Of Right-fal-Lara-whack !

" It is these broad and over-palpable jocularities
that hit modern audiences hardest. Smart writing,
keen satire, and hard raps at social abuses, though
they look well in print and are admired of critics and
habitués, fail to elicit the loud roars of laughter that
follow an ingeniously audacious pun, or a happy
paraphrase or parody.

" With the rehearsal of the burlesque the author's

8

perplexities begin. The scenic artist wishes to introduce the limelight in a scene where it is more than usually inappropriate. Possibly he thinks the dialogue will be the brighter—it will light up the puns, and make the jokes more brilliant. The ballet-master requires to cut the story into two halves in such a place that it will be impossible to reunite the thread of interest; and last and worst difficulty of all, the performers have to be reconciled to their parts, and to the parodies allotted them.

" As with tragedy, so with burlesque.

" ' I am engaged in this theatre,' said a French tragedian, ' for tears. My speciality is tears. Unless I weep I cannot act; unless I weep the audience will not recognise me. There is not a tear in my part. I pray you, then, dear monsieur, to permit me to curse my daughter, and then subside into heart-rending sobs.'

" ' Now, my dear Mr. Charade, I must have a serious talk to you,' says the young lady who plays Kaled.

" The author moves uneasily.

" ' About the songs,' continues Mdlle. Kaled. ' I hope that I'm to have one to the air of " Ribstone Pippins "? '

" ' Well, to tell you the truth, I had intended that for Lara.'

"'Oh dear me! You surprise me. Mr. Oddjaws always has the best of everything. Last year he had "The Little Baker's Boy." It's very inconvenient to me to have to "colour" for this Caleb.'

"'Kaled.'

"'Kaliz—what d'ye call it? And "Ribstone Pippins" has such a good chorus. I think with a dance I could make it go down.'

"'No doubt you could, my dear Miss Gigwell; but——'

"'Now, I must have no "buts" about it. Either I sing "Ribstone Pippins" or you must get Miss Chillgrim to play the part. Good-morning, Mr. Charade.'

"And Miss Gigwell glides away.

"When the author informs Lara that he thinks a medley will be suited to him, that gentleman immediately breaks out with:

"'Oh, nonsense, my dear boy—nothing of the sort! "Ribstone Pippins" must be mine, or—— It has such a stunning chorus, you know, my dear boy—

"'With my
Rip-pip-pip, my rip-pip-pip,
My rip-pip-pipstone pippins,
Rip-pip-pip-pi-pip, rip-pip-pip-pi-pip-ip-pip-ip-pip,
My ribstone pip-ip-pippins.'

Oh, it's the very thing for me.'

"'I'll make a swop with you,' says the author. 'Let Miss Gigwell have "Ribstone Pippins," and you shall have "Hot Codlings."'

"'What a fellow you are! No, my dear boy; I must have it. Sooner than go without my "Ribstone Pippins," I'd go without my Christmas pudding.'

"'Or your Christmas goose,' says the author to himself, not to Mr. Oddjaws. To make which piece of esoteric satire intelligible, we must inform our readers that 'goose' is theatrical *argot* for hissing.

"The 'Ribstone Pippin' difficulty for a long time agitates the theatre. Negotiations fail, a congress is held, and eventually a compromise effected. 'Ribstone Pippins' is sung as a duet. On Boxing Night the audience demand its repetition and its re-repetition.

"'I told you how I could make "Pippins" go,' says Miss Gigwell to the author, as she receives his congratulations.

"'I was right about the "Pippins"—wasn't I?' says Mr. Oddjaws.

"'I knew "Ribstone Pippins" would be best as a duet,' says the author to his wife, as they drive home together, after the delighted lady has heard her husband called for, and seen him make his bow from the stage.

*   *   *   *   *   *

" It is understood that these pages treat of none but those actors and actresses whose calling is that of actor and actress only; that is, our types are theatrical, and nothing else. We speak only of those who embrace a hard-working and ill-paid career for the purpose of earning an honest livelihood, of following an artistic calling, or gratifying a pardonable vanity. Of the man who has emoluments or half-pay, or a rich wife or relations; or the woman to whom the stage is the mere pastime for an idle hour, a peg whereon to hang rich clothes, or a means of advertising purchasable charms, we do not speak.

" In the days of the performance of the old comedies —works whose absence from the stage we should regret the more did we not remember their utter conventionality and unnaturalness—there used to be found in most dramatic companies a short, somewhat stout, white-toothed, sweet-breathed, snub-nosed, black-eyed, broad-hipped Hebe who played the class of character called in green-room parlance ' the Chambermaid.' She possessed a good voice, could sing by ear, and had a saucy way of tossing her head that was half boyish, half hoydenish, and wholly captivating. A Chambermaid was the motive power of comedy, the female factotum or Figaro in petticoats, who advised her young mistress to oppose her father's will and to elope with the ' Captain '; who abused her old master, counselled his wife to deceive him, took guineas, and sometimes kisses, from the ‘ Captain ’—that eternal officer—behaved with hideous insincerity to all the *dramatis personæ* over the age of forty, secured to herself a competence, and all the while loved and was beloved by the Captain's own man, Mr. Tagg, the valet. The dialogue she spoke was sometimes not only broad, but coarse ; but there was a fresh, vivid humanity in her and about her. She was a high-mettled wench, with great natural wit and small education, who loved and hated with equal ardour ; in brief, she was feminine, exaggerated and natural. *Mais nous avons changé tout cela.* About the same time that the art of acting—as an art— began to be degraded, the Chambermaid gradually assumed French airs and vaudeville graces. It was as Mr. Square, the philosopher, said, ‘ in the eternal fitness of things ’ that, as our stage became a school-boy vulgarization of the Parisian theatres, that pert Betty should be transformed into *piquante* Lottee, and that the good old English oaken-staircase, candlestick-carrying, cherry-brandy sort of word ‘ Chambermaid ’ should be abandoned for ‘ soubrette.’

“ The soubrette is highly genteel. Oh ! so genteel that she has velvet ribbons at the pockets of sky-blue satin aprons, and travels over Europe in a Mechlin-lace cap the size of a crown-piece. She would not break a silver sixpence with her sweetheart ; to halve a £5 note she would consider low. She sings, too, scientifically ; and in costume, character, coquettishness, and contralto voice is a queer combination of reality and impossibility—of theatre and opera ; neither fish, flesh, fowl, nor good red herring.

" The public is indebted for the introduction of this hybrid to those women whose resources are obtained outside and not in the theatre. It is easier to find ear-rings than talent ; money will purchase ribbons by the yard, and the power of delivering smart repartee and delineating character is *not* sold at the haberdasher's ; but, as it has been already stated that this subject is forbidden, it cannot be pursued.

" With the change of feeling, taste, and fashion, the theatre—that cheap mirror with a Dutch metalled frame, that *inverts* all that it reflects—must change too. The Chambermaid is gone—gone with the oillamps, the sheet-iron thunder, and the green carpet, stowed away as useless lumber, unfit for the consideration of a speculative dealer in marine stores. The soubrette, too, is very nearly off the stage ; and we shall bear the loss of that genteel gimcrack with considerable fortitude. Those two divinities of the gallery, powers over the pit and pets of the boxes, have been eclipsed by a more vivid, more dazzling, more spangly star—the Burlesque Actress, who now rules the hours between nine and twelve p.m., as sure as legs are legs.

"The Burlesque Actress is young, elegant, and accomplished in more than the usual sense of the word. She is generally handsome, and when her features are irregular she more than atones for them by expression — expression that combines good humour, malice, intensity of feeling, Bacchante-like enjoyment, and devotion. She can sing the most difficult of Donizetti's languid, loving melodies, as well as the inimitable Mackney's ' Oh, Rosa, how I lub you ! Coodle cum !' She can warble a drawing-room ballad of the ' Daylight of the Soul ' or ' Eyes melting in Gloom ' school, or whistle ' When I was a-walking in Wiggleton Wale ' with the shrillness and correctness of a Whitechapel bird-catcher. She is as faultless on the piano as on the bones. She can waltz, polk, dance a *pas seul* or a sailor's hornpipe, La Sylphide, or the Genu-*wine* Transatlantic Cape Cod Skedaddle, with equal grace and spirit; and as for acting, she can declaim à la Phelps or Fechter ; is serious, droll ; and must play farce, tragedy, opera, comedy, melodrama, pantomime, ballet, change her costume, fight a combat, make love, poison herself, die, and take one encore for a song and another for a dance, in the short space of ten minutes.

" The young actress in possession of all these
abilities wakes up the morning after her appearance
in London to find herself famous. The men at the
clubs go mad about her. She is almost pelted with
bouquets and *billet-doux ;* enthusiasts crowd round
her cab to see her alight or waylay her in omnibuses ;
old gentlemen send her flowers, scent-bottles, ivory-
backed hair-brushes, cambric pocket-handkerchiefs,
and parasols ; matter-of-fact barristers compose verses
in her honour ; and photographers lay their cameras
at her feet. Half Aldershot comes nightly up by
train. She is a power in London, and theatrical
managers drive up to her door and bid against each
other for her services. Fortunate folks who see her
in the daytime complain ' that she dresses plainly '—
' almost shabbily '; but, then, they are not aware that
she has to keep half a dozen fatherless brothers and
sisters and an invalid mother out of her salary—
which intelligence, when known to the two or three
men who really care for her, sends them sleepless
with admiration. Here is a household fairy who can
polk, paint, make puddings, sing, sew on buttons,
turn heads and old bonnets, wear cleaned gloves,
whistle, weep, laugh, and perhaps love.

*   *   *   *   *   *

" The Stage-Manager is the man who should direct
everything behind the scenes. He should be at one

and the same time a poet, an antiquarian, and a costumier; and possess sufficient authority, from ability as well as office, to advise with a tragedian as to a disputed reading, to argue with an armourer as to the shape of a shield, or to direct a wardrobe-keeper as to the cut of a mantle. He should understand military science like a drill-sergeant, and be as capable of handling crowds and moving masses as a major-general. He should possess universal sympathies: should feel with the sublime, and have a quick perception of the ludicrous. Though unable to act himself, he should be able to teach others, and be the finger-post, guide, philosopher, and friend of every soul in a theatre, male or female, from the manager and author to the call-boy and the gas-man, from the manageress and principal soprano to the back row of the extra children's ballet and the cleaners.

" Above all, he should be endowed with a perfect command of his own temper, and the power of conciliating the temper of others. The art of stage-management consists chiefly in a trick of manner that reconciles the collision of opposing personal vanities.

" That is what he should be; what he is is a very different affair.

" Some Stage-Managers are appointed to their office for curious reasons : because they have gray hair, or a fatherly-looking stomach, or because they once wrote a piece which failed, or because they know nothing of stage business, or because they know nothing *but* stage business, or because they are deferential, or because they have a large family, or because they wear a heavy gold watch and chain, or because they knew the late Charles Kemble, or any other good theatrical reason.

" One man, who for many years was Stage-Manager of the patent theatres—a position for which he was totally unqualified—was appointed solely because he was well acquainted with the hours at which the coaches started from one town to another. . . .

" Then there is the Cruel Stage-Manager, who hates everybody in the theatre and out of it, and who abuses his power in the largest spirit of the smallest tyranny, and, while he fawns on public favourites, is the bane of the actors of inferior parts, and the terror of the ballet. If a poor girl be one minute late by the Cruel Stage-Manager's infallible chronometer (which, with the green-room clock, he always keeps five minutes before the Horse Guards), he directs the Prompter to fine her—' Fine her, fine her, Brooks !'—and the girl, who walks twenty miles a day, and, being a clever dancer, earns eighteen shillings a week, is mulcted of one shilling. . . .

" The Affectionate Stage-Manager is a flint-musket of a different bore. He lives but to employ adjectives agreeable to his hearers, and is of an incompetency compared to which ordinary inability soars to genius. With him every male is his ' dear boy,' every woman his ' darling child,' every manager ' a splendid fellow,' every actor ' a first-rate man,' every actress ' a charming creature,' every supernumerary ' a good chap,' and the world in general a Bower of Bliss and Home of Happiness. Whatever is is best, and his *bonhomie* is supposed by actors—an easily-persuaded and credulous race—to spring from a kind heart, whereas it is only pure, simple, unadulterated blarney. He could not live by his ability, so he ekes out his thin, weak, conventional knowledge with a mouthful of tender words.

" The Traditional Stage-Manager is the man who knew Charles Kemble, and whose knowledge—dramatic, artistic, literary, and general—ends there. To the stupidity of this creature no tongue could do justice; to the density of his intellectual powers lignum-vitæ is as a transparent soap-bubble.

" The Muddle-headed Stage-Manager is a donkey of another colour. He will listen to every suggestion and understand none. In the inmost recesses of that cerebral pulp which in his skull does duty for brain, he has a confused notion that the Act of Parliament forbidding marriage with a deceased wife's sister somehow or other affects the probability of the plot

of ' Hamlet.' Under his auspices—and be it always remembered that the deeper his incapacity the prouder he
is of his ' experience '—rehearsals progress but slowly.

*   *   *   *   *   *

" The Scene-painter is usually one of the pleasantest
men in the theatre. King in his snug painting-room,
high above the stage, he recks not of the whirl of
passions and vanities below. It is a great power the
theatrical Scene-painter holds between his pliant
thumb and fingers. He copies Nature on a large
scale. It must be high delight to look upon a broad,
flat, white surface, and choose whether it shall be
converted into an Emir's palace, all pillars, curtains,
gold tassels, fringes, and polished-mirror marble floor,
the hot sun shining on a fountain in the distance; or
into an Alpine gorge, with blocks of snow-covered
stone and funereal fir-trees, with plains of ice conducting to a frosty horizon; or into a magician's
cavern, where the dark rocks, cut in fantastic forms,
loom into sight in the shape of squatting demons,
petrified giants, and ghostly vertebræ of huge and
hideous reptiles; or into a sparkling, rippling sea,
with but one white speck of sail between it and the
clear dome of blue sky above it. These are great
privileges. But the great charm of the Scene-painter's
life is to take off his well-cut, well-brushed garments,
and don his painting suit; then he revels in dirt and

daubs and spots, that are of his clothes, and not of him. How? That very faultlessly got-up gentleman, who just now asked for letters in the hall; that exquisite in the black frock-coat, pearl-coloured trousers, fashionable hat, and perfect boots—can he be this canvassy creature in a wideawake which a thriving farmer would be ashamed to see upon his scarecrow? That dirty jacket, those grimy trousers! Is it a beggar who has made himself a suit out of old sail-cloth? No! It is an artistic gentleman, who owns a villa in the neighbourhood of Hampstead, who has choice wines in his cellar, and is a captain of Volunteers. These are his working clothes.

" In these present days of scenic display, when even no poor ghost can walk undisturbed by scientific satellites, lime-lights, mirrors, and the like, the Scene-painter is a far more important person in a theatre than the Tragedian—not that the bearing of those gentlemen would impress a stranger with the fact—for by so much as the Tragedian is pompous, blatant, and assuming, the Scene-painter is easy, natural, and polite. Perhaps the Tragedian takes his tone from the brigand-chiefs and aspiring patriots whose characters he assumes; and the Scene-painter, with his keen eye for the glories of colour and knowledge of the combinations of natural beauty, knows how to blend himself harmoniously.

" The Stage Carpenter is a singular creature. He is the victim of a delusion, by which he is bound hand, and foot, and brain. It is a belief, as deeply rooted in his mind as is his two-foot rule inserted in his trousers-pocket, that while he is in the theatre he is ' at work.' If he is what, in theatrical parlance, is termed a ' day man,' he reaches the theatre at a quarter to ten if the rehearsal be at ten, at a quarter to eleven if the rehearsal be at eleven, at a quarter to twelve if the rehearsal be at twelve, and so on. Once in the theatre, his first proceeding is to hide himself in the scene-dock, where nobody can find him. He then takes off his coat, puts on his ' working ' canvas-jacket, sticks a hammer in his girdle or apron pistol-wise—after the fashion of bold buccaneers in penny plates—uses his coat-sleeve as a pocket-handkerchief, sits down in a corner and goes to sleep. And here commences his delusion. It is his firm belief that while he has on his canvas-jacket and his hammer stuck into his girdle that he is hard at work—nay, perspiring copiously. He will even carry this delusion out so far as to wake up after an hour and a half's nap and feel fatigued, so much so as to be compelled to adjourn to the nearest public-house and recruit exhausted nature with half a pint—for he is also the victim of half a pint, or, rather, the victim of a pint and a half, not to say two gallons—

and in three days, when not an interval of labour, not the screwing out of an old nail from a rusty hinge, has occurred to vary the tedious monotony of slumber, he will declaim in the taproom on the wrongs of the working man and the tyranny of employers. It has been said by a popular novelist of the day that no set of men can idle as nautical men can. From this observation it is evident that the servants of a theatre have never passed under that popular novelist's eye.

" The Stage Carpenter works but once a year—for the production of the pantomime—and then he works *con amore ;* for during the run of the pantomime the genius of stage carpentry is properly estimated, and authors, actors, composers, musicians, and such mere idlers sink into their proper insignificance.

" The Property Man—*i.e.*, the man who looks after the chairs and tables and things movable by hand, and who manufactures the sheep, fish, carrots, and huge chamber-candlesticks used in the pantomime— is a mysterious mechanic, whose habits are unclean, predatory, and mendacious. His complexion is a singular compound of the perspiration of the Mid-summer before last with the dust of the preceding Christmas. Dust rests upon his eyelashes as moss rests on the boughs of an old tree. If ever he wash himself—which is doubtful, save on his wedding-day —his ablutions are made in the glue-pot. He is so

sticky that, were he to lean against a wall, portions
of his garments would adhere to it when he sum-
moned up sufficient energy to walk away. Why does
this gifted getter-up of gnomes, salamanders, dragons'
heads, and fairies' wings abjure cold water and ignore
all crystal streams, save the pantomime fountains
framed of wire, blue gauze, white Dutch metal, and
spangles ? Would his fingers lose their cunning if
occasionally polluted by the use of soap? his tongue
its power of ready excuse, or his brain its in-
ventive faculty, if fluid touched his external man ?
The cause of this dramatico-mechanico-hydrophobia
is inexplicable, and ever must remain a mystery, to
be solved only by a treacherous member of the craft,
who, converted to cleanliness by a Turkish bath, shall
renounce the property-room and divulge its secrets.
The Property Man has the same peculiarity as the
oldest inhabitant—he never remembers anything ;
nor will he, no matter how familiar the object, confess
that he has ever seen a specimen, or that it is pro-
curable, save by the expense of large quantities of
money, time, difficulty, and danger.

*   *   *   *   *   *

" But the limit of our space is near, and there are
many other specimens that must be left undescribed.
There is the Costumier, who is a sort of cross-legged
mixture of milliner and magician, and who thinks

9

that the north star would shine the brighter if thickly spangled. There is the Call-boy, a clever imp of mischief, who recognises no aristocracy but that of talent, and no talent but that of the actor. There are the Wig-makers—hold ! The mere English word requires an apology. If tailors are Costumiers, wig-makers must be Perruquiers, who weave dead men's hair into false scalps, and brush out cataracts of blonde ringlets without a thought of the beauty of the soil on which they grew. The rank grass that grows in churchyards has been called ' the uncut hair of graves.' Does no sexton association occur to the wig-maker as he plaits, and weaves, and oils, and curls the terribly human-looking silk ? It is to be supposed not. Custom hath made it in him a property of greasiness.

" Then there is the Gasman, who, though his trade be odorous, manages to keep a clean face and hands. He runs about the theatre, nimbly correcting cross-grained taps and bursting batwings with his pliant pincers. Then there is the Hall Porter, who is invariably old ; is an Irishman, and has served in the Peninsula in an Irish regiment, and fought at Waterloo, and whose jaws have a grim rigidity, suggestive of barrack-life ; whose speech is a stiff civility, redolent of discipline, and whose gray, rat-like whiskers are perfumed with whisky. There is the

Gentlemen's Dresser, who has also been a soldier; who informs the actors that when he was in the marines 'he were off the Gold Coast in the *Devastator*, and they had no shoes on them, sir; and Captain Dawbarn, as was the captain, was an awful severe man, and drink—oh, how he did drink! He says to us one day on parade, "You marines," he says, "I'll work you down to ile"; and he nearly did, and he would have been broke only he died off Sumatra, thank goodness! for if ever there was a beast he was.' Time works wonders, and the warrior mariner has tamed down into a dramatic valet, and hooks and eyes doublets, and pulls off yellow boots, as deftly as he used to polish bayonets and pipeclay belts.

" The Ladies' Dresser has usually seen better days, and is of the same ascetic, rusty, musty type as the pew-opener at a church, with perhaps a sprinkling more dust. She is invariably a widow, and her late husband was either the greatest wretch on record or the most perfect of his gay, perfidious sex. Last of all there is the Supernumerary—a dreadful trade, strange to say, pursued only by men and boys with thin legs. A muscular Supernumerary is a phenomenon that has never been known to occur even in the experience of the oldest, most experienced, and stupidest of Stage-Managers.

" There are many other types of theatrical character. . . . To the outer world theatrical life is a deep, dark well, whose troubled waters are much feared and little understood; but Truth lived in a well, and a large amount of Truth and Goodness dwells in the Theatre, and few looking at the green froth of vanity that stagnates on its surface would guess the richness of the pearls that lie beneath.

" 'That some very bad man should want something to which he has no right—a kingdom, duchy, throne, estate, title, house, lady, watch, soup-ladle, or leg of mutton—is. the starting-point of every tragedy or drama; and without a villain—and the worse he is the better—no tragedy or drama could get on. He is as fuel to the steamboat; and not only fuel, but machinery, paddle-wheels, wind and water.

" 'These despotic Dukes, malevolent Marquises, and bad Barons in the illogical world behind the scenes (which, if remarkable for nothing else, would be so for false classification) are called 'heavy' parts, and are played by 'heavy men.' It must be understood that the word 'heavy' has no avoirdupois signification; on the contrary, the Heavy Man is generally slight and slender. Villains should be thin; no audience would believe in a fat murderer. The stage arbitrarily presumes a physical organization of its own, totally independent of the laws of nature. In theatrical pathology, remorse absorbs all the adipose matter in the bodies of bad men. The worse the heart, the more active the secretions. The word ' heavy ' is doubtless intended to express the weight on the spirits of the auditors of the villain's presence, appearance, conversation, and soliloquies.

" For he is a dreadful fellow to soliloquize, is the Heavy Man! No sooner has the meek old noble whom he means to murder, or the high-spirited heir whom he intends to dispossess of his broad lands, or the amiable heroine he destines for a fate worse than death, gone off to their respective towers, bowers, or rendezvous, than he advances to the front, plants his right toe between the two centre footlights, and, contracting his eyebrows and clenching his fist —that fist already red with the blood of a twin-brother—looks at the audience as if he said: ' *You*, at least, cannot escape me; you have paid your shillings at the door; miserable miscreants, *you* are in my power, and *shall* hear me!' He then, after rolling his eyes, carefully informs his hearers, in tones that must disturb the meek old Baron on his couch, the high-spirited heir at his rendezvous a mile off, and the amiable heroine at her latticed casement, that he considers parricide rather a creditable thing than otherwise if a man be urged to it by an un-governable temper, a father's rebuke, an impatient thirst for gold, or the desire of vengeance. According to him, vengeance is the chief object of a man's life; and he enlarges on this delightful subject until the Gallery is rapt with admiration, the Boxes considerably bored, and a stout old lady in the Pit—Mr. Arthur Sketchley's friend, Mrs. Brown, perhaps—exclaims in a Camberwell gurgle: 'Oh, the wretch!'

" With an audience, villains are an acquired taste, and the article depends on locality. There are apricots and nectarines for Covent Garden Market, and pickled whelks for the south side of the river Thames; so there are elegant brigands, murderous marquises, and fascinating forgers, for the postal district marked W., and absconding stewards and pirate captains for that marked S.

" Among many other things dramatic which we owe to the French—or, rather, to the Parisians, for there are two nations, the Parisians and the French—we are indebted for the cool, fashionable villain, the villain *à la vanille*, the refrigerated rascal, whose costume is confined to the coats and trousers of modern days, and whose unamiable weaknesses are francs and females. This is the 'mildest-mannered man' that ever cut throat in kid gloves. He is all diamond studs and devildom, and finishes an act by saying in a silvery tone, ' Having poisoned my mother and stabbed my sister to the heart I will bathe, and then to breakfast with the Marchesa.'

"One of the favourite fopperies of the High Life Heavy part is a coat elaborately trimmed with fur. It would seem as if, this garment being in his confidence, and knowing all his villainies, the knotted and combined locks of the fur parted, and each particular hair did stand on end like quills upon the fretful porcupine, aghast at the terrible complications of his guilt. The rose-scented ruffian is always an accomplished duellist, a dead shot, and a crack swordsman, and usually brings upon himself his inevitable end by overdoing his rascality. There should be limits to all things, even to stage villainy.

" With the pickled-whelk class of audiences the Heavy Man's lapses from the right path are invariably more innocent than in the arena visited by opera-cloak and fan ; but they are more openly avowed and more coarsely delineated. The absconding steward or the rascally lawyer—two favourite varieties of scoundrel east of Temple Bar and south of Waterloo Bridge—have in their marble hearts no spot of love. They care not for the old farmer's daughter or the honest cotter's wife. They aspire, respire, and perspire, but for GOLD ! Forged wills, fabricated codicils, hidden mortgage deeds, and unexpected parchments are the tools with which they work.

They are invariably cowards, and tremble like aspen-leaves when an honest tar only threatens to 'keel-haul' them. Keel-hauling, by the way, although a mode of punishment long since abolished in the British navy, is constantly alluded to by the theatrical British tar. When the false steward or corrupt lawyer consorts with thieves, highwaymen, smugglers, coiners, and the like, he is invariably treated by them with the greatest contempt. He, on the contrary, is always civil and apologetic, even to the most abandoned outlaw, whom he addresses as ' Mister.'

"' Don't " mister " me!' thunders out the Pirate Captain. ' Death's head and cross-bones ! but you make me feel as if a cr-r-rawling snake were twining his slimy folds around me! My name is Ruthven Rudderblood, captain of the *Ocean Helldog.* Yonder lies my bark, and never has this hand failed a friend in guilt, or spared a foe when on his knees for mercy !'

* * * * * *

" Character parts are those that do not positively belong to any of the usually recognised lines of business. Ruffians with dialects, such as broken-hearted farm-labourers, who object to work, and set fire to ricks because they are not kept sumptuously at the parish expense, or idiots, who say cleverer things than the people presumed to have possession of their intellectual faculties. The marked and singular personages found in dramas adapted from popular novels, and comic villains, belong to this category. They are too exceptional to require any detailed description.

*   *   *   *   *   *

" A crowd of well-dressed gazers; a sound of music, low, languid, and sensual; a swell of harmony, celestial in the pagan sense of the word, melting, luxurious, passionate, emasculating, flooding the senses with emotions, no single note appealing to the intellect—music of the syrens, not of the spheres. The curtain rises cumbrously: a cool, sparkling, stalactite, coral grot is disclosed to view—a sub-aqueous retreat, half cavern on the coast, half barley-sugar temple—the Abode of the Fairy Corallina, and Haunt of the Nymphs of the Lurley.

" The music undulates, swells, grows louder, louder yet, fills the arena, and then changes its character with a crash that seems to shake the glittering crystals sparkling in the magic rocks.

" Down four different coral banks four different troops of fairies enter, dancing joyously. Their eyes, arms, feet, and figures glisten with shining corals, and their hair is bound with seaweeds. They are mermaids with human continuations to their figures —living mermaids, whose glances reflect the many

lights thrown on them, whose white arms bear coral-
branches, whose bosoms heave and whose nostrils
tremble with the execution of the dance.   They form
bowers with their coral garlands; triumphal arches,
of which their arms are pillars, and the bent garlands
the dome; then they separate to meet again, and meet
again to separate.   Tiny fairies appear in the far-off
alcoves and snowy caves. . . . The music changes
again, and becomes noisy and billowy.   The nymphs
leave off dancing and throw up their arms, then run
from side to side, and by feature and gesticulations
express—something, but what no mortal conundrum-
guesser could ever divine.

" But the answer to it is that there is a storm
above, and they hear the wrecking of a vessel.

" Crash, smash music, lifted arms, fingers pointed,
hurry, scurry, and alarm; and down at the back falls
a spar, a rope, and a shipwrecked mariner pendant
therefrom.   The shipwrecked mariner falls upon the
stage in the whitest of shirts and the most graceful of
attitudes.

" There is dreadful consternation among the fairy
Lurleybergians, who have been brought up in the
strictest submarine seclusion and the coral-grottiest
horror of a man; they avert their faces and extend
the palms of their hands, as in horror and disgust.
They would fly and leave him to his fate; but the

Queen signifies, by stamping her foot and tapping her bosom, that the rights of hospitality are sacred. She desires that the drowned mariner be succoured, and herself approaches him, looks on him, and falls in love with him that moment!

" Corallina's penchant for the objectionable stranger being obvious, the nymphs give him to drink from crystal streams, using shells instead of saucers; and thus the mariner is, as it were, weaned from his mortality.

" No sooner does the shipwrecked mariner recover and express his convalescence by two pirouettes and an entrechat, than everything goes wrong in Coral-grottia. Sirena, a nymph of impressionable nature, dares to rival Corallina; the young mariner is impulsive and inconstant, and the feature of the evening is a 'Grand Pas de Trois de Jalousie.' It is never known how matters are ultimately made up, but that is of no consequence. The shipwrecked mariner becomes a river-god by the simple process of changing his dress, and dances—ugh! how he dances! He is an ugly old man, with naked, skinny arms, and a wig and a common French face of the common French ugliness, and he grins as if he felt himself the young Apollo. Out on all *male* operatic dancers! for they are an abomination and an eyesore.

" A ballet is a wonderful conglomeration of grace

and nonsense, and, it is to be presumed, is concocted
for the purpose of puzzling as well as of delighting
the outer world. Much has been said and written
of the dancers who form what is called in the play-
bills the Corps de Ballet. The stories told of
them are more or less true, and very much less than
more.

"Some say the members of the Corps de Ballet are
in the habit of dining with dukes daily; of living at
the rate of about £1,000 per diem; of having sets of
diamonds for every week in the year; two broughams,
four footmen, three lady's-maids, and a boudoir of
white velvet and lilac satin, with mother-of-pearl furniture, and a solid silver fireplace with a gold fender
and fireirons *en suite*. Others protest that she is
the possessor of rather more good qualities than all
the famed heroines of ancient or modern times:
rather prefers linsey-wolsey to satin; thinks porter a
nicer drink than champagne; is never irritable with
her father, mother, or the nine brothers and sisters
whom she supports by her earnings; has not in her
composition one particle of envy, hatred, malice, or
uncharitableness; and is exactly like those most impossible and disagreeable persons—the heroines of
small novels and the 'ideals' of lads of sixteen.

"This last opinion is the sentimental one circulated
by those idiotic men who go about calling themselves

'friends of dramatic art,' and who, by asseverating that everything and everybody connected with a theatre is best, more best, and most best, do the calling they say that they admire more real injury than the attacks of silly, conscientious, and ignorant fanatics. They prove too much with their sham chivalry, these gushing *gobemouches*.

"There are ladies of the ballet who have broughams though they do not dine with dukes daily. There are ladies of the ballet who have fine clothes, equipage, and luxury, for reasons connected with anything but merit.

"But these gorgeous creatures are, happily, but few. The majority of them live by the industry of their feet and fingers. Dancing and the needle is their sole support, and their virtues are as many and their faults as many, their goodness and their foibles as oddly mixed together, as in others of their sex of the same age and station, and are worthy as much honour, pity, consideration, and reproof. . . . Theirs is not a luxurious life; it is not sensual. It is laborious, unpleasant, comfortless, wet, sloppy, and sore-footed. Its monotony is seldom broken except by the happy intervals when a piece has a 'long run,' and there are no rehearsals. But this is but a poor compensation for the terrible amount of fatigue and danger incurred at Christmas for the gratification of ardent-minded scene-painters, money-loving managers, and a sensation and splendour loving public.

" The transformation-scene—an ingenious piece of cruelty introduced some ten or fifteen years ago—is a pleasure to the audience, but death to the ballet. The poor, pale girl is swung up to terrific heights, imprisoned in and upon iron wires, dazzled by rows of hot flaming gas close to her eyes, and choked by the smoke of coloured fires. Sometimes the silver-robed victim faints or goes into hysterics, and so incurs the odium of affectation. The scene-painter is relentless, the stage-manager is relentless, and the manager must make a fortune speedily. ' Hoist 'em up, carpenters!'—fill their minds with fear, their lungs with foul vapour. They are young and strong ; and it won't kill 'em, unless, indeed, a rope break or a wire give way ; and if so, the spirited and enterprising lessee will behave with that accustomed liberality which has ever characterized, etc., etc. He will bury the girl at his own expense, and for the parents' tears, they may be d——d—with a £5 note. Against all this the ballet feel an enormous pleasure in the exercise of their calling. While dancing they are happy."

Comment on the foregoing sketches is needless. Every line is instinct with truth ; and it is very pleasant to note how jealous Robertson was for the honour of the profession that had for so many years used him badly. He could put his finger on all its weak spots, he loved to ridicule its foibles ; but for its artistic value, and the reputations of those who in all its branches, low or high, worthily worked in it, he entertained the most intense regard and respect. If a set of similar types, dealing with the high-class theatrical productions of to-day, were written, we should see how much he did to eradicate the tawdriness and the conventions of thirty years ago.

CHAPTER III.

THE time for a change in Robertson's fortunes at
length arrived. The enormous popularity that had
deservedly attended Sothern's remarkable impersonation of "Lord Dundreary" at the Haymarket had
begun to wane, and the comedian was anxiously
looking out for a new piece. Always imbued with
the idea that tragedy rather than comedy was his
forte, he wished to appear in one of a serious
type; but his friends advised him that, for the present, he could only be accepted as a "character"
actor; and it was not until Robertson appeared with
his delightful version of "Sullivan," entitled "David
Garrick," that a happy compromise was effected.
Sothern expected to make an enormous success out
of the opportunities for earnest acting that the first
and third acts afforded, and his well-wishers felt
certain that he would do wonders with the sub-

sequently world-famous scene of simulated intoxication.

A note on the origin of a play that is as popular
to-day as when it was first produced, and which
seems likely to hold the stage for many years to
come, will not be out of place here; and in this connection we cannot do better than quote Mr. Moy
Thomas.

"The play," says that authority, "is an acknowledged version of De Melesville's 'Sullivan,' one of
a long series of dramas turning upon the same idea,
which was described by Théophile Gautier as 'the
everlasting story of Garrick, Talma, or Kean curing
some foolish girl of a passion for them as actors by
exhibiting themselves in private life under the most
repulsive conditions.' This description occurs in a
criticism by Gautier in 1842 on a vaudeville called
'Le Docteur Robin,' which happens to be the original
of the little piece called 'Doctor Davy,' in which Mr.
Hermann Vezin has won renown. Gautier further
tells us that this piece was based on a story by his
friend and comrade of the famous 'Gilet-rouge'
fraternity, Joseph Bouchardy, and that seven or
eight playwrights had at that time already laid their
hands upon it. We have been at some pains to trace
the story here referred to, and have found it in a
novelette entitled 'Garrick Médecin,' published in

Paris in an obscure weekly paper called *Le Monde Dramatique*, in April, 1836. Somewhere about the same time M. Fournier produced a one-act piece called 'Tiridate,' which is founded on the same notion, the only difference being that in this case it is not an actor, but an actress, who, at the sacrifice of dignity and personal inclinations, undertakes the weaning process. It was in this piece that Mr. Charles Reade found the substance of his novelette and play entitled 'Art,' wherein Mrs. Stirling has so often played the part of the heroine, Mrs. Bracegirdle. Several other versions of 'Tiridate' hold the stage, thanks to the energies of Mrs. John Wood, Miss Geneviève Ward, and other impersonators of the heroine; and traces, more or less distinct, of the dramatic idea worked out in 'Garrick Médecin' are to be found in numerous modern pieces. It has, we are aware, been said that 'Sullivan,' the direct original of 'David Garrick,' was itself merely a translation of a German play; but in this there is, we believe, some confusion of fact. The German play referred to is probably Deinhardstein's 'Garrick in Bristol.' Of this piece we are not able, unfortunately, to give any account; but it is certain that there is an acknowledged translation of Melesville's 'Sullivan' by the dramatist Edward Jermann, which is well known on the German stage—a fact which

would be hardly possible if ' Sullivan ' had been only
a Frenchman's version of a German play."

It was through his old schoolfellow and Robertson's stanch friend, Charles Millward, that Sothern
heard of the existence of " David Garrick "—and he
at once desired to read it.   But, alas for our luckless
author! the piece was held in bond by Mr. Lacy for the
magnificent sum of ten pounds !   On hearing of this
dilemma, the ever open-handed, open-hearted Sothern
at once produced the money, and at his chambers in
Regent Street the play was read to him by its
nervous, anxious writer.   Nothing could be more
satisfactory.   Sothern was delighted with the idea of
playing Garrick ;   Buckstone, who was present,
thought he could make a success of Squire Chevy ;
and when Robertson wended his happy steps home-
wards he had a cheque for £50 in his pocket,
and the promise of handsome royalties whenever
the piece should be played at the Haymarket or elsewhere.

Prior to its production in London, " David Garrick " was tentatively produced at the Prince of
Wales's Theatre, Birmingham, with Miss Edith Stuart
as Ada Ingot, Mr. G. K. Maskell as Squire Chevy, and
Mr. Bellair as Simon Ingot.   After the performance
Sothern, who was most keenly anxious about his new
part, and never satisfied with his own acting, em-

phatically declared that the whole thing was a failure, and, as far as he was concerned, would never be heard of again. Luckily, his own judgment was overruled by that of his friends and advisers, and, as every play-goer knows, Garrick became one of the most success-ful of his impersonations. No doubt the wonderful drunken scene, clever in its conception and perfect in its detail, was the great feature of the piece ; but though some critics took exception to his acting in the love-scenes with Ada Ingot, he gained in them a multitude of admirers. Generally willing to accept the verdict of the press, Sothern was always rather sore with regard to this alleged defect in his perform-ance, and on one occasion, when, on his benefit-night in a provincial town, he made one of those little before-the-curtain speeches for which he was famous, he said : " The local critics have unanimously de-clared that, unfortunately for my career as an actor, my voice is wholly unsuited to ' love-making.' With some compunction, and with my hand appropriately placed on my heart, I should like to inform those gentlemen that, following in private life that most agreeable of pursuits, I find that *I get on as well as most people.*"*

When " David Garrick " was first produced at

* *Vide* " A Memoir of E. A. Sothern," by T. Edgar Pember-ton.

the Haymarket, Sothern (still thinking that he had made a failure) generously declared that the piece was saved by the exquisite acting of Miss Nellie Moore in the character of Ada Ingot; but long after that charming young actress was dead, he continued to play Garrick to crowded and enthusiastic audiences in London, in all the large provincial towns of England, Scotland, and Ireland, and in America.

To-day the part is honourably identified with the name of Mr. Charles Wyndham, who has gone still further, and, with the most gratifying and extraordinary success, has played it in the German language at Berlin, St. Petersburg, and Moscow.

Robertson had unlimited faith in the pretty love-story that forms the chief theme of " David Garrick"; and he wrote it in narrative as well as in dramatic form, but (for reasons that are only too apparent) the novel did not find a publisher until the success of the play had made the name of its author famous. It appeared in March, 1865, and contained the following graceful dedication:

" MY DEAR SOTHERN,

" I dedicate this little book to you for reasons which will be obvious to those readers who do me the honour to peruse the preface. Though the offering be small, it is made with as much kindly feeling as if the matter contained in this single volume were as weighty and well arranged as the contents of a large dictionary.

"Accept it then, my dear Sothern, with all its faults, though they are neither few nor far between ; a circumstance which should not surprise you when you remember that it is the work of

" Your very sincere friend,

" THE AUTHOR."

In the preface, Robertson tells, as follows, the story of the origin of the play, as far as it concerned him :

" Having seen the drama of ' Sullivan ' acted by a company of French comedians at the St. James's Theatre, I was struck by the compactness of its story, its contrast of character, and dramatic effect. Its moral was good and wholesome, and the piece was entirely free from that objectionable element which, though acceptable to a French audience, is, happily, exactly the reverse with an English one. I adapted ' Sullivan,' and christened it ' David Garrick ' for these reasons :

" Garrick was a great actor ; he had been dead a century, had no living descendants, and his name was public property. He was much admired ; his impressionability, versatility, and, above all, his wonderful impersonation of drunkenness, marked him out as the proper hero of the tale.

" 'The next step was to submit the drama to several managers of theatres and to several actors.   Each and all of these gentlemen declared that the piece—when produced—would be a failure.   For about seven years the manuscript slumbered in a drawer ; until, in the course of a casual conversation, I happened to mention the plot of the play to Mr. Sothern. He was struck with it as I had been, in particular with the fact of Garrick, who was so estimable a man in the private relations of life, refusing to take advantage of the affections of an heiress, and advising her return to her father.   The admirable acting of Mr. Sothern, and of the members of the Haymarket company, made the piece a success ; and its reception in town and country has falsified the predictions of the managers and actors to whom it had been previously submitted.

" Let me here say that, though the incidents of this little book are not in accordance with biographical and historical fact, they are not for that reason untrue.   They might have happened.   The real, actual Mr. David Garrick was not married until the year 1749.   Whatever adventures may have occurred to him before that time are a legitimate theme for speculation ; and the novelist may claim his privilege."

The novel follows very closely the lines of the play; but in several instances the names are different. Squire Chevy figures as Mr. Robert Raubreyne; Alderman Ingot is Alderman Trawley; and a Lady Shendryn (the name, it will be remembered, was again used by Robertson in " Ours ") is introduced as Ada's great-aunt and chaperone in society. Of course the story (it is nowadays unknown, and we may therefore be pardoned for quoting from it) gives scope for an abundance of descriptive matter. The fatal night on which Ada first saw Garrick on the stage is thus graphically described :

" The playhouse was full, and the conversation of the patrons of the pit was coarse ; but it was a coarse age, and the pit critics would have done well to imitate the decorous silence of the occupants of the footman's gallery. Ada glanced round the house ; saw its tawdry decorations—a badly lighted platform, a large curtain of dirty green, a candle-snuffer going his greasy rounds, the people of fashion in the neighbouring boxes—and heard a roar of exultation from the gallery at the sight of some men who, with musical instruments in their hands, seemed to emerge from the earth beneath the platform. Her eyelids fell ; if this were a playhouse, it was not a playhouse that the expression of her face had seemed to seek."

" Hamlet " was, as we all know, the play of the

evening ; and the following was the cast of the characters :

Hamlet - - - - -	Mr. Garrick.
Ghost - - - - - -	Mr. Delane.
Claudius - - - - - -	Mr. Ryan.
Laertes - - - - - -	Mr. Hallam.
Horatio - - - - -	Mr. Havard.
Polonius - - - - -	Mr. Taswell.
Osric - - - - - -	Mr. Neale.
Guildenstern - - - -	Mr. Green.
Rosencrantz - - - - -	Mr. Yates.
Gravedigger - - -	Mr. Macklin.
Queen - - - -	Mistress Pritchard.
Ophelia - - - -	Mistress Clive.

" ' Nosey !' shouted a man in the gallery.

" ' Play up !' screamed another.

" ' Catgut !' yelled a third.

" And fifty pair of lips began to whistle ; and the men who had emerged from the earth with the musical instruments began to play.

" Suddenly it grew dark upon the platform, and Ada was startled by the dead silence that followed the cessation of the music. The green curtain was drawn up, and discovered a number of old and young beaux seated at the side of the stage, holding their canes and snuff-boxes in the most approved fashion ; for it was the custom of those days, not only for gentlemen to frequent the side-scenes regularly, but for them to be accommodated with chairs upon the stage, to the inconvenience of the actors and the disillusion of the auditors. Romeo and Juliet plighted their vows amid a swarm of wide-skirted, spindle-shanked macaroni; Iago soliloquized aloud with a spectator on either side of him, and then picked his way off that he might not tread upon diamond buckles and patrician toes. Nor was this the only nuisance, for these fine gentry would sometimes show themselves at the wings, speak out in tones as audible as the actors, and walk about to exchange snuff, compare the cut of a ring or the pattern of a steinkirk, while some necessary question of the play was being acted out by the performers, and thought out by the audience.

"No sooner did Mr. Delane—an actor of fine figure and dignified presence—stalk solemnly upon the stage as the Ghost, than the attention of Ada was riveted. A new feeling seemed to rush into her heart and mind; her eyes dilated as though to drink in the darkness of the space before her. When the scene ended, she gave a sigh of relief; the tension on her nerves had been too strong, and she was pleased to see the stage grow lighter, and to hear the sound of drum and trumpet.

"It was her first play.

"There was high expectation in the front of the house, and even a movement and a flutter among the fine gentlemen seated on the stage, as the second scene was disclosed to view, and Taswell as Polonius, and Ryan and Mrs. Pritchard as the King and Queen, marched statelily on, and the playhouse shook with applause as the new Hamlet—Mr. Garrick— made his dejected, melancholy entrance.

" Mr. David Garrick was a small, handsomely-formed man, of a singularly graceful deportment. He was apparently made up of sympathy; his voice was so flexible and well modulated that it charmed the ears of listeners with a sound as of a slowly rushing brook. The expression of his features varied with every line he spoke, and this without mechanical trick or intentional art, but as if his apt, elastic features followed the workings of his mind. His face *rippled* with thought; and his quickly-moving brow, and black, far-darting eyes, commanded his hearers as completely as they dominated his plastic mouth and restless nostrils.

" At the end of the second act Mr. Garrick walked impatiently to his dressing-room, and threw himself into a chair. He was ill-tempered, vexed, irritated, mortified, but not so much as to forget to look into his mirror, to note the expression of his face under these feelings, and register it in his memory."

Then follows an account of how a certain Mr. Smirker (" one of those men who make capital of knowing theatrical celebrities; who lived to admire and to praise, and was a sort of dramatic ivy or artistic creeping-plant") visited the dissatisfied actor's dressing-room, accompanied by the objectionable Mr. Robert Raubreyne ; and the reader is taken on to the account of the third act, in which :

" Again Mr. Garrick tried his utmost to arouse the lethargic sympathies of his audience. He recited the speech on suicide, and obtained some little applause, but still he thought his hearers cold and unwilling ; this roused him to fresh exertions, and he resolved to *force* them to acknowledge the power of his genius. The scene with Ophelia, his instructions to the players, and observations on the play delivered, the audience were silent as if a spell hung over them.

" When the conscience-stricken Claudius rose from his throne, and called for ' lights,' Garrick sprang from the stage, and cried exultantly :

> " ' Why, let the stricken deer go weep,
>   The hart ungallèd play;
>   For some must watch, while some must sleep;
>   So runs the world away,'

and rounds of acclamation followed. At this moment the actor caught sight of the face of a young lady ; she was leaning over her box, her folded hands clasped tightly to her breast, her brow contracted, and her lips apart. Their eyes met, and for some seconds they looked into each other's minds. A current of electric sympathy shot from one to the other ; they were not in Drury Lane playhouse, but far above in cloudland ; they were not surrounded by beaux and reigning toasts, but alone in an ideal world. Though there was space between them, they met, pulse to pulse and heart to heart."

The story goes on in much the same way as the play, except that Alderman Trawley (the Alderman Ingot of the stage) does not ask Mr. Garrick to call upon him, but presents himself at the actor's rooms in Southampton Street, Strand. Here Garrick, in his dressing-gown and nightcap (by the way, one of the characters in the book has said of him that " he would be a great player if he would but learn to stand still," which strikes one as a thoroughly Robertsonian piece of criticism), is musing in his arm-chair. "The expression of his face, always the bright and varying index of his thoughts, was one of high good humour. Complimentary letters were in his hand, complimentary journals at his feet. A ring had been sent to him by a fair unknown ; the applause he had received the night before still rang in his ears ; every pulse that beat within him seemed congratulating him on his individuality, and he felt convinced that the art of acting was the highest of all arts, and that of that art Mr. David Garrick was king and kaiser."

The scene that ensues between Alderman Trawley and the famous player is thus ushered in :

"'Rupees and Russian tallow!' thought Commerce; 'here is a fellow now who passes his life in mimicking emotions he don't feel, painting his pale face, and talking nonsensical words written by fools bigger than himself for poor wages.'

"'Mask, bowl, and dagger!' thought Art; 'here is a man who spends his existence in a musty counting-house casting up figures, who cares neither for life nor the belles-lettres, recks not a jot for the passions or feelings of any but himself, and considers the accumulation of guineas to be the *summum bonum* of earthly happiness.'"

And so the pretty and familiar tale runs on. Garrick accepts the Alderman's invitation to dinner (the invitation that he himself has suggested), finds that his daughter Ada is the girl who has fascinated him at Drury Lane, realizes the fact that they are not only passionately but truly in love with each other, and yet, faithful to his word, disgusts her with his scene of pretended intoxication. But there are passages in the narrative that, for obvious reasons, cannot be reproduced on the stage, and from which it is interesting to quote.

The famous dinner is followed, in the hearty, old-fashioned style, by a sumptuous supper. Mr. Garrick has, of course, gone, and poor Ada, pleading "headache" (so often the feminine pseudonym for "heartache"), has retired to her own room. Availing herself of the opportunity, the vulgar Mrs. Smith, after upbraiding Alderman Trawley for allowing his daughter "to sit down to *meal* with a player," gives way to reminiscences of her own courting days; and of this Robertson says :

"It was strange that so prosaic and commonplace a person as Mrs. Smith should that night have indulged in these retrospections ; for though invariably garrulous, her shop, kitchen, and children were the usual themes of her discourse. Strange, too, that, after years of courtship, that night of all others should have been chosen by cruel Miss Araminta Brown for an acknowledgment of mutual feeling for the devoted Jones ; or, perhaps, if we understood psychological chemistry, mental electricity, and those subtle affinities that link soul to soul, and charge the atmosphere with sentiment as with gas, not strange at all. Ada and Garrick were the cause. Love was in the air, and infected those who breathed it : old Alderman Trawley thought of his departed wife ; Mistress Smith recalled her days of courtship ; Araminta returned Jones's protestations of the palm

with interest; perhaps downstairs the cook and the
footman sat silent side by side, and revolved projects
of eating-houses and settlements in life. Love, like
fire, or steam, or compressed air, is a terrible,
capricious power—a whirlwind that involves all
objects, great and small, within its wilful, passionate
vortex.

" The supper was a great success. The awful eyes
of Mr. Garrick were no longer upon the vest and
breast of Mr. Smith. Mr. Brown had slumbered
during the process of digestion. The host knew
that his daughter's passion was effectually crushed.
In the absence of Ada, Araminta was the belle of the
table, and Jones felt himself beloved.

" And the poor girl upstairs, hugging her pillow
in ecstasy of agony, each sob shaking her fragile
frame, hard dry sobs, unrefreshed by tears—all this
supper-table happiness was distilled from her grief.
In this material world there is no waste. There is
natural economy even in sentiment, which is turned
to account and made useful to others."

And so the story goes on. Disgusted with
Garrick, poor Ada consents to marry her cousin; the
elated Raubreyne shows Alderman Trawley the difference between real and simulated intoxication; and
Garrick finds out the dire consequences of his successful masquerading. In due course the actor tells

his story to a friend, and through this channel it reaches the ears of Ada. At first the dutiful girl has no notion of running counter to her father's wishes, or of breaking off her engagement with the dissolute Raubreyne, but on the eve of her wedding her courage fails her.

" Standing in the centre of her own room, the candle in her hand, she looked round the apartment as if it were the first time she had seen it. She examined the comfortable furniture, the snow-white hangings, and the tasteful evidence of feminine occupation, with a strange interest and reflective curiosity. She had been very happy in that room. As a child, she had eaten secret sweetmeats in it with the intense relish peculiar to the enjoyment of stolen fruit. Since she left the far-off fairyland where the sun was hot, and there were troops of coloured servants, she had known no other abiding-place, save for a few weeks at Lady Shendryn's. Her bed was her stronghold— the vantage-ground to which she could retire from the material world of 'Change, bulls, bears, stocks, the Smiths and the Browns, to a kingdom of fancy, in which she had too often revelled. . . . The room was her own, the bed was her own. The carpet was sacred to her feet, the mirror to her form—and to hers only. She was the Robinson Crusoe of this lonely island of romance, sentiment, and maiden meditation—monarch of all. She possessed a humble friend and familiar Friday in the cat, who sometimes shared her couch. But the days of security and peace had passed; upon the shore was stamped the footprint of a savage.

" And her chamber was to be given up, and her maiden meditations and the solace of her fancies, and she was to consign them—her duty, love, obedience, sentiment, feelings, heart, person, and future life—to the man who was making himself so happy in his friend's chambers in King's Bench Walk in the Temple. An odour of punch and of tobacco stole across her senses as she thought that, at that hour the following night, she should no longer be her own; that *he* would have a right to demand a strict account of her every thought; that he would be her lord and master—she the slave of his will, caprice, and temper; that she was to swear in church that she would cleave to him for ever !

" She had unfastened her dress as the bitter pang smote her. She looked into her mirror, and her face flushed red; and she relaced her bodice swiftly, cruelly, and sternly."

The denouement of the novel runs very much on all-fours with that of the play. Ada seeks refuge with Garrick, and the necessary explanations are made; but the pretty love-scene that has always proved so effective on the stage is in the book shirked in the following fashion :

" The confession was made—the tale was told. From that moment neither doubted the other.

" Then followed a dialogue to which no pen could do justice. The limner of old covered the face whose grief he could not paint ; let the struggler with poor, colourless words leave a blank space for the happiness he cannot depict. It is only for the great to describe First Love, Maternal Tenderness, and Rainbows."

And soon after this, hat in hand, the repentant Alderman Trawley says : " Mister Garrick, will you do me the honour of accepting my daughter's hand ?" and, somewhat abruptly, the story ends.

To account for this, we must again refer to Robertson's preface :

" Poetical justice," he wrote, " could not be awarded to the loves of Mr. David Garrick and Miss Ada Trawley, as detailed in the following pages. They could not, with any regard to known and undisputed facts, have been united. It has, therefore, been thought better to let each reader finish the story as he or she pleases. The cynical and sceptical may think that Ada and David, when allowed to see each other daily, grew weary ; that the gentleman found his inamorata a spoiled, forward girl, and the lady discovered her hero to be a mere vain player, who had no thought but for himself, and of the shrugs and starts that procured him applause at the theatre; that mutual disgust set in, and the lovers became unloving. The romantic may suppose the marriage broken off by the interposition of Lady Shendryn, and the lovers doomed to separation and unmitigated woe; and the sentimental may imagine that Ada, warmed by the sun of Garrick's love, rallied, but that the dart had stricken too deeply, and the actor had the unutterable anguish of smoothing the death-pillow of his promised bride. It is permitted to us all to fashion the clouds into the shapes most pleasing to our mental vision."

With one more quotation from its concluding chapter, we shall leave "David Garrick" in its interesting narrative form. As indicative of Robertson's frame of mind at the time that the book was penned, the following is surely worth preserving:

"'There is nothing,' says the proverb, 'so successful as success.' But, then, success is only successful—it is no more. A town taken, a victory of any sort won, a triumph of any kind achieved—the hero, victor, or gainer does not live happy ever after. He is still susceptible to catarrh, coughs, corns, east winds, rheumatism, the oppressor's wrong, the proud man's contumely, the pangs of despised love, and other of the million ills to which flesh is heir and executor. But of all the compensatory strokes of affliction that sting the successful, none are so terrible as those that strike to the heart, centre, or bull's-eye, as it were, of their success. The man who has toiled all his life to amass a gallery of pictures, built his gallery, secured his masterpieces, and is stricken blind; the keen sportsman, who has dragged through the drudgery of City life, that he might enjoy the country and the meet, and who, the means to the end attained, is made prisoner to his chamber for the remainder of his life; the duck who rears her shelled brood, and conducts them, cackling, to the pond, only to see them drown, feel a keener pang than those who fardels bear, and are habituated to their inconvenience and burden."

Struck with the combined power and humour of Sothern's acting in "David Garrick," Robertson immediately conceived for him the character of a gentleman of the day, with a strong dash of Bohemianism in his nature, well suited to the easiness of manner for which the actor was famous, and giving him a scene in which he, overwrought by nerves and a little champagne, becomes heroically and sentimentally intoxicated. When finished, "Society" (as the play was named) was read to Sothern, who was delighted not only with the play, but with the part (of course it was that of Sidney

Daryl) intended for him. The other characters were all written with a view to performance by the Haymarket company—Chodd senior for Buckstone, Lord Ptarmigant for Chippendale, Tom Stylus for Howe, and so forth.

When Buckstone heard the piece, he characteristically declared that it was "rubbish." Sothern, with a truer eye to the requirements of the times, but not yet an "actor-manager," disagreed with him, but induced Robertson to accept £30 as a retaining fee, telling him he would play it on the first opportunity, although it would have to be in the country, as Buckstone would not hear of it at the Haymarket, declaring it "couldn't run three nights." Shortly after this Sothern wrote to Robertson, saying that if he could find a home for "Society" he might do so, as the prospects of his producing it were very remote; so it went first to Miss Herbert, then to Benjamin Webster, after that to Alfred Wigan, and finally was refused everywhere.

How sore all this made poor Robertson may easily be imagined. One day a friend met him in the Strand, a brown-paper parcel in his hand, his head aloft, teeth grinding, nostrils dilated, and eyes aflame.

"What's the matter, Robertson?" he asked. "Is the house on fire?"

"No, no; but *I* am!" was the reply. "I've just

been reading this play—a splendid play, a magnificent play, to Sefton Parry! What do you think he said?"

" Don't know."

" Why, he said it was 'rot'! What do you think *I* said?"

" Can't guess."

" I told him that until that moment I was in doubt as to whether the play was a good one or not; but now that he had pronounced it to be a bad one, my assured conviction that he was an idiot had convinced me that the play was a good one!"

That play was " Society."

H. J. Byron believed in the piece thoroughly, and recommended it to Alexander Henderson, then manager of the Prince of Wales's Theatre, Liverpool. The fates seemed to have combined against "Society," and with regard to the appointment made to read it one Sunday evening, a curious little incident nearly robbed Robertson of his chance. Henderson was in town on the Sunday, and, being compelled to leave for Liverpool early on the Monday morning, had no other opportunity of hearing it. Robertson had lent his friends Mr. and Mrs. John Billington the only manuscript of the play to read, and immediately set out to obtain it. They had been in possession of the piece for some weeks, and, being thus suddenly asked for it, knew not where to find it. Ashamed to confess the real state of affairs to the impatient author, Mrs. Billington commenced a vigorous search while her husband kept him engaged in conversation. After about an hour and a half of fruitless labour, and just when hope was being given up, the precious manuscript was unearthed; and little knowing of the peril that he had been in, and setting down poor Billington as the greatest bore of his acquaintance, Robertson took his departure.

Having listened attentively to the reading of the piece, Henderson said that he believed that it would succeed, and there and then offered to produce it in Liverpool, an offer that was immediately and joyfully accepted. Without saying a word, and with the manuscript in his pocket, Robertson went to his good friend Byron to tell him the news and the dilemma that he was in. Nothing would induce him to let the piece be played unless he could repay Sothern the £30 that he had advanced upon it. Could he help him ?

Byron pulled his silky moustache : " I can't help it, Tom, but I can't help you; I haven't got it. What's to be done?"

" I don't know," said the perplexed dramatist. " I know nobody I would care to ask, and very few who would be likely to have such a sum !"

After a long but fruitless talk on the subject, the two parted; and on the Monday, depressed and in anything but his usual spirits, Robertson strolled into the Arundel Club. Sitting in the memorable bow-window was genial William Belford, and as a matter of course the author told his story. When he had finished, Belford said : " Tom, my boy, cheer up; I'll get it for you. I've heard about the piece; and how in the ' Owls' Roost' you have hit us all off to the life." The next day Robertson had the money, sent it to Sothern, and " Society" was free to spread its wings. Kind-hearted Belford is no more ; but those who remember the warm-hearted comedian, to whom the Arundel Club was as home itself, will understand how like him this good-natured act was. Belford was repaid with the first cheque that, on his own account, Robertson ever drew.

And so, after all these vicissitudes, " Society" was, on May 8, 1865, produced at the Prince of Wales's Theatre, Liverpool; and to Alexander Henderson belongs the credit of giving the greatest dramatist of his day, and the founder of a new school, his first real chance.

In this original production, Mr. William Blakeley appeared as Lord Ptarmigant; Mr. Edward Price as Sidney Daryl; Mr. Lionel Brough as John Chodd junior; Mr. Edward Saker as Tom Stylus ; Miss

Sophie Larkin as Lady Ptarmigant ; and Miss Teresa Furtado as Maud Hetherington.

It will thus be seen that **Mr.** Henderson's stock company numbered many who have since risen to fame.

In Liverpool, both by press and public, the intrinsic merit and value of the literary portion of the comedy, dominating as it did the natural dialogue and unconventional method necessary for the proper delineation of the characters, which might easily have been mistaken for want of power and lack of technique, was frankly and freely acknowledged. The Bohemianism of the piece proved infectious and irresistible, and roars of laughter and applause accompanied the development of the scene in the "Owls' Roost." Then, again, the delicacy of the love-scene in the first act, taking place in a London square at twilight, wherein the lovers tenderly plight their secret troth, was so unlike the traditional fevered impetuosity of the stage love-making to which playgoers had grown accustomed, that it made an effect as immediate as it was—by London managers—unexpected ; and out of it grew that which came to be known as "a Robertson love-scene."

It is here interesting to note that before the production and during the rehearsals of "Society" in Liverpool, Robertson and John Hare were first introduced to each other ; and it is hardly necessary to say that from that day they were the best of friends, their successes being mutually bound up in a common cause. Writing of Robertson, Hare has said : " From the day I met him till the day of his death, I found in him always a gentle, kindly, and sympathetic friend, whose memory I shall ever cherish with affection and gratitude."

Being present at the first performance of " Society," Hare, then a very young actor, took a strong fancy to the part of Lord Ptarmigant, the elderly aristocrat, and had a great ambition to play it, " little thinking," as he subsequently said, " that it would be my good fortune to create the part before a London audience, and by so doing laying the foundation for my reputation as an actor."

In theatrical circles the success of " Society " in Liverpool was of course immediately known, and it was with very little difficulty that Byron induced Miss Marie Wilton (Mrs. Bancroft) to hear the piece read with a view to its production at the Prince of Wales's Theatre, in Tottenham Street, of which (with Byron for a partner) she had but recently become the manageress. A great drawback to the success of the piece in London was foolishly supposed to exist in the delightful " Owls' Roost " scene, it being thought that the journalistic world would condemn the sketches of the well-known men who were Robertson's comrades in the land of Bohemia. Mrs. Bancroft, however, boldly declared that danger was better than dulness, and when she heard the comedy read, at once determined that it was a piece to be produced. " This," she has recorded, " was my first acquaintance with Mr. Robertson ; and I cannot describe the charm with which he read his comedy. I remember how he impressed me as being of a highly nervous temperament : he had a great habit of biting his moustache and caressing his beard ; indeed, his hands were rarely still. He was at that time thirty-six ; somewhat above medium height ; rather stoutly built ; he had a pale skin and reddish beard, with piercing brown eyes, which were ever restless. The rehearsals advanced, and I liked the play more and more. My views of acting so entirely agreed with Mr. Robertson's that we encountered no difficulties whatever, and everything went smoothly and merrily, although to the last Byron dreaded the effect of the ' Owls' Roost ' scene. My faith remained unshaken, and acquaintance with the author soon ripened into friendship."

And so, on November 11, 1865, " Society " was produced in London; and on November 12 Robertson awoke to find himself famous.

The success of the piece was, indeed, instantaneous,

and soon became the talk of the town. Not to have seen Marie Wilton as Maud Hetherington, Bancroft as Sidney Daryl, John Hare as Lord Ptarmigant, John Clarke as John Chodd junior, Fred Dewar as Tom Stylus, and Miss Sophie Larkin as Lady Ptarmigant (this, it will be noted, was her original character), was to argue yourself unknown; and so at one and the same moment the fortunes of a comparatively new, and so far not very prosperous, theatre, and a hitherto misunderstood dramatist, were made. How much of this success was due to Robertson may be told in Mr. Bancroft's own words : "As the part I first played in Society,'" he says, "was a very important one to entrust to so young an actor as I then was, bearing as it does much of the burden of the play, I would like to note how much the success I was fortunate enough to achieve was due to the encouragement and support I received from the author, who spared no pains with me, as with others, to have his somewhat novel type of characters understood and acted as he wished."

In connection with this interesting first night Mr. Clement Scott says :

" There was a great gathering of the light literary division at the little theatre in Tottenham Court Road on the first night of Tom Robertson's new play. It was dear old Tom Hood, who was our leader then, who sounded the bugle, and the boys of the light brigade cheerfully answered the call of their chief. I remember that on that memorable night I stood—for there was no sitting for us on such an occasion —by the side of Tom Hood at the back of the dress-circle. The days of stalls had not then arrived for me. Suddenly, as the play advanced, there appeared on the stage what was then an apparition. Bancroft had delighted us with his cheery enthusiasm and boyish manner, for he was the lover in this simple little play—well dressed, and, for a wonder, natural. Think what it was to see a bright, cheery, pleasant young fellow playing the lover to a pretty girl at the time when stage-lovers were nearly all sixty, and dressed like waiters at a penny ice shop! Conceive a Bancroft as Sidney Daryl in the days when W. H. Eburne played young sparks at the Adelphi, and old Braid was the dashing military officer at the Hay-market! But what astonished us even more than the success of young Bancroft was the apparition that I spoke of just now. A little, delightful old gentleman came upon the stage, dressed in a long, beautifully-cut frock-coat, bright-eyed, intelligent, with white hair that seemed to grow naturally on the head— no common, clumsy wig with a black forehead-line—and with a voice so refined, so aristocratic, that it was music to our ears. The part played by Mr.

Hare was, as we all know, insignificant. All he had to do was to say nothing, and to go perpetually to sleep. But how well he did nothing! how naturally he went to sleep! We could not analyze our youthful impression at the time, but we knew instinctively that John Hare was an artist. Had 'Society' been accepted at the Haymarket—which, luckily for Tom Robertson, it was not—the part of Lord Ptarmigant would have been played by old Rogers, or Braid, or Cullenford. Chippendale and Howe would certainly have refused it as a very bad old man. No; Tom Robertson's lucky star was in the ascendant when 'Society' was refused by the Haymarket management with scorn. Had it failed there, I believe my old friend would have 'thrown up the sponge' and never worked for the stage any more. The refusal of 'Society' by Buckstone, and the keen and penetrating intelligence of Marie Wilton, who was determined that Tom Robertson should succeed and that his plays should be acted, were the turning-points in the doubtful career of a broken-hearted and disappointed man.

"I don't think I ever remember a success to have been made with slighter material than that given to Mr. Hare. And it was a genuine success. We of the light brigade could not work miracles. We might have written our heads off, and still have done no good for the new school. Luckily, there was at that time as critic to the *Times* a man of keen and penetrating judgment. John Oxenford knew what was good as well as any man, and he knew how to say it into the bargain. He was not a slave to old tradition, and when he had a good text what a wonderful dramatic sermon he could preach! Luckily, also, the new school had the constant support and encouragement of the *Daily Telegraph,* whose leading proprietor and director, Mr. J. M. Levy, never missed a first night in the company of his artistic and accomplished family. All that was liberal and just and far-seeing was in favour of the new Robertsonian departure—of a dramatist who was not old-fashioned and dull, and of actors so new, so fresh, so talented as Bancroft, Hare, and their companions. The heavy brigade of influential writers, led by John Oxenford, patted the new movement on the back ; the light division, led by Tom Hood and others, lent their enthusiasm to the good cause. Gilbert, Prowse, Leigh, Millward, Archer—all of us, in fact, who knew Robertson and appreciated his talent were the first to step forward and back up our friend's success in every way that was possible."

In view of the contemptuous manner in which "Society" had hitherto been treated by London managers, and Robertson's firm and even touching

faith in the value of his own original work (a faith
so amply justified by his subsequent productions),
we may, perhaps, be excused for here quoting some
of the opinions of the leading critics of their day on
what may be definitely called "a new departure."

Writing of "Society" in the *Times*, John Oxenford
said of the much-dreaded "Owls' Roost": "The scenes
in which the 'Owls' figure are indeed the best in the
piece, not only because they are extremely droll, but
because they constitute a picture of the rank and file
of literature and art, with all their attributes of fun,
generosity and *esprit de corps* painted in a kindly
spirit. A report has reached us which, if true, is
only the more absurd on that account, that some thin-
skinned gentlemen have objected to these scenes as
derogatory to the literary profession. Never was
'snobbery' more misplaced. The 'Owls' are emphatically described as 'good fellows' who are unable
to rise in the world, and have nothing whatever to do
with the men who are recognised as magnates of the
republic of letters. If on Saturday last the world
learnt for the first time that there are still persons
who prefer grog to Clos Vougeot and 'long clays'
to choice Havannahs, the world is in a state of
appalling darkness, and a larger field is open to mis-
sionary enterprise than was ever anticipated even at
Exeter Hall. . . . The piece was vehemently ap-

plauded from beginning to end. Success could not be more unequivocal."

In its second notice, the outspoken *Daily Telegraph* said : " The new comedy of ' Society,' which has just been produced with so much *éclat*, is evidently the work of a shrewd, observant writer, who has looked at life from his own point of view, and who prefers saying smart things about the weaknesses of humanity to the utterance of solemn homilies bewailing their existence. Those who demand a subtle analysis of human motives, and require an elaborate dissection of the various component parts of the social body, must seek opportunities for acquiring knowledge elsewhere ; but people who care about seeing a clever, sketchy picture of modern men and manners, dashed off in a spirited style, and giving, perhaps, a new view of some of the gradations in the social scale, may include themselves among the throng who nightly gather round the portals of the cheerful little theatre in Tottenham Street, and make sure of not coming away disappointed. The lower as well as the upper sections of society will find some familiar features quickly to be recognised, and whilst the plebeian occupant of the gallery will readily appreciate the very intelligible humour of the comedy, the most aristocratic patron of the stalls will decidedly approve the moral lesson it enforces."

It does not appear that the comedy owed any of its success to the elaborate and perfect way of "mounting" plays for which, when Robertson's influence was an acknowledged factor, the theatre subsequently became justly famous.   From the notice given in the *Pall Mall Gazette* on November 17, 1865, it would appear that—"with the exception of the 'Square' scene "—" Society " would have been " more effective if it had been 'mounted' with a more liberal hand and with a better sense of the exigences of the scenes. In a comedy which aims at realism, and the essential character of which demands *vraisemblance*, the furniture and accessories are of great importance.   For these the author is not altogether accountable.   Few dramatists are allowed to be stage-managers, and one does not expect to find in Tottenham Court Road the elegance which Madame Vestris exhibited at the Lyceum; but we may reasonably expect to see a fashionable drawing-room in the 'noble mansion' of Lord Ptarmigant furnished with more than one chair and with a carpet of visible proportions, especially as there are some allusions to the wealth of the British nobleman."

The *Daily News* also commented on the want of improvement in the scenic department.   But these things are only mentioned here to show that it was by the sheer force of its own merit—backed up, of course, by admirable interpretation—that " Society " won its brilliant first-night reputation.

And so, after countless disappointments and perpetual misunderstanding, Robertson's strong faith in himself was justified. For his own original work he had at last obtained a hearing, and press and public valiantly declared that he was right.

Henceforth all London theatres were open to him, and the new dramatic school—the natural as contrasted with the artificial school—that he had striven so hard to found, had become in a single night an established fact.

How he saw through and detested the old but universally accepted style of acting cannot be better shown than by quoting from the foot-notes appended by him to the manuscript of his comedy of " War."

Of the French Colonel de Rochevannes, he said :

" The Author requests this part may be played with a *slight* French accent. He is not to pronounce his words absurdly, or duck his head towards his stomach, like the conventional stage Frenchman. Colonel de Rochevannes is to be played with the old pre - Revolutionary politeness — knightly courtesy, with a mixture of ceremony and *bonhomie*."

Of the German Herr Karl Hartmann, he noted :

" This part to be played with a slight German

accent, and not to be made wilfully comic. Herr
Karl Hartmann is to be a perfect gentleman, with a
touch of the scholar and pedant in his manner—but
always a gentleman."

And of Captain Sound, R.N. :

"Captain Sound is not to be dressed in uniform,
but in the morning dress of a gentleman. His
manner is to be hearty, but not rough ; in every
respect that of a captain of a man-of-war, and not of
the master of a halfpenny steamboat."

To the West-End manager of to-day such author's
directions would, no doubt, be deemed superfluous,
but Robertson lived in different times, and knew from
bitter experience what the dramatist might from his
interpreters expect. How that experience was gained
we have endeavoured in these pages to show. The
perception that enabled him to detect glaring faults
and inconsistencies where others were content to
accept recognised stage types can only be explained
in the words *Poeta nascitur, non fit.*

The unqualified success that attended "Society"
brought about great changes in the theatrical world,
and we may here appropriately take a glance at the
programmes of the other London theatres at the time
of its production at the little house in Tottenham
Street. It will, we think, show that a Robertson
was sorely needed. At Drury Lane, Shakespeare

appropriately held the boards, and Mr. Phelps, Mr. Swinbourne, Mr. James Anderson, Master Percy Roselle, Miss Atkinson, and Miss Rose Leclercq were appearing in an excellent, but it is to be feared unremunerative, representation of " King John."   At the Haymarket, in an amazing programme that included an adapted comedy, " Three Weeks after Marriage," the familiar " Used Up," Planché's " The Golden Fleece," and a Spanish ballet entitled " Fans and Fandangos," there were to be seen Mr. and Mrs. Charles Mathews, Mr. W. Farren, Mr. Chippendale, Mr. Compton, Mr. Charles Leclercq, Mr. Howe, Miss Nelly Moore, Miss Snowdon (Mrs. Chippendale), Mrs. E. Fitzwilliam, Miss Louise Keeley, Miss Fanny Wright, and a *corps de ballet.*   At the Princess's, Charles Reade's " It's Never Too Late to Mend," with Messrs. Vining, G. Melville, T. Meade, Dominick Murray, S. Calhaem, J. G. Shore, G. Murray, R. Cathcart, Miss L. Moore, and Miss Katherine Rodgers in the cast, was in full swing.   The Strand was announced to reopen with the burlesque by Mr. F. C. Burnand, happily enough entitled " L'Africaine ; or, The Queen of the Cannibal Islands," with parts specially designed for Mr. J. D. Stoyle, Mr. David James, Mr. Thomas Thorne, Miss Swanborough, Miss Raynham, and Miss E. Johnston.   At the Adelphi (here truly was an attraction : although regarded as literature, the play, in its play form, was perhaps of little account) Jefferson, supported by Mr. and Mrs. Billington, Mrs. Alfred Mellon, and Mr. Paul Bedford, was giving his inimitable impersonation of Rip Van Winkle.   At the Lyceum, Fechter, with a company that included Mr. H. Widdicomb, Mr. S. Emery, Mr. C. Horsman, and Miss Elsworthy, was to be seen in a now forgotten drama called " The Watch-Cry."   At the Olympic there was another miscellaneous programme that included " A Sheep in Wolf's Clothing," " A Cleft Stick," and " Prince Camaralzaman," and the names of H. J. Montague, J. Maclean, R. Soutar, Henry Neville, Horace Wigan, F. Younge, Miss Kate Terry, and Miss E. Farren figured in the bills.   At the St. James's, Mr. and Mrs. Frank Mathews, Mr. Walter Lacy, and Miss Herbert were acting in pieces of an ephemeral type, and at the Royalty another of Mr. Burnand's burlesques, " Widow Dido," was the attraction.   That there was abundant variety in all this cannot be denied, and many of the names that have been quoted will ever hold honoured places in theatrical annals—but where, among it all, was an original comedy by an English dramatist ?   Who, indeed, in those days, when almost everything " worth listening to " was " taken from the French," believed that an English dramatist lived who could write an original comedy ? Robertson, conscious, no doubt, of the power within him, and still more conscious of the difficulties that would stand in the way of the production of his play, had ventured to devote the time, that to him meant money, to the writing of " Society," and, when once he obtained a hearing, secured attention.

But the public triumph upon which he had set his heart, and for which he had so long laboured, came at a time when poor Robertson could not only find no pleasure in it, but was even inclined to resent it as the cruel irony of a bitter fate. The manuscript of " Society " is dated August 12, 1864, and was written at 16, Duke Street, Manchester Square, where Robertson and his little family communed with the stars on the fourth floor; but just at this time, encouraged by the success of " David Garrick," and full of hope concerning his new play, he ventured to take a tiny house at Gospel Oak Village, Kentish Town. In those days this was by no means an unpleasant spot. The sanguine author's windows looked out upon the common that then existed, and in the diminutive summer-house and strip of lawn that constituted the chief attractions of his " garden," many a pleasant Sunday afternoon was spent with such congenial companions as the Broughs, H. S. Leigh, Andrew Halliday, E. C. Barnes, H. J. Byron, Dr. Strauss, and

other good friends from his favourite land of Bohemia.
But housekeeping, even when it is conducted on a
very modest scale, costs money—"Society," as we
have seen, was not snapped up by the first London
manager to whom it was offered—and in order
to bring grist to the mill, Mrs. Robertson, who was
by no means in good health, continued, in spite
of doctors' warnings, to fulfil her duties at the
various theatres at which she found lucrative employment.

To this no one was more strongly opposed than her
devotedly attached husband, and it is on record that
when she was fulfilling her last engagement (at
Astley's Amphitheatre) he even threatened that if she
would persist in acting he would persuade his friends
to go to the theatre and hiss her performance.   As
far as sending his friends to the theatre was concerned,
his little plot was carried out, but they came back and
told him that she looked so sweet, and played so well,
that, in spite of themselves, they could do nothing
but applaud.

Poor Robertson ! He soon found a more trust-
worthy confederate than his friends. It was not long
ere the brave and loving woman had to own her
defeat, and come home to the little house, of which
she had been so proud, and which she so longed to retain, to die.   On August 14, 1865, at the age of

twenty-nine, the poor creature breathed her last, leaving her husband to be both father and mother to their two young children. This, it will be noted, took place just three months before the success of " Society " in London told Robertson that he had won his goal, and it is said among his intimate friends of those days that his anguish was a terrible thing to witness. He had won the fame for which he longed, the fortune that might have saved the life of his devoted wife was within his grasp, and she, the loving helpmate of his stormy, struggling days, could take no share of the one or of the other. It is thought that he was never in actual health from that grim hour, and it was surely with this great trouble in his mind that he was wont in later days to say, with the bitter satire of which he was a master, that he would like " to have the world as a ball at his feet that he might kick it."

Fortunately for the sorely stricken author, and for the welfare of the English stage, he had his little children, Tom and Maud, to think of and care for, and his sorrow found in work its surest alleviation. The enduring success of " Society " brought him both money and friends, his hitherto despised plays were on all hands eagerly inquired for, and a new life in which " he began to live and ceased to exist " was before him. It was, however, with a heavy heart that be commenced writing his new comedy for the now popular and fashionable little playhouse in Tottenham Street.

In conjunction with his old friend H. J. Byron's burlesque on " Don Giovanni," " Society " ran for one hundred and fifty nights, and on the occasion of the one hundredth performance the author (who, if truth must be told, never forgot an intentional or un- intentional slight) placed a private box at the disposal of Buckstone, at the same time reminding him of his opinion and prophecy.

It was about this time that Frederick Clay's opera of " Constance," with a libretto written by Robertson, was produced at Covent Garden. The work did much to enhance the reputation of its gifted composer, but was not an enduring success.

It has been said that Millais's beautiful and well- known picture " The Black Brunswicker " first sug- gested the theme of " Society's " successor, " Ours." Be that as it may, it is certain that in this play Robertson's love of soldiers first clearly shows itself ; and it may be noted that nearly all his subsequent pieces contained, in the form of incident or character, something of the military element. To him a story of love and honour was ever seen at its best when associated with a soldier's uniform.

It was arranged that " Ours " should have its trial

trip (in much the same way as " Society ") at the Prince of Wales's Theatre, Liverpool, but with the difference that Miss Wilton and her London supporters should replace Mr. Henderson's company. In common with most successful plays, the production gave its anxious author abundant trouble. The first reading of the play caused some disappointment to those who were to appear in it, and Mr. John Hare stoutly objected to the part of Prince Perovsky (subsequently one of his most notable successes), only undertaking it on Robertson's assurance that it could do him no harm, and that he would regard it in the light of a personal favour. Then, again, the character of Mary Netley did not come up to Miss Wilton's expectations, and she has recorded how the author suggested that she should " build it up," begging her to do all she could in the scene which concerned her in the last act, " for somehow he felt unable to make Mary as prominent as he wished." " So at the rehearsals," continues this pleasant writer, " I set to work and invented business and dialogue which, happily, met with his approval ; he declared I greatly helped the act, which was not only improbable, but in parts very weak. The audience laughed at the fun, and forgave the rest. I must confess that I often felt a little ashamed of the expedients I was obliged to adopt, and was fully conscious that it was not art, and only fun and frolic, where we pretended to be soldiers going through their exercises."

This frank admission on the part of the first Mary Netley explains away a great deal of the incongruity which undoubtedly exists in the final act of an otherwise charming play. Now, there is no doubt that at the first reading some dismay was felt by the admirable little company at the length and importance of the character of Hugh Chalcot (by the way, in the original manuscript Chalcot is named Draycote, Shendryn is Lysart, and Prince Perovsky is without a title)—an importance which seemed likely to overshadow the play, and make small the chances of those who were to appear in its apparently subordinate characters. But it was not so, and therein became manifest the great ability of the author; for, magnificent as the part of Chalcot is from the actor's point of view—length—it does not constitute " Ours " a one-part play, but is merely the necessary pivot on which the remaining characters turn one after the other in delightful contrast. Anyone reading the piece for the first time might easily regard Chalcot as its " be-all and end-all"; but in acting the truth comes out, and it is found that though Chalcot does most of the hard work, " honours," on the fall of the curtain, are very fairly " divided."

Of course Robertson went to Liverpool, to superintend the rehearsals of his play; and in letters that he wrote to his life-long friends, Mr. and Mrs. Colman Burroughes, he frequently alluded to his perplexities concerning it. Mr. and Mrs. Burroughes were at that time taking care of his children, and that in the midst of his work and worry they were ever uppermost in his thoughts is abundantly manifest. The tender words of affectionate solicitude that in these letters he used in speaking of his motherless boy and girl are both beautiful and touching. The letters also show that when he was not at work at " Ours " he was busily writing for Lacy, Beeton, and other publishers.

" I read the piece to-day to the company," he wrote, " and many of them are dissatisfied with their parts;" and a little later, when the rehearsals had commenced: " I am very tired of Liverpool, as I have so many annoyances at the theatre." Of the first-night performance he said nothing except, " I am going to alter the last act of my comedy." But that the evening of August 23, 1866, when " Ours " was first acted at the Prince of Wales's Theatre, Liverpool, brought him another triumph, and gave the English stage an enduring success, is now a matter of theatrical history. In the course of a lengthy notice that appeared in the *Liverpool Daily Post* the next day, a keen critic said : " Always a pleasant event to the public, the production of a new piece becomes doubly so to the critic when he is compelled to hail it as a welcome addition to our stock of comedies, and a strong confirmation of the abilities of the author. Great were the anticipations indulged in by the theatrical public regarding 'Ours'; and we are confident everyone's expectations must have been realized. The performance of Mr. Robertson's piece last night was in all respects a triumph—literary, histrionic, and scenic."

Of the sensitive author's anxiety in connection with that fateful first-night, his friend Charles Millward has given the following account: " Robertson was fearfully nervous at the rehearsals, and not sanguine of success. After the final rehearsal, on the day of production, I persuaded him to join me in a sail on the river, and Clarke and Dewar readily agreed to accompany us. We accordingly took the steamer for New Brighton, and on arriving there proceeded to the best hotel, and ordered the best dinner that could be provided. And how we all enjoyed that delightful impromptu banquet, the pleasant balcony (facing the sea) upon which we sat, and the exhilarating after-dinner talk ! Robertson was in his very best form, and no longer shaking with nervousness ; but just as we were thinking about returning to the theatre he fell fast asleep. I would not have him disturbed, poor fellow! so he slept soundly until within one hour of the time fixed for the commencement of the memorable performance. It then became necessary to arouse him; and the painful duty devolved upon myself. We reached the theatre just in the nick of time, and then it was unpleasantly evident that Robertson's nerves were again unstrung.

" The theatre was crowded in every part; but Robertson positively refused to occupy the box the manager had reserved for him. He would first take a smart walk, he said, 'to blow the steam off.' He must have accumulated a large quantity of superfluous steam, for he was *non est* during the performance of the first and second acts, and although he had been vociferously called for by the audience, he was nowhere to be found. When the third act commenced, every soul in the theatre, save the author, knew that 'Ours' was a thumping success. But where was Tom Robertson? Surely not still blowing the steam off? As we knew there would be a tremendous call for him when the curtain fell, we were bound to find the missing author dead or alive.

" Messengers were despatched in all directions in search of him; and as I had frequently seen him during his nervous attacks, I joined in the pursuit. I dreaded the prospect of the play terminating before

the author turned up; so I sought for him in the
streets around the theatre.   Ultimately I encountered
him in Bold Street, walking at a furious pace, mop-
ping the perspiration from his brow, in evening-dress,
and *bare-headed.*   He had been pacing the streets,
' blowing off,' more than two hours.   With great
difficulty I induced him to return with me to the
theatre, where we found the last scene on.   When
the curtain fell, a tremendous shout arose for the
author ; and Marie Wilton dragged him across the
stage, pale as a ghost, as limp and flabby a specimen
of a successful dramatist as one could wish to see."

Well—although that troublesome last act had to
be altered—the discussions and anxieties were over
at last.   Mr. and Mrs. Bancroft were delighted with
their new parts; and neither they nor the other members of the company had reason to grudge Mr. John
Clarke the undoubted success he made as Hugh
Chalcot.   The dubious Mr. John Hare had to own
that he had done admirably as Prince Perovsky; and
even Robertson must have felt at ease with himself
and the world.

On the following September 16, at the Prince of
Wales's Theatre, "Ours" was submitted to a London
audience.   Mr. Frederick Younge replaced Mr.
Dewar as Sergeant Jones; but otherwise the cast
was the same as in Liverpool, and the reception of

the piece was never for one moment in doubt.   Concerning this eventful evening, Mrs. Bancroft has written : " The success of the play was immediate and remarkable, and did much to decide the ultimate fortunes of the theatre and the fame of its author. The effect of the second act, where the troops leave for the Crimea, on the first night's audience was extraordinary, the same enthusiasm being kept up nightly for a long time; and in the Crimean hut great surprise was caused by the realistic effect of the driving snow each time the door was opened."

Robertson's fame as a dramatist was now secure. His work was no longer treated as a surprise, but as a serious theme for encouragement, and the long and exhaustive notices that appeared in all the London papers, bidding welcome to the reputation he had made, and expressing approval of the admirable acting to be seen at the Prince of Wales's theatre, conclusively showed the keen interest taken in the future of all concerned in the production.

How " Ours " has been reproduced on London boards over and over again need not be recorded here ; neither need much be said of its immense popularity in English provincial towns, the colonies, and America (where, by the way, Mr. Lester Wallack was an excellent Hugh Chalcot) ; but it is interesting to note that on the occasion of its first revival at the

Prince of Wales's, Robertson was so delighted with the performance that he wrote to the Bancrofts: " For the first time in my life I felt grateful to the folks on the stage-side of the footlights, and I am not given to that sort of gratitude." Mr. Bancroft, on the evening to which this refers, made a great hit as Hugh Chalcot, and Mrs. Bancroft excelled herself as Mary Netley.

When the time came for these deservedly successful managers to say good-bye to the Tottenham Street house which they had so worthily controlled, " Ours" was once more revived in its first London home. " It was only right," says Mr. Bancroft, " that the last bill at the little house should bear the name of Robertson, to whom we owed so much of our success there. In these words we announced the farewell revival at this theatre of ' Ours' : ' Mr. and Mrs. Bancroft's last appearance prior to the opening of the Theatre Royal, Haymarket, under their management at the beginning of the new year' (*i.e.*, 1880). This oft-tried friend again stood by us, and served to fill the little theatre until we left it."

CHAPTER IV.

THE undoubted success and great popularity of "Ours" brought Robertson as many commissions as he could wish for, and the managers who had previously refused his plays were now only too eager to secure them. The immediate result of this was that he undertook rather too much, promising to provide, in addition to a new comedy for the Prince of Wales's, new plays for the Princess's and the St. James's.

At the former house, under the management of Mr. George Vining, "Shadow Tree Shaft," a drama in three acts, was produced on February 6, 1867, the cast including Mr. Vining, Mr. J. G. Shore, Mr. H. Forrester, Mr. R. Cathcart, and Miss Katherine Rodgers. It was a pleasant and picturesque drama, and it contained one situation which, for intensity, has rarely been surpassed ; but it was marred by an unsatisfactory third act, and a too willing sacrifice at

the shrine of the scene-painter. Herein, no doubt,
lay the great difficulty. At the Princess's the author
was hampered by tradition, and had to abandon
much of the fascinating simplicity that had made his
plays so popular at the Prince of Wales's. Melodrama was expected by the audience—melodrama
was in the minds, in the attitudes, and on the
tongues of the actors—melodrama, no doubt, was the
aim of the dramatist who was now writing for a
melodramatic house—and it is to be feared that the
fanciful touches and dainty episodes that he put into
his work interfered with its chances of prolonged
success. Of all classes of playgoers, the lovers of
melodrama are the most conservative, and it must
have startled many a stanch patron of the Princess's
of those days to find an idyllic love-scene like the
following in the semi-sensational "Shadow Tree
Shaft":

KATIE. Stay, Michael, let me tie this bit of ribbon round your
wedding-finger (*takes a red ribbon from her hair and ties it round the
finger of Michael's left hand*). That makes you mine, and shows
that we are plighted. See (*sweeping snow into her hand from the
corner of the booth*), as my mother did before me, and as do many
in this wild country, I roll this ball of snow. We clasp it in our
right hands, and as sure as it melts, so sure will our hearts cling
together, and as we love each other truly, so through our wedded
life shall we have but one thought, one mind, one heart.

[DARKYN * *has entered during this, and comes down between them.*

---

* "Darkyn" was the inevitable melodramatic villain.

KATIE *lets go* MICHAEL'S *hand.   The ball of snow falls to the ground.*]

KATIE. Oh, Michael !   See, the snow has fallen unmelted ! We shall never be wed !

This episode is certainly pretty both in idea and execution, but it and similar graceful scenes were sadly out of place in the melodrama of those days, and were thrown away upon audiences far more eager concerning the beautiful and elaborate scenery provided by Mr. Lloyds, than the grace and finish of Robertson's dialogue.   So it was with more than one of the characters, and notably with that of one " Sampson," who was much given to Latin quotations, coupled, in the author's manuscript, with scholarly English translations for the benefit of the comedians destined to play the part.   Had he been equally thoughtful for the requirements of his audiences, his play would probably have had a better chance of popularity.   As it was, " Shadow Tree Shaft," although by no means a failure, was coldly received, and (with one or two exceptions) unfavourably criticised, and after a comparatively brief run it was withdrawn.

Still less gratifying was the fate of " A Rapid Thaw," a two-act comedy adapted from " Le Dégel " of Victorien Sardou, and produced, under the management of Miss Herbert, at the St. James's Theatre on March 2, 1867.   In the cast were included the manageress, Miss Ada Cavendish, Miss Carlotta Addison, Miss Eleanor Bufton, Mrs. Frank Mathews, Mr. Frank Mathews, Mr. E. Dyas, and Mr. Henry Irving, who, as an Irishman named O'Hoolagan, contributed a valuable character-study. The character played by Miss Herbert had been "created" in Paris by the famous Madame Déjazet; but there is no doubt that in its English dress the play was a failure, and that Robertson attached little importance to it, either one way or the other, is proved by the fact that he (usually so methodical in such matters) did not retain the manuscript or any reference to the production. In the same month Mr. and Mrs. German Reed were supplied by him with a two-act piece of the class associated with those popular entertainers, entitled " A Dream in Venice," in which the famous John Parry made a notable success.

Keen was the excitement among theatrical critics and playgoers when it was announced that a new and original three-act comedy by the author of " Society " and " Ours " was to be produced at the Prince of Wales's. The productions at the Princess's and the St. James's had somewhat shaken the faith of the ever-wavering public in the powers of the new dramatist. The doubtful shook their heads ; the envious talked of a " flash in the pan"; even the hopeful were uncertain. "Would Robertson succeed again?" was the question asked by everyone interested in the stage. "Caste" was the reply, and it was not to be challenged. From the moment of the production of this delightful comedy on the evening of April 6, 1867, its author's name was permanently established in the category of acknowledged English dramatists. Of course, the conditions were favourable. To begin with, the author knew his company, and they had implicit faith in him. "I vividly recall," says Mrs. Bancroft, "the effect he produced by his exquisite reading of his work to the little band of players who had the delightful task of first acting it; for I don't know of such cleverly-drawn and powerfully-contrasted parts in any other modern play. The rehearsals were a labour of love." In the second place, he was his own stage-manager.

In speaking of Robertson in this capactity, Mr. W. S. Gilbert says: "I frequently attended his rehearsals and learnt a great deal from his method of stage-management, which in those days was quite a novelty, although most pieces are now stage-managed on the principles he introduced. I look upon stage-management, as now understood, as having been absolutely 'invented' by him." To which Mr. John Hare, a master of this delicate and all-important part of modern theatrical art, adds : " My opinion of Robertson as a stage-manager is of the very highest. He had a gift peculiar to himself, and which I have never seen in any other author, of conveying by some rapid and almost electrical suggestion to the actor an insight into the character assigned him. As nature was the basis of his own work, so he sought to make actors understand it should be theirs. He thus founded a school of natural acting which completely revolutionized the then existing methods, and by so doing did incalculable good to the stage."

It was under these happy conditions that "Caste," generally held to be its author's masterpiece, was launched.

The germ of the play is to be found in a short story entitled "The Poor Rate unfolds a Tale," contributed by Robertson in 1866 to "Rates and Taxes," a Christmas volume, edited by Tom Hood the younger ; and in calling attention to this fact, Mr. Clement Scott maintains that, "Here we find that echo of the spirit of Thackeray which has so often been detected in Robertson's works, especially 'Caste.' Who," continues this keen critic, " can doubt it, who reads the following ?

" 'Fairfax Daubray (George D'Alroy) was a brave, stupid, good-natured young man, and adored by the men under his command. A finer-hearted gentleman, *or a more incapable officer*, never buckled on a sword-belt. .He fought gallantly at Alma, and wrote after the battle. His wife, who was again in the little house at Stangate, read part of his letter to her sisters, who cheered, and wept, and hurrahed as she read. *She took them all with her to church on the following Sunday.* . . . It was in a hot skirmish that Ensign Daubray found himself in command of his company. His captain had been shot, and the lieutenant borne wounded to the rear. He saw the enemy above him. He knew that it was a soldier's duty to fight, and he led on his men up the hillside. "Dib! Dib! come back!" shouted two or three old officers from the main body of the troops behind him. Daubray turned round to them. "*Come back be damned!*" answered he, waving his sword above his head. "*You fellows come on!*" . . . The wounded man smiled again, pressed his friend's hand, sank back and died, as the General of Division galloped up and said to a bleeding major, "Beautiful—beautiful! Like men, by God!" . . . Major Swynton (Hawtree) returned to England with one of his coat-sleeves empty.'

"How thoroughly all this is in the very spirit of Thackeray! and who can wonder that Robertson's favourite 'bit' in 'Vanity Fair,' which he was never tired of reading to his friends, was the picture of the

Battle of Waterloo, and 'Amelia praying for George, who was lying dead with a bullet through his heart'? We seem in 'Caste' to be reading of Becky, and Jos, and Amelia, and George, and Dobbin, not of Polly, and D'Alroy, and Hawtree, and Esther. That incident of Hawtree returning from the Crimea with his 'coat-sleeve empty' is very characteristic of the writer, who was so passionately attracted by soldiers and their English pluck. Mr. Bancroft, as he tells us in his Memoirs, wanted to introduce a maimed Hawtree with an empty coat-sleeve in the last act of 'Caste.' Why has it never been done?"

That on the first night Robertson was once more the victim of overwhelming nervousness may be shown by the following anecdote :

"We were standing together," says one of his friends, "at the back of the circle of the old Prince of Wales's Theatre, leaning on the barrier, when, at the end of the second act, I unnerved him by a premature congratulation, he being still naturally anxious for the result. In my thoughtless friendship I foolishly slapped him on the shoulder; and when all was over, and success assured, he told me, in his original way, the story of the man who carried a chest of oranges on his head from Botolph Lane to Covent Garden for a wager. The poor wretch was killed by a 'pal,' who, just as the wager was being won, gave

him a slap on the overweighted spine—*and broke it!*
Robertson insisted that my felicitations, coming so
near his triumph, came almost as a death-blow to it
and him."

Only those responsibly connected with the production of a new play understand the misery of these
first nights ; and perhaps the poor author is in the
worst plight of all. Unlike the actors, he has nothing
to do, and with his reputation trembling in the balance,
and with an ear terribly keen for any little slip in his
dialogue on the part of the nervous performers on the
stage, or any apparent want of appreciation on the
side of the critical audience, he can do nothing but
watch and wait and listen until the curtain finally
falls and his fate is sealed.

On the first night of " Caste " Robertson was
evidently on the outlook for anything that could be
construed into a shortcoming. In his manuscript,[*]
in the final scene of the last act, where the lovers are
made happy, and Esther and Polly—just, in short,
before the end of the play—the following lines occur:

ESTHER (*aside*). And she will live in a back room behind a shop.
Well—I hope she will be happy.

POLLY (*aside*). And she will live in a fine house, and have a
carriage, and be a lady. Well—I hope she will be happy.

---

[*] On the opposite page we give a specimen of this manuscript
in facsimile.

Peebles. Once proud and prosperous.
I am now poor and lowly.
Once the master of a shop
I am now by the pressure
of circumstances over which I
have no control, driven
to seek work and not to find
it. Poverty is a dreadful —
monster, for a man as has
once been well off.

~~Snap. Before toby~~
~~Poverty worketh a ruin to~~
~~took of himself is a sad thing~~
~~sort to be heard of~~

Snap. I dare very ~~wonderful Heart~~

Peebles. Sighing ah. wis, the poor
and lowly is often hardly used.
What chance has the working
man?

Hawk. None ascete. when he don't
work.

Peebles. ◊ I am sorry, gentlemen that
I cannot offer you any refreshment
but luxury and me has
long been strangers.

When the comedy was printed, the following foot-note was inserted :

"These last two speeches of Esther and Polly were omitted in representation. For what reason on earth—or behind the footlights —the author cannot imagine."

But sensitive as he was, Robertson must after this notable first-night have been abundantly satisfied, and one can fancy the gratification with which he read the verdict of one of the most eminent critics of the day. Surely those hard-working fingers of his never had a pleasanter task than when they inserted the following into his carefully-kept record of " Press Notices ":

" ' Society ' and ' Ours ' prepared the way for a complete reformation of the modern drama, and until the curtain fell on Saturday night it remained a question whether Mr. Robertson would be able to hold the great reputation which those pieces conferred upon him. The production of ' Caste ' has thrown aside all doubt. The reformation is complete, and Mr. Robertson stands pre-eminent as the dramatist of this generation. The scene-painter, the carpenter, and the costumier no longer usurp the place of the author and actor. With the aid of only two simple scenes—a boudoir in Mayfair and a humble lodging in Lambeth—Mr. Robertson has succeeded in con-centrating an accumulation of incident and satire more interesting and more poignant than might be found in all the sensational dramas of the last half-century. The whole secret of his success is—truth!"

But although the scenery was subordinate to the play, in it some important innovations were made, as witness Mr. Bancroft, who says : " It was in ' Caste ' that we made a distinct stride towards realistic scenery. The rooms, for the first time, had ceilings, while such details as locks to doors, and similar matters, had never before been seen upon the stage."

Mrs. Bancroft has recorded that the success of " Caste" " passed her wildest dreams," and further says : " This comedy is specially endeared to me by the dedication, ' To Miss Marie Wilton (Mrs. Bancroft) this comedy is dedicated by her grateful friend and fellow-labourer, the author.'"

It is not the purpose of this book to criticise the acting of those who took part in the first or subsequent representations of Robertson's plays, but in the case of " Caste " he had so perfectly fitted his company, and the impersonations of one and all concerned in the production were so excellent, that it is impossible not to say something concerning them. As Captain Hawtree, Mr. Bancroft was admirable ; and although this accomplished actor has virtually retired from the stage, it is to be hoped that the performance will be seen again. It was—and is—

the perfection of acting, and in the highest sense a most artistic assumption. Mr. John Hare, as Sam Gerridge, was inimitable. "Mr. Hare," said a leading critic of those days, "is so refined and perfect an actor, so true an observer of life, that we were not surprised to find him made up as a sharp, wiry, veritable working-man who might have stepped out of any carpenter's shop in England. The scene in which he reads to his 'intended' the trade circular he has just composed is the most exquisite and unforced bit of comedy we have seen for years." Another critic ventured to predict that one day Mr. Hare would be "the greatest ornament of the London stage." To-day we know that this was no false prophecy. Some censors would have it that George Honey's marvellous performance of Eccles was somewhat out of the picture; but though he may have been almost too realistic in his desire to present a perfect portrait of the old pot-house orator who " didn't work as much as he used to do, but liked to see the young uns at it," the faults were (if any), and as Robertson told him, "all on the right side." The make-up, the voice, the manner, the savagery in one part; the hypocritical maudlin grief in another; the toadying to wealth in another; the disgust and abuse when wealth refuses to deposit even a sovereign; the exits and entrances of this wonderfully delineated character, are things to be gratefully remembered. Of course since the days of 1867 the character has been played by many of our best comedians (notably by Mr. David James), and it is now regarded in the light of a stage classic, and is as well known to the public of 1892 as were Shakespeare's characters to the playgoers of the so-called " legitimate" days. In proof of this we may quote Mr. William Archer, who not long since said : " I have mentioned Mr. Oswald Crawfurd's suggestive article in the *Fortnightly*, and may possibly return to it another time. Here let me note an ingenious misprint which has been allowed to creep in : ' There have been times,' Mr. Crawfurd is made to say, ' when plays were written to please it' (the gallery) 'in the " Eccles vein."' One cannot but suspect that the intelligent compositor must himself have been somewhat in the ' Eccles vein ' when he achieved this muddle." Here, probably, Mr. Archer is in error. No doubt " the intelligent compositor " was more familiar with his Robertson than his Shakespeare, and thought that he did Mr. Crawfurd good service when he transformed his " Ercles " into his own " Eccles."

The Esther Eccles of Lydia Foote, with her expressive face, and the exquisite pathos of a voice which brought tears to the eyes of all when she read the manly letter sent by Hawtree, enclosing her a cheque for thirty pounds, will always be remembered. The Marquise de St. Maur, played by that highly-accomplished and appreciative actress, Miss Sophie Larkin, was replete with finish and refinement; and the elocutionary decision evinced in the second act, when the estimable, though worldly, old lady narrates the chronicles of Froissart to her eldest son, did much to secure the marked success of a difficult scene. And what is to be said—that has not already been said—of the Polly Eccles of " Marie Wilton"? Writing as Mrs. Bancroft, this charming actress is somewhat inclined to underrate her achievement in what is undoubtedly a most difficult character.

" I am under the impression," she says, " that among many lovers of the old plays, Polly Eccles may be thought to have been my favourite character. No—it was not. I love Polly for the innate fine qualities of her nature; her devotion to her dissolute, worthless father; her filial desire to screen the worst side of his nature (if there could have been a worse), by trying to make him appear a little better in the estimation of others. Her love for her sister; her real goodness under a rough exterior; the undercurrent of mischief, and real appreciation of humour : all these genuine qualities appealed to me largely; and I hope I understood them, otherwise I do not

think I could have made the impression in the part
which I am told I did. I thoroughly enjoyed the
boundless love of fun, the brisk gaiety of Polly's
happy nature, and I felt acutely the pathos of her
serious scenes.

"The character is very dramatic in parts, and
requires all the nervous acting I could bring to
bear upon it. The last act of 'Caste' is the longest
I ever appeared in, and I believe one of the longest
in the whole range of the Drama; for it often played
nearly an hour and a half, and Polly is but seldom
off the stage throughout it. Almost every word
she has to say is a pearl, so to speak, and affects the
audience more or less. Hers is always a welcome
presence, for every one loves Polly. I am naturally
very proud of my success in the part, and feel happy
in all that is now left to me—the remembrance of it.
Success *must* bring pleasure, and 'labour's light as
ease when with cheerfulness 'tis done'; and although
Polly is not my favourite character, still I love her
for her strange mixture of boisterous fun, tenderness
and affection. The sudden transitions, too, from
broad comic humour to deep feeling pleased me, and
my heart was therefore in my work. In the situation
where George D'Alroy suddenly returns from India
when he is thought to be dead, I felt the reality of the
scene so thoroughly that I cried every night when

acting it. Polly Eccles, as a work of art, did me more credit than all the others, and doubtless, as an artistic effort, stands first in the rank, for she is a difficult part to play; the range of feeling must be very wide to fully reproduce the intentions of the author. 'Caste' is assuredly Tom Robertson's *chef-d'œuvre*, and one of the cleverest plays written in my time. Well then, why, in the face of all this, was not Polly Eccles my favourite part?

"I fear I can only give a woman's reason, and say that 'it was not.'"

Mrs. Bancroft finds but few who on this point agree with her. Her Polly was exquisite, and will ever live in the memories of those who were fortunate enough to see her play the part. Though Frederick Younge was by no means juvenile in years or appearance, he was a perfect George D'Alroy, as those will testify who remember the scene with Polly Eccles in the third Act, when, in order that George may see his little son for the first time, she carries in the baby. At this point his acting was inexpressibly touching; but, then, Younge *was* a father, and, like Robertson, adored children. On the first revival of the play, in 1868, the part, somewhat modified by the author, was taken by handsome and all too short-lived H. J. Montague. This popular young actor had previously played in Robertson's drama " For

Love," at the Holborn Theatre, and, no doubt, to that circumstance owed his introduction to a theatre and a company in which he did so much good service.

Frederick Younge's absence from the Prince of Wales's is accounted for by the fact that by this time, with the author for his ally, he was managing these successful Prince of Wales's comedies in the provinces. The phenomenal popularity of " Caste " was, indeed, the cause of the system of travelling companies as against the " stock " country companies then in existence. When Frederick Younge and Robertson made up their minds to send a properly organized company into the provincial towns to represent ' Caste," they met with considerable opposition from country managers. Many refused to receive the company at all, except on a prohibitive percentage, but in these cases public halls were taken, and when it was found that the admirably rendered representations of the comedies given in them emptied the recognised theatres, the obdurate managers gave way. There was a good deal to be said on both sides. In England custom dies hard. Provincial audiences loved to see their local favourites on the boards, country managers liked to reign supreme in their own theatres, and the stock companies were the recognised preparatory schools of the dramatic profession. From

this point of view a distinct loss has to be acknowledged, but, on the whole, it must be granted that
country playgoers have benefited by the change;
though few of them know that it is to Robertson that
their thanks are really due.

The " Caste " company did not cease its labours in
the artistic representation of the famous series of
comedies for fourteen consecutive years, under the
successive managements of Frederick Younge, Richard
Younge (his brother), Frederick Craven Robertson,
T. W. Robertson (the dramatist's son), and later on
of T. W. Robertson and H. A. Bruce.

The younger Robertson's appreciation of, and
delight in, his father's works have done much to
make the public, both in England and America,
familiar with them, and have been pleasant to witness.
Under his management the pieces were invariably
admirably stage-managed and perfectly performed—
he has acted in them with marked distinction—and
under his banner many raw recruits have qualified
themselves for the leading positions that they now
hold on the London stage. Never had worthy father
more loyal son.

That like most other permanently successful ven-
tures the new touring departure had to be " built
up " may be shown by an extract from the following
letter written by Robertson, in the early days of the

provincial " Caste " company, to his friend and partner :

" DEAR FRED,

" I'm glad that you lost no more at Bradford than £10, and hope that the end of this week may make up for the beginning.   Please let me know how ' Ours ' goes."

The continuation of this note bears painful witness to the fact that, even at this period, its writer was a martyr to patiently-borne ill-health.

" I was better last week," he says ; " but on Monday night I had one of my old attacks, and I have been, and am, queer since.   Sometimes I feel very much depressed, at others hopeful.   The new comedy gets on but slowly ; however, I shall finish it by Christmas.   When I suffer the pain is so acute that it leaves an echo in the bones after it has passed away.   Having done little or no work, of course I am full of plans, notions, schemes, etc."

In another letter to Younge, he alludes to his old comrade, H. J. Byron's, appearance at the Globe Theatre as Sir Simon Simple, in his comedy " Not Such a Fool as he . Looks," a part that had been essayed, but (somewhat too hastily) thrown over by Sothern.

" The business at the Globe," he writes, " has, I hear (and believe), improved, and may still continue to go up. I hope it will ; but it can never be a success. The piece is too weak, and Byron has too little ' go ' in him as an actor. His acting was a false step, and I knew it would be."

Inasmuch as subsequent events justified this prophecy on the part of one of Byron's best friends, it is worth quoting.

It would be as unnecessary as it is impossible to allude in these pages to the number of times that " Caste " has been reproduced on the London stage, but some reference may be pardoned to the famous revival at the Prince of Wales's of 1879, of which a leading critic wrote :

" Robertson, the dramatist, long before he obtained fame, might well have said with Milton, ' By labour and intent study (which I take to be my portion in this life), joined with the strong propensity of nature, I might, perhaps, leave something so written to after times as they should not willingly let it die.' To very few amongst modern authors who struggled painfully to succeed, and who, after years of misdirected energy and unappreciated genius, woke up one morning to find himself famous, was ' labour ' more truly ' a portion of this life '; in the recorded works of very few do we see the fruits of so much

' intent study ' of contemporary life ; in the picture
poems of favourite authors we seldom find painted in
such vivid colours the ' strong propensity of nature,'
coming out, as it does, in the women Robertson so
well understood and loved, in the men he so
thoroughly appreciated and admired, in the bravery
for which he had so much reverence, in the modesty
he so much respected, in the humour which was so
sympathetic to his kindly nature, or in those scenes
of English life, English feeling, and English sentiment, which he reproduced for us with a master hand.
And in ' Caste ' Robertson has bequeathed to us and
to our stage one of those pure fresh evergreens which
the public and his friends will not ' willingly let die.'
Seven years have passed away since this favourite
play was revived in its old home, and a new generation of playgoers have sprung up since Robertson
wrote for us.   In other circumstances such a new
generation, fresh entering upon pleasures which most
of us have appreciated, tasting for the first time the
sweets that come unaccustomed to the palate, would
be the subjects of considerable envy.   But it is not
so with ' Caste.'   Familiarity breeds no contempt
here.   Old stager and young stager are on the same
platform.   The mind, familiar with every scene, every
movement, and every situation, is animated with the
freshness of a new delight. . . . And so it turns out,

when we consider the delicacy of the author's conception and the finished care of its treatment, that neither age nor custom can change or wither the variety of a familiar plant. Such plays as these—so pure in sentiment, so English in tone, so wholesome in effect—are like the dreams and books described by Wordsworth. Concerning them, we may truly say, ' Round these, with tendrils strong as flesh and blood, our pastime and our happiness will grow.' "

In speaking of the popularity of the play another writer said : " Mrs. Bancroft has not appeared at the Prince of Wales's in her admirable impersonation of Polly Eccles since 1871, but it may safely be said that since its first production in 1867 a year has never elapsed without ' Caste ' being somewhere upon the stage. The present law of copyright has enabled the sale of most of Mr. Robertson's comedies, which, as literary works, are well worth dissemination, to be stopped in England ; but they have a considerable vogue in America. We have in this country a provincial band of players formed, under the title of the ' Caste ' company, expressly to represent the eleven pieces by which Mr. Robertson is known to the public. ' Caste ' has also made its way to Germany, for its influence must assuredly be recognised in the successful play by Julius Stinde and George Engels, produced last September at the Wallner Theatre in Berlin, under the title ' Ihre Familie.' "

It is in connection with the production of 1879 that Mr. Bancroft says : " It may here be mentioned, as an instance of the great change that had come over things theatrical, and for which we were chiefly responsible, that Mr. Honey, when he first played Eccles in 1867, received £18 a week, while for this revival—we guaranteed also a six months' engagement—his salary was sixty. . . . The favourite old play was marvellously welcomed, and the receipts equalled even the early days of a new production."

That the author's fees had not been advanced in proportion to the actor's salary was not the fault of Mr. and Mrs. Bancroft may be shown by the following episode, creditable alike to manager and to dramatist. It was after the revival of " Ours " in 1870 that the Bancrofts, seeing that the play had settled down for a long and profitable run, decided to offer Robertson an increase on the fees originally agreed upon and paid ; and to a letter requesting him to accede to this he sent the following characteristic reply :

" Don't be offended that I return your cheque. I recognise your kindness and intention to the full; but, having thought the matter over, I cannot reconcile it to my sense of justice and probity to take more than I bargained for. An arrangement is an arrangement, and cannot be played fast and loose with. If a man, say an author, goes in for a certain sum, he must be content with it, 'and seek no new'; if he goes in for a share, he must take good and bad luck too. So please let 'Ours' be paid for at the sum originally agreed on."

With a reference to the memorable night at the Haymarket when "Caste" was played for the last time under the management of Mr. and Mrs. Bancroft, we shall take leave of this admirable play.

On that occasion Mr. Hare came from his own theatre (the St. James's) to play his old part of Sam Gerridge to the Captain Hawtree and Polly Eccles of his former managers, and the greatest enthusiasm prevailed both before and behind the curtain.

"The evening of Friday, April 13, 1883," says Mr. Bancroft; "will long be remembered by us, and is not likely to fade easily from the memory of anyone present. It was apparent directly the curtain rose that the audience was exceptional, and that some strange magnetic influence affected both auditor and actor. The reception of all the familiar characters was very prolonged ; while of Mr. Hare, the moment he appeared as Sam Gerridge, and of ourselves, no other word will so express the demonstration as 'affectionate.' It would look like exaggeration to describe the enthusiasm which followed the comedy, or the scene that occurred at the close of it."

But the evening was nevertheless overshadowed by a tinge of regret. If only the author—who, conscious of the power within him, had so bravely surmounted the cruel anxieties of his early days—could have been present to witness the sustained triumph of his evergreen play!

*   *   *   *   *   *

Very soon after the first production of "Caste," Robertson, accompanied by his friend E. C. Barnes (the well-known artist), went on the Continent for a much-needed holiday. With characteristic solicitude for his children, he left before starting, and "in case of accident," the following statement of his affairs with his friends Mr. and Mrs. Burroughes:

" May 2, 1867.—Shares : Abney Park Cemetery Company, £200. Albert Levy, for investment, £300. Insurances: Norwich Union, £300 ; European, £500. ' Caste,' £3 a night. Copyrights: ' Shadow Tree Shaft,' ' Ours,' ' A Rapid Thaw,' ' David Garrick,' and ' The Cantab '—half with Lacy. Other copyrights of little value. MS. of dramas finished, and various MSS. Hardly any debts — certainly under £20. Various sums lent, about £100. All papers, securities, will, etc., are at the London and South-Western Bank,

Park Street, Camden Town. The key of the box containing the securities is in my desk, labelled."

When we consider how short his time for saving money had been—that he received but £1 a night for "Society," £2 a night for "Ours," and that "Caste," at its £3 a night, had only been running about a month—we realize how wonderfully careful for those depending on him he was. In those days his author's fees were no doubt considered ample; and that he was well satisfied with them is certain. To-day our dramatists take—as no doubt, up to a certain point, they are entitled to take—other views.

The fellow-travellers visited France, Germany, Switzerland, Italy and Savoy, and after an absence of five weeks Robertson returned to London in good spirits, in invigorated health, and with a new life before him.

At this time E. C. Barnes was one of Robertson's most intimate friends; he helped him to design the scenes for many of his plays, and painted the only portrait on canvas of him that exists. From this the etching by R. W. Macbeth, A.R.A., was taken, and in connection with it a touching little story is on record. As it confers honour on all connected with it, there can be no harm in relating it in these pages. As evidence of the affection inspired by Robertson in the hearts of those who knew and loved him, it has great value.

Of " sitting for his portrait " he entertained a perfect horror, but on the occasion of an idle happy
Sunday morning spent in company with congenial
spirits in Barnes's studio, he laughingly consented to
be " taken in oils." The little picture, hastily painted
though it was, developed into an admirable likeness,
and for many years it occupied an honoured position
on the studio walls. When Robertson died, nothing
would induce his artist friend to part with this
treasured record of their close companionship, and in
the troubled days that were in store for him he clung
to it as to his most valued possession. All too soon
poor Barnes died, too, and, his deft fingers being still,
those dear to him felt the pressure of a needy hour.
Friends there were ready and willing to help ; but
how was this to be done in a fashion that would not
appear obtrusive ? Robertson's son—remembering the
portrait, and anxious above all things to possess it—
thought that by offering to purchase it he might not
only secure a long-coveted prize, but be of service to
his father's old friends. But no ! Anxious concerning the future though they were, the dead artist's
relatives would not sell his most cherished treasure ;
but they would gladly *give it* to him to whom it
seemed by right to belong.

Going away with his prize, young Robertson wondered what he could do to show his appreciation of

the gift, and at the same time render the help that he had in view when he went in quest of it; and it suddenly struck him that if an etching of the portrait from the hand of some well-known artist could be produced, there were many of his father's old friends who would be glad to purchase copies. Obtaining an introduction to Mr. Macbeth, he told the story and the artist, without hesitating for one moment, and in the kindest possible manner, undertook the task. One stipulation, however, he made. He was to receive no payment; it must be a labour of love. By this means an appreciable sum of money was amassed; and thus it came about that by tenaciously clinging to the portrait of his friend poor Barnes unconsciously made some provision for those so near and dear to him.

We have said that Robertson came home from his holiday with a new life before him—and it was, indeed, for a new life that he earnestly longed. His position as a dramatist was now permanently assured; he felt that he was prosperous, and he knew that if he had continued health and strength (and these blessings were not yet denied him) he was in a fair way to become rich. What more natural than that he should wish to blot for ever from his memory the painful struggles, the heart-breaking disappointments, and the necessarily sordid expedients of his dark early days? Robertson always cordially hated the memory of those old times. Even with his earliest and most intimate friends he disliked to speak of them; and between a cruel past, a peaceful present, and a prosperous future he wished to draw a firm and ineffaceable line. Since his wife's death, too, he had experienced a terrible sense of loneliness. Of this he often spoke to his closest companions, and no one was surprised, and all were glad, when he announced the news of his engagement to the niece of one of his sincerest well-wishers, Mr. Joseph M. Levy (of the *Daily Telegraph*), to whom he dedicated his comedy "Ours." It was at an evening party given at the house of Mr. Edward Levy (Lawson) on Christmas Eve, 1866, that Robertson first met Miss Rosetta Feist, a young German lady from Frankfort-on-Maine. They were at once attracted towards each other, and with the permission of the young lady's parents they became "engaged" in the following August, thanks, in a great measure, to the friendly mediations of the Levys, who helped to overcome some slight objections as to religion and nationality raised by "mein Herr Papa!" In a letter addressed to his future wife, Robertson speaks in the most affectionate terms of the Levys generally, who from the day they met him were his attached and sincere friends.

The letters from Robertson to his *fiancée* are in existence, and from them we may here and there quote. To publish these love-letters in their entirety would be little less than sacrilege, and yet the temptation to do so is strong. The language in which they are couched is most beautiful. His intense and almost fatherly affection for the young girl who has consented to leave her own friends and country, and entrust her life and happiness to his care, is as tender as it is manly, and his thought for her in a hundred little ways infinitely touching. Well, we all know how Robertson could write love-scenes for the puppets in his plays. Picture, then, his love-letters to the mistress of his heart! But, beautiful though they are, they were meant for one eye, one ear, and in sanctity must lie. We wish that more of Robertson's letters had been preserved. He was a fascinating correspondent, and we believe in what Dr. Newman said when, in 1863, he wrote to his sister, Mrs. John Mozley : " It has ever been a hobby of mine—though perhaps it is a truism, not a hobby—that the true life of a man is in his letters. Biographers varnish, they assign motives, they conjecture feelings, they interpret Lord Burleigh's nods ; but contemporary letters are facts." Southey, too, has said : " Letters often tell more of the character of the man they are to be read by than of him who writes them ;" and from this point of view extracts from Robertson's correspondence would have been interesting. We must, however, do the best we can with the material at our command.

In the early days of his courtship Robertson appears to have been somewhat embarrassed with regard to German ways in such delicate matters, and in June he (with characteristic consideration) wrote to Miss Feist : " The manners and customs, habits of thought and fashions, of the Continent are so widely different from those of England that I may be excused for not understanding Continental modes, and I may be pardoned if, through ignorance, I unwittingly appear unconscious of a received *convenance*. Having given your mother your promise that I am not to hear from you further at present, you must, of course, keep your promise. If, however, any circumstance should arise which should induce your mother to permit you to send me a few words, I hope you will indulge me with a line or two. . . . I am glad to be able to tell you that I shall be able to leave England early in August, and so I may reasonably hope to be in Nanheim by the tenth of that month— about seven weeks from the present time. For this alteration of dates I am indebted to a lucky accident ; so if I do not hear from you, I shall have the happiness of seeing you a month before I expected.

As you are kind enough to finish your letter by saying that you would like to hear from me now and then (by which I understand that I may be permitted to write to you), I shall certainly avail myself of the permission, and send a letter or two (or more !) during the weeks that have to elapse before I see you. I am as busy as I can be, but I can never be so busy that I cannot find time to write to you."

With matters so far arranged he settled down to steady work, and the second week of July, 1867, saw him at Garlinge, a little village outside Margate, with his two children, and in a small farmhouse, called by courtesy Guildford Villa, he finished the drama entitled " For Love." There he would write most of the day at his desk in a bay-window facing the sea, and in the evening it was his custom to walk the mile separating Garlinge from Margate and spend an hour or so with his friend, E. P. Hingston, who managed the newly-erected Hall by the Sea.

From Garlinge he wrote the following characteristic and manly letter to Miss Feist : " Having received a note from your father saying that he wished to see me, I went up to London yesterday. I cannot in the brief space of a letter tell you all that he and I said, but I can give you its purport. Your father said that, much as he felt gratified by the attention I had paid you, there were impediments to our union. I asked what they were. He said three : First, that you had no money ; secondly, that you had been reared in a different faith to me (although he admitted that he himself thought but little of that) ; and, thirdly, that I had a family. I replied that I never thought you had money ; that I did not care for money, as I was sufficiently prosperous to maintain a home comfortably and elegantly. That for the question of creed, I considered it no obstacle to sensible and intelligent minds ; but for his last objection I said I had no answer. It was a good and valid objection. I could, therefore, only reply that I had but two young children ; that, although I had that responsibility, I had *made* my way in the world, that I had not to *make* my position, and that it was a question of feeling for the contracting parties ; that if *you* did not make that an obstacle, I thought it but a very small one. I then entered into a description of my circumstances. The final reply was that he must ' consider the matter, and would write to me ' ; and so, dear, the matter stands. I need not tell you that I await your father's letter with anxiety, and that I am by no means sanguine as to his decision."

As we have already seen, his misgivings were groundless, and having finished his play, and entered into negotiations for its production, he set out for Nanheim with a light heart.

Before starting he had to make arrangements for his children, and from Garlinge wrote as follows to Mrs. Burroughes:

"What do you think of my leaving Tommy and Maud here with the Ralphs for the month of August while I am in Germany? The air is doing them immense benefit. I do not know whether Mrs. Ralph would have them—particularly Tommy, who has painted the pigs with gas-tar."

The story of this terrible misdemeanour runs as follows: The outhouses of the farm were being given a new coat of tar, and while the workmen were away at their dinner, Master Tommy took upon himself to paint not only the insides of the piggeries, but the pigs themselves. Thus uncomfortably decorated, the poor creatures rubbed themselves against the walls of their houses, and so, to the dismay of their owner, gave themselves a very fair second coating, in, as the painters' contracts have it, "a workmanlike manner."

A letter that Robertson wrote to Mrs. Burroughes immediately after his arrival at Nanheim again shows his wakeful solicitude for his children. It winds up in characteristic fashion. "I am happy to tell you that I am quite well," he says, "and 'gathering copy

every day from every opening tourist.' Give my
kindest regards to inquiring friends, particularly to
those who don't like me!"

At Nanheim all arrangements for the marriage
were made, and after a naturally pleasant holiday,
Robertson travelled to England by way of Baden,
where, for copy-gathering purposes, a short halt was
made. Here it was that he learnt, to his infinite
delight, that it was generally believed that not only
was he already married, but that the principal attraction of his bride was her power of being able to
"translate from the German." The manner in which
he at once conveyed this startling piece of intelligence
to Miss Feist showed how thoroughly he enjoyed the
joke, though no doubt he attributed the report to
those (if any such existed) who " didn't like him."

On September 4 he arrived in London, and his
first letter to Nanheim enclosed a beautifully-worded
one from his father to his future daughter-in-law,
which, if such things did not seem sacred, it would be
pleasant to quote at length. Its purport was, of
course, to express his satisfaction with regard to the
forthcoming wedding, but it contains one passage that
is of general interest :

" My son," wrote William Robertson, " has had
some annoyance since his return to town, arising out
of an injustice that is practised upon his literary work

in America, and which will, I think, terminate in an international law for the future protection of all authors in that country. The affair is creating much excitement in the States. To my son it will prove a temporary loss, but it will not compromise the cheering prospects that are opening to him at home."

This alluded to the now well-known incident of the scandalous piracy of " Caste " in America. The disagreeable story has been told before, and need not be here repeated. It caused Robertson intense annoyance and heavy loss, but he bore both with dignity, and the publicity given to the proceeding no doubt had something to do with the better and more honourable state of things that to-day exists.

And so in England Robertson not only found renewed toil, but unexpected worry, and it is easy to enter into his feelings when he wrote : " I am full of business. My hand is with my work, but my heart is with my beautiful little wife." But he had his new play " For Love " to rehearse and produce before he could return to what he whimsically termed his " Vater (in-law) Land."

And yet, busy as he was, his mind was always, and in some ways amusingly, running on his marriage. In one letter he says : " *A propos* of our wedding, of course we shall be married at the Consul's. Please tell me in your next letter whether in a case of that sort a bridegroom is expected in Germany to be dressed as we dress in England for a marriage in church. Don't forget to answer me on this point, as I shall have to order *my trousseau!* I yearn for the day that makes you mine, and changes Rosetta Feist to Rosy Robertson."

" For Love; or, The Two Heroes," the drama in three acts written for the New Holborn Theatre, then under the management of Mr. Sefton Parry, was produced on October 5, and in a letter written to Miss Feist the following morning Robertson said : " The piece was a success, and in my opinion it will run six months. I may be wrong ; but I judge as I think, without being over-sanguine or over-despondent. The first act went gloriously, the second splendidly. The third act did not go well (but not so badly as the third act of " Shadow Tree Shaft "—still, it dropped a little). We shall alter that, and then I have no fear of a long run."

The cast included Henry Widdicomb, H. J. Montague, Charlotte Saunders, and Fanny Josephs, and William Telbin provided some exquisite scenery, but the piece did not realize the fond anticipations of its author. It was the old story. Charming in comedy, Robertson's delicate touch and pointed style were unsuited to, or, at all events were misunderstood in, the melodrama of five-and-twenty years ago ; and the situation was cleverly summed up as follows by one of the leading critics :

"It behoved the manager to open his second campaign with flying colours, and he naturally had recourse to the brilliant author of 'Society,' 'Ours,' and 'Caste.' No wonder that the assembly of Saturday was most select and generous—select in comprising what is most notable in the literary world, and generous in hearty appreciation of all that was sparkling in dialogue and moving in incident. The title 'For Love,' though it might remind old playgoers of Sheridan Knowles's comedy of 'Love,' and play-readers of Dryden's 'All for Love,' was sufficient to arrest attention. The curiosity awakened by the title was stimulated by the opening act. . . .

"The delight that Mr. Robertson takes in repartee threatens to be the chief obstacle of his success in drama. The scenes are invested with an artificiality which ill prepares the listener for a tragic denouement. We may well doubt if the appalling catastrophe of the sinking of the *Birkenhead* is not too recent an event to be, under any circumstances, parodied by half a dozen supers on a pasteboard ship. Although Mr. Robertson's new drama is not, in our opinion, so artistic a piece of workmanship as the sparkling comedies with which his name is chiefly associated, it contains abundant evidence of his highly original talent and striking dramatic skill. For instance, the contrast between the pathetic complaints of poor Bridget that she could not go out with her drunken husband, and the insignificant doings of titled folks, which go on in antiphonal sequence, is admirably managed and highly effective. It was not an easy task to make both his heroes propose to the same girl —both in fear and trembling — and yet each in separate fashion. But Mr. Robertson has here had his customary success. By far the best scene in the play, however, is that in which Lieutenant Tarne and Mabel, leaning over the bulwarks, and playing nervously with the ropes, look down into the deep blue waves, and surprise, each in the other's trembling voice, the mutual secret of their hearts. Mr. Robertson is accused of being cynical, but if he be so his cynicism is of the right sort. He is cynically contemptuous of all snobbishness and show, and he heartily admires what is real and true. Like all genuine humorists, he finds the source of humour to be very near the fount of tears, and as we listen to his dialogue, our laughter is checked of a sudden by a serious thought, and our sympathy is speedily brightened by a smile."

In calling attention to the fact that the plot of "For Love" was founded on the well-known and pathetic story of the "Wreck of the *Birkenhead*,"

Mr. Clement Scott says : "I shall never forget Robertson's description of the 'Wreck of the *Birkenhead*,' which he always wanted to make into a grand play. It made me thrill to listen to him. He had the genius of the dramatist; he was alive with pathos and situation ; but he could not do impossibilities, and make houses without material. The Holborn Theatre and the company there were not suited to tackle the 'Wreck of the *Birkenhead*.' . . . Robertson had, no doubt, a power of description in which he distanced most of his contemporaries. Oxenford, George Rose, Charles Coleman, J. C. M. Bellew, and countless others, were all able conversationalists, but they were distanced by Robertson in the club-room and at the dinner-table. He could read a play as well as he could write one. I have seen a room full of clever men interested with his conversation. I have been present at literary gatherings when he electrified us with a reading of one of his short stories, and I have seen a company in tears when he read to the assembled actors and actresses one of his plays. It must have been this gift that inspired the artists of the little Prince of Wales's Theatre. But the description of the play he wanted to write on the subject of the 'Wreck of the *Birkenhead*' I shall never forget."

Well, it is pleasant to know that Robertson was

satisfied with the first-night success of his new play, and that it was with a light heart that he hurried off to Germany " to press the dear hand on which I have to place—in token of love, esteem, sovereignty, and subjection—a wedding-ring."

The marriage took place at the English Consulate at Frankfort on October 17. The honeymoon was passed in Paris ; and a little later on, at his new home—No. 6, Eton Road, Haverstock Hill—the new life for which Robertson had longed commenced in earnest. Once more happy in his domestic life, he devoted himself to the labour that he loved, and although in 1868 only two pieces from his pen were produced, the amount of work that he did was extraordinary, as the record of 1869 will show.

The next comedy produced at the Prince of Wales's Theatre (the date was February 15, 1868) was in four acts, and entitled " Play." Its popularity was in a great measure due to a charming love scene, admirably played by Mrs. Bancroft and Mr. H. J. Montague, which had been thought out by Robertson during his recent stay in Baden, and after a visit to the " Alte Schloss," a ruin standing on an eminence in which Æolian harps had been placed. Other characters were admirably sustained by Miss Lydia Foote, Mrs. Leigh Murray, Mr. Bancroft, Mr. William Blakeley and Mr. John Hare. " The parts," Mr.

Bancroft says, " seemed wonderfully adapted to the company—a quality in which Robertson was perhaps pre-eminent."

" The success of the production," he continues, " passed our best hopes—demanding, in fact, an addition to the number of stalls. Hawes Craven painted some really beautiful scenery—-the old ruined castle, with an effect of the sun dancing on the flowing river far below, being an ambitious attempt upon so small a stage. Robertson was fresh from Baden-Baden, and supplied a great deal of local colour with regard to picturesque detail outside the springs and in the gaming-room ; so all went merrily on both sides the curtain. ' Play ' went gaily on its career until some time in May, when its good-fortune received a sudden check, like all things theatrical in that year, which was that of the great drought and most exceptional heat."

To Robertson the reception of the piece was most gratifying, and he especially valued the opinion of a critic who said :

" There is an impression of reality about the personages he has introduced, which helps us to a belief in the probability of their actions ; and in their speech we catch an echo of the tone of modern life, not always so distinctly heard within the walls of a theatre."

It was for this reform that Robertson had so long and so earnestly striven.

To the pretty love scene on the Alte Schloss he was evidently, and with good reason, much attached. Later on in the year—and while his wife was staying with her parents at Nanheim—he was again at Baden, and wrote to her : " I should have liked to have shown you the Alte Schloss, where I thought out the scene between Rosie " (the source of his heroine's name is not far to seek) " and Frank." He visited the spot over and over again, and on one occasion was accompanied by his friend John Hare.

The only other play written and produced in 1868 was " Passion-Flowers," a drama in three acts, adapted from the French. This was tentatively brought out on October 28 at the Theatre Royal, Hull, with his sister, Madge Robertson, in the principal part. Since then it has for some unexplained reason remained on the shelf. It is a pretty play, and deserves to be revived.

Robertson's dramatic works were now in request wherever the English language is spoken, and it was just at this time that he wrote as follows to Frank Younge, concerning their production in Australia :

" I know that you are sure to do the best you can for me in Australia, and I agree with you that ' certain ' terms are best. ' Caste ' is always more liked the more it is seen, and I think £5 per night might be got in your best theatres for a successful play of mine. 'Play' has been sent off to you. I shall shortly send you other pieces. I have four coming out immediately, among others a sensation drama of the most sensational type. I shall send assignments out of all the plays I send you, that you may be armed with full legal authority in case of piracy. I need not tell you to look after your MSS. Of course I shall send you all my pieces, for what is a miss here may be a hit in the colonies. Produce 'Ours' after 'Caste,' if you can ; then 'Society'—but this, of course, you will judge of best yourself on the spot. In arranging with managers, remember that you are selling the rarest article in the world, *i.e.*, successful plays—the article that is more valuable from its scarcity than diamonds, for the diamond is not reproducible, whereas a play can 'run on for ever.' This, of course, does not apply to *good* plays, but only to *successful* ones ; so carry matters with a high hand with managers, for they *must* have the article—they *cannot* do without it."

This shows that Robertson had learnt to put a proper value on his work, and that he had views of his own with regard to " good " as compared to " successful " plays. It was in 1868, too, that Robertson was the means of bringing Mr. W. S. Gilbert's first dramatic work under the notice of playgoers. " It was entirely through him," writes Mr. Gilbert, " that I obtained an introduction to the stage. He believed that I had a capacity for dramatic writing, and at first strongly urged Sothern to commission me to write a piece for the Haymarket. This, however, did not come to pass, but in 1868 Miss Herbert, the then lessee of the St. James's, asked him to write her a Christmas piece of a fanciful description. He was too full of work to undertake the commission, but suggested to Miss Herbert that she would do well to entrust the work to me. She acted on his suggestion, and commissioned me to write my first piece, ' Dulcamara,' a burlesque on the ' Elisir d'Amore.' "

So what Byron did for Robertson, Robertson did for Gilbert, and better examples of good judgment could hardly be cited.

A remarkable series of plays from Robertson's rapidly and now happily working pen flooded the stage in 1869.

On January 14, at the Haymarket Theatre, "Home," a comedy in three acts, written expressly for E. A. Sothern, was a conspicuous success, both for dramatist and for actor. Sothern, who was never sanguine about a piece unless he was cast for one of those purely romantic parts in which, oddly enough, he never quite succeeded, was exceedingly nervous about this production ; but after the first night he wrote : "'Home' is a great hit, everyone giving me far more praise than I deserve. I played so nervously that I fully expected a cutting-up in the papers. However, the public is satisfied, and I always acknowledge the verdict it gives, *pro* or *con.*" "Home," which was an adaptation of Emile Augier's "L'Aventurière," became exceedingly popular. Sothern excelled himself as Colonel White ; Miss Ada Cavendish made a notable impression as Mrs. Pinchbeck ; Mr. Chippendale was excellent as Mr. Dorrison ; and no one who saw it will forget the Mountraffe of Henry Compton. Under the famous management of Mr. Hare and Mr. Kendal, "Home" was very successfully revived at the St. James's. The managers played Mountraffe and Colonel White, Mrs. Kendal was the Mrs. Pinchbeck, and great interest was attached to the occasion, inasmuch as the boyish character of Bertie Thompson was admirably impersonated by the author's son, the younger T. W. Robertson.

By the way, it ought not to be forgotten that one of the most artistic productions and greatest successes of the Hare and Kendal *régime* was the revival of " The Ladies' Battle," which Robertson wrote—or rather adapted — in his struggling days for Lacy. It is sad to think that he did not live to see the

16

exquisite acting of Mrs. Kendal as the Countess D'Autreval ; the incisive, vigorous Montrichard of Mr. Hare ; the humorously-conceived De Grignon of Mr. Kendal, and the perfect taste in which the piece was staged.

It was only two nights after the production of " Home " at the Haymarket that " School," a comedy in four acts, was produced with phenomenal success at the Prince of Wales's—a success which has been continually repeated on its reproductions. Although Robertson acknowledged its indebtedness to a German source— Benedix's " Aschenbrödel " (the prototype of the more familiar " Cinderella "), there is very little in " School " that is not original. Play and players were alike the success of the season, and Mrs. Bancroft's Naomi Tighe, Miss Carlotta Addison's Bella, Mr. Bancroft's Jack Poyntz, and Mr. Hare's Beau Farintosh, are historical performances. From an audience-drawing point of view " School " was the most successful of the brilliant series of comedies that Robertson wrote for the little Tottenham Street Theatre, and its first run was an absolute triumph. To quote Mr. Bancroft : " ' School ' ran on through frost and snow, through fair weather and foul, to the same record of crowded houses, owing, doubtless, some share of its popularity to the success which had attended previous productions by the same author; for although it grew to be the greatest favourite of all Robertson's works, it cannot be compared in a dramatic sense with ' Caste,' nor does it contain a scene to equal the second act of ' Ours.' The public, however, being masters of the situation, chose to raise it to this position, and it was not for us to quarrel with so pleasant a verdict."

From a strictly critical point of view this is, no doubt, right; and yet the play is a charming one, and Mrs. Bancroft has admitted that in Naomi Tighe she found the part that she loved the best.

" I affectionately hug the memory of 'Nummy,'" she says, " and wear her in my ' heart of hearts ' as freshly as though I were still representing her. The artless simplicity and sunny nature of ' Nummy '; the utter ignorance of the existence of any sadness in the whole world except what school discipline enforces; her fearless and open avowal of her romantic adoration for Jack Poyntz, make her a lovable thing. She is one big slice of sunshine, and " (this is, of course, in contradistinction to Polly Eccles) " she had no drunken father ! It was a delight to act Naomi Tighe; she is as fresh as country butter, and every word she utters breathes the unladen atmosphere of a bright green spot ' far from the madding crowd.' "

" School " remained in the bill until the end of the season, and on the last night of its first run—

August 28, 1869—it was resumed on September 11
—Charles Dickens paid his last visit to the Prince of
Wales's Theatre, and expressed his delight in the new
comedy. In his "Life of Dickens" Forster speaks
of the high estimation in which he held Robertson's
stage work, and records that on the introduction of
the new dramatist to the veteran novelist the latter
said "that to himself the charm of the comedies was
their unassuming form, which had so happily shown
that real wit could afford to put off any airs of pre-
tension to it."

Much of "School" was written in the summer of
1868. Robertson's son was then at a boarding-school
a short distance from home, and he would often call
in the afternoon and take the boy out for a walk,
asking him as they strolled along what answers he
would give to certain questions if he wished to be
mischievous. Many of the answers to Dr. Sutcliffe's
interrogations in the examination scene were obtained
in this way, and the astronomical answers given by
Bella were both supplied by "Master Tommy," who
received in payment various sums varying from sixpence to two shillings. During these strolls from
Belsize Park towards Hampstead, Robertson would
talk to his son as if he were an old friend, recounting
stories of his early life from boyhood to manhood,
and particularly impressing upon him that if he in

his turn drifted into the theatrical world his father would have nothing to do with him, and would let him struggle for himself. On the other hand, should he fall in with his father's views as to his future, he should never want his aid or help. Unfortunately for poor Tommy, his father died while he was a mere child; but in any case, it is pretty certain that under any circumstances, being a Robertson, he would have " drifted." Fortunately he did this to good purpose, and in spite of his sound advice (fathers are very fond of warning their boys against their own professions) Robertson would have been proud of his son's marked abilities as an actor; and certainly nothing would have been sweeter to him than the affectionate pride ever taken by him in his father's plays. On this point more will be said by-and-by.

The letters that so soon as they were able to read, and when occasion demanded them, Robertson was in the habit of writing to his children, are brimful of affectionate solicitude, and his pride in his boy and girl and the rational way in which he treated them will be seen from the following characteristic anecdote :

On an occasion when " Tommy," conscious of sundry school-boy peccadilloes, was inclined to be unduly on the alert for admonition, he and his sister were sent for to see a friend of their father's, and as they entered the room the guilty young ears thought they heard the warning parental words, " Ils sont mauvais enfants." Nothing coming of this, the young gentleman plucked up courage, and, in the retirement of his school, and probably under the stimulating influence of renewed "good marks," he penned a letter of serious protest against a charge at once sweeping and unjust. To this the father replied : " You are wrong. If your ears were as sensi-tive as your feelings you would have heard that I said as my children entered the room, ' Ils sont beaux —mes enfants ?' to which Mr. —— assented. Be quite sure of what you hear another time."

" School " has already held the stage for twenty-one years, and its recent acceptable revival at the Garrick Theatre, under the management of Mr. John Hare, and the stage-management of the author's son, will be fresh within the memory of playgoers.

Concerning this production, it is pleasant to quote the words of an eminent dramatic critic—Clement Scott—a critic who believed in Robertson from the first, who saw him grow famous, mourned his death, and who has lived to see that his expressions of early encouragement were well and wisely given.

" The faith of Mr. John Hare," said this writer, " in past and present alike was put to a pretty severe test, and in his absence, on Saturday night.*

* September 19, 1891.

"'Faith builds a bridge across the gulf of death,
   To break the shock kind nature cannot shun,'

and the popular manager-actor virtually asked the public to decide for him two important questions: 'Was the Robertsonian comedy a thing of the past; a dust-covered relic to be shut up for ever in the lumber-room or the china-closet with the old tea-cups and saucers?' That was the first question. The second was: 'What truth is there in the hereditary theory as regards our youngest aspirants for honour on the stage?"

"Mr. John Hare came into court fully prepared with evidence and witnesses. He brought 'School,' a play written by his old friend Robertson; a play that has never failed, no matter when or where produced; a play that brought more money to the Bancrofts on production and revival than any of the famous Robertsonian series; a play that gave us those delightful memories, never to be effaced by time or circumstance, of Harry Montague as Lord Beaufoy, John Hare as Beau Farintosh, Mr. Bancroft as Jack Poyntz, and Mrs. Bancroft in the character she has elected to love the best of all in her delightful repertoire—the warm-hearted, impulsive, witty and womanly little 'Nummy' Tighe. The play-bill—one of the most interesting documents ever presented to the playgoer in our time—contains the names of Mr. Hare's witnesses to the fact that histrionic talent is distinctly hereditary. Play-bills of centuries past have proved this beyond all dispute, but here is one dated Saturday, September 19, 1891, containing the names of a young Irving, a young Hare, two of the youngest Denes, two Grattans, the youngest of the Robertsons, and more than one representative of the united families of the Robertsons and Kendals. The Garrick play-bill of Saturday is a document well worth preserving, and on it may be written, as briefly as possible, the record of the unanimous public verdict : ' Robertson, in spite of the pessimists, is not a lost memory ; the younger generation of players has inherited the distinct talent, if not the genius, of the old.'

" The curtain had not been up five minutes before it was proved that the nature and art of Robertson are as true to-day as they were yesterday. It was not the enchanting picture of the wooded glade ; it was not the fantastic grouping of the schoolgirls ; it was not the fascination and nature of the scene—it was Robertson who won, as he has won wherever ' School' has been played. ' What is love ?'—that was the theme. We all know the dialogue by heart. But when it came to Naomi Tighe's summing-up of the question : ' You don't suppose love is to be taught like geography or the use of the globes, do you ? No ;

love is an extra!' at once and without effort down came the roars of laughter in one sound and compact volley. It was the triumph of the dramatist. Once more came another test-point out of scores of them. The repulsive Krux is making love to Bella in this same sunlit woodland glade. The evil-minded, mean-souled creature is insulting the word ' love ' with the declaration of a mercenary passion. ' Got married ! Who got married ?' asks the wonder-struck girl. ' You to me—me to you ; Mr. and Mrs. Krux, of Cedar Grove House. I love you, Bella !' hisses the worm-like Krux. ' Oh, don't !' screams the girl, as if some horrible thing had stung her ; and then comes the exquisite reflection, a masterpiece of observation, ' Oh, don't !—*on such a nice day as this !'* The audience was not slow in appreciating a poem wrapped up in seven words of simple prose. Emphatically was it proved that even in an unsentimental age the humanity of Robertson has not died out."

It is interesting to note that in this revival the author's sister and early playmate, whose name has already been seen in this book—Miss Fanny Robertson—distinguished herself as Mrs. Sutcliffe ; and that Miss Kate Rorke, the gentle, persuasive, and gracious Bella, was originally one of the school-girls on the occasion of the revival of the play at the Haymarket in 1880.

Almost immediately after the production of 'School' at the Prince of Wales's, Robertson went to Liverpool to rehearse and produce his four-act drama entitled " My Lady Clare," with Herr Bandmann in the dual *rôle* of father and son, and his wife, Miss Milly Palmer, as the heroine. From Liverpool he wrote to his wife : " The Charles Mathewses are here. They want me to write a piece for them. *Old Ben Webster has written to me for a piece!!!*" " My Lady Clare " was produced at the Alexandra Theatre on February 22, and scored an immediate success. On March 27 it was produced under the altered title of " Dreams " at the Gaiety Theatre, London, and there ran for ninety nights, the principal characters being played by Alfred Wigan, John Clayton, Robert Soutar (in the part created in Liverpool by that admirable comedian, Edward Saker), Miss Rachel Sanger, and Miss Madge Robertson.

The Lady Clare of Miss Robertson was an exquisite performance, and John Clayton made his first substantial success as Lord Mountforestcourt. Alfred Wigan was not so happy in the characters of the father and son as to receive unqualified criticism ; and why the author required the two parts to be played by one actor has always been a matter for some astonishment, for as there is no reference in plot or dialogue to points of resemblance between the two, it might easily have been otherwise arranged. A capital scene between two old men—one a duke, and the other a servant—in which the pair talk on a perfect ground of equality of the days gone by, was perfectly acted by John Maclean and Joseph Eldred, and gained for each the heartiest recognition.

After Robertson's death several writers expressed an opinion that away from the Prince of Wales's Theatre he never achieved great financial success; and it was in connection with "Dreams" that Mr. John Hollingshead, then the manager of the Gaiety, gave the report flat and public denial:

" In many of the obituary notices of the lamented Mr. Robertson," wrote this well-known and matter-of-fact *entrepreneur*, " the writers have assumed that he failed as a dramatist in every other theatre except the Prince of Wales's. This is not true as far as the Gaiety is concerned. His drama of ' Dreams ' was played here for ninety-six nights to receipts that most managers would consider excellent. Mr. Robertson, let me say, was the most liberal and amiable dramatic author I have had to deal with. He consented readily to any managerial alteration likely to increase the popularity of his drama, and freely acknowledged any such service rendered him."

The comic drama entitled " A Breach of Promise," which would nowadays be described as a " farcical comedy," was most successfully produced at the Globe Theatre on April 10, 1869.

Some genuinely funny acting on the part of Miss Maggie Brennan and John Clarke helped to secure for it a very favourable reception. The eccentric part of Philip was originally meant for Sothern, who never had an opportunity of trying it; and when Sefton Parry, the manager of the Globe Theatre, went to Robertson for a comic piece, with Sothern's consent he finished it for Clarke. There were two other pieces written for Sothern and never produced—namely, " Post Haste," a farce in three acts; and " Which is It ?" a piece of extravagance in two acts.

In the last-named he foreshadowed, in a speech to be delivered by Sothern " as himself," the growing tendency of people (how it has " grown " since then!) to " adopt the stage."

The dialogue is supposed to take place between Sothern and the landlady of a country-town hotel. He has come down to this obscure place to play for the benefit of the daughter of an old professional friend, but on his journey he has lost the wigs and costumes necessary for the performance :

SOTHERN. I don't mean to play to-night.
MRS. THRODDLE (*the landlady*). No !
SOTHERN. No.
MRS. THRODDLE. Why not?

Sothern. I haven't a rag to my back, except what I stand up in ; all my costumes are in the river, all my wigs——

Mrs. Throddle (*interrupting*). La ! Do you wear wigs ?

Sothern. Yes. (*Aside*) So do you.

Mrs. Throddle. La ! Mr. Sothern.   I do so well remember seeing you on the stage at the Haymarket, that night I went in with the order you gave me.   I do so love a play—when I go in with an order.

Sothern. Yes, many people like that way of getting in—as a rule they prefer it.

Mrs. Throddle. But I should never have thought you would have come down to act here, the place is so small.

Sothern. I know. I only came down to act for Miss Chepstow's benefit.   You see, I knew her father.   He was an old friend of mine, a very good fellow.   Well, one day he died, leaving a widow and a large family ; when good fellows die—they generally do die —they always leave widows and large families.   It's a rule. And they leave 'em totally unprovided for—that's another rule. Well, this girl Clara, who is the eldest, came upon the stage. When people can do nothing else they come upon the stage— that's another rule.

A short comedietta, entitled " Dublin Bay," the rights of which had been disposed of in early days, was produced at the Theatre Royal, Manchester, by John Knowles, the then lessee of that house, with some success, on May 18.

The next comedy from Robertson's pen produced during this busy year of 1869 was " Progress," in three acts, adapted from Victorien Sardou's " Les Ganaches."   Although played at the Globe on September 18, with Henry Neville, John Billington,

Charles Collette, John Clarke, Lydia Foote, and Mrs. Stephens in the cast, it had been written specially to order for Buckstone and the Haymarket company. When Robertson read the play to Buckstone, the veteran comedian looked aghast and said : " My God, they are all old people in it !" " Certainly," said Robertson ; " I've written a play for your company." At that time the principal actors at the Haymarket were Buckstone, Howe, Chippendale, and Compton, and they were by no means juveniles. The capital part of Bunnythorne was meant for Buckstone, and that of Bob Bunnythorne for Buckstone's son, who was then about to make his first appearance on the stage.   But the old actor was very angry with Robertson, and would have nothing to do with his idea of " Progress " at the Haymarket.

At the Globe the piece was very well received. It has been frequently and successfully revived, and has an honoured place in the stage triumphs achieved by Robertson in 1869.

CHAPTER V.

It would perhaps have been well for Robertson if he had treated Benjamin Webster's suggestion that he should write a drama for the Adelphi in the jocular spirit in which it struck him when he wrote about it to his wife : "*Old Ben Webster has written to me for a piece!*" He was, however, an insatiable worker— perhaps—who knows ?—he had already begun to think that his time would be short ; he accepted the commission, and " The Nightingale," a drama in four acts, was quickly written, and produced at the recognised home of realistic melodrama on January 15, 1870. It was a failure, and (though it must be confessed that the plot is not what one would have expected of the author) for the old reason. His delicate and scholarly style was not suited to the house ; his notions of acting were opposed to the traditions of those who played in it. Take, for example, his directions for the character of Ismael-al-Moolah, the part taken by Benjamin Webster : " Ismael *to be a man about forty-five. He wears a frock-coat and red fez ; his beard half gray, half black ; his manner amiable and agreeable, perpetually smiling. (No* Iago-*glances at the pit, and private information to the audience that he is a villain, and that they shall see what they shall see.) A suave, bland Oriental, with the old Oriental dignity.*" Now what was Webster or any other actor to do with an Adelphi pit of 1870 ? " Iago-glances " and " private information " were expected, and not being supplied were missed—the omission being resented in the usual undignified and reprehensible way. Nor must it be forgotten that Webster (who was supported by Mr. Arthur Stirling, Mr. J. D. Beveridge, Mrs. Alfred Mellon, Miss Eliza Johnstone, and that charming actress Miss Furtado) was hardly at that period of his long and brilliant stage career when he could expect to make a great success as an amiable man of " about forty-five."

In connection with this ill-fated venture, we may perhaps be permitted to quote one of those droll and satirical summaries of new plays that in those days Mr. W. S. Gilbert contributed to the pages of *Fun.*

It is pleasant to think that when the first sting of

disappointment was over, Robertson would be the
first to smile at the humour of his old friend.

THE NIGHTINGALE;

OR, THE TERRIBLE TURK AND THE GREAT TIDAL WAVE.

ACT I.—MARY'S *house.* *Enter* HAROLD.

HAROLD. As I am now forty, it is high time I began to think
of choosing a profession.   I shall go to Cambridge, and then take
orders.

(*Enter* CHEPSTOW, *in high spirits.*)

CHEPSTOW. Harold! Congratulate me! I have just been
gazetted to an ensigncy in the Twenty-second!

HAROLD. I do. We were at Rugby together. My early education having been neglected, it occurred to me, at the age of
thirty, that it would be well if I went to school. And that is
how I came to know you. (*Aside*) Heavens! I love Mary.

(*Enter* ISMAEL, *a terrible Turk, and* WILLIAM WAGE.)

WILLIAM. Ismael, you are my tutor.
ISMAEL. I am.

(*Enter* MARY.)

MARY. William !
ISMAEL (*aside*). Take her hand. (*He does so.*) Bless you both.
HAROLD (*aside*). All is lost !

ACT 2.—*The Italian inn.* MARY (*now married to* WILLIAM) *discovered with a roguey-poguey in a cradle. Also an impertinent
but faithful female servant,* KEZIAH.

MARY. My dear husband is dying in the next room. I am
convinced that Ismael is poisoning him ; but I will not interrupt
them.

17

(*Enter* ISMAEL.)

ISMAEL. There is no hope. He can't live through the night.
When he is dead will you marry me ?

MARY. Villain ! Know that the pure English wife seldom (if
ever) listens to overtures of marriage until her husband is quite,
quite dead. (ISMAEL *quails.*)

(*Enter* WILLIAM, *very poorly.*)

WILLIAM. Villain ! You have poisoned me. You have insured
my life heavily, and you have committed forgeries in my name.

ISMAEL. Pardon me, you err. (*But he has, the bold, bad man !*)

WILLIAM. You—ha ! I die (*wriggles and dies*).

(*Enter* ADELPHI JOHNDARMES.)

JOHNDARME. I arrest William Wage for forgery.

ISMAEL. It is too late. He is dead.

ACT 3.—*A Portsmouth attic. Fine sea view. Enter* MARY, KEZIAH,
and ROGUEY-POGUEY.

MARY (*explains*). After the death of my husband, I took to the
operatic stage, and came a dreadful cropper. Failing abjectly as
a prima donna, and having nothing in my pocket, I put my pride
in it, and accepted an engagement in the Portsmouth chorus at
two pounds a week. Hence I am known to the world as the
Nightingale.

KEZIAH (*aside to* ROGUEY-POGUEY *in a whisper*). Hush, then, it
mustn't make faces at the audience and spoil its mother's best
scenes. It must be a good boy, den, and concentrate its little
attention on the business of the stage.

MARY. The sea view is charming, but as the sea comes right
up to the attic window-sill in calm weather, it is not pleasant to
think of the consequences of anything like a gale of wind. Thank
heaven, we are not on the ground-floor !

[*Exeunt, leaving* ROGUEY-POGUEY.

(A boat is rowed up to the window, and ISMAEL *enters through that aperture. Flight of steps conveniently placed for that purpose.)*

ISMAEL. Now to steal the child and insure its life. But first to give it an anticipatory dose of poison. (*To child*) Oh, nicey, nicey, nicey! (*Gives the child a tablespoonful of arsenic, and exit into the sea.*)]

(Re-enter MARY *and* KEZIAH.)

MARY. Where is the child?

KEZIAH. I don't know. (MARY *rolls her eyes.*) Ha! Missus is mad! I will run away and leave her all alone. (*Does so, like a faithful creature as she is.*)

*(*MARY *steps out of window into a boat. Enter the Great Tidal Wave. The house is swamped and disappears.* MARY *alone on the wild waste of waters in a boat. The sea rises very much indeed. Happily the presence of a limelight suggests that human aid is not far off. The sea runs mountains high, but the boat behaves well. Tableau.*)

ACT 4.—*A London square—real gas-lamps and actual pillar-post. Showy house, with fashionable ball going on. Adelphi guests arrive on foot, and all at once. This is accounted for by the fact that they had been spending the earlier part of the evening with* "Ethel; or, Only a Life," *but were summarily dismissed from that lady's house in consequence of her sudden death on the piano. Enter* MARY, *very poorly clad, but quite sane again.*

MARY. If it had not been for the limelight-man I had perished! I have lost my situation in the Portsmouth chorus, and consequently I am no longer known as the Nightingale. Ha! I faint. (*Does so.*)

(Enter ISMAEL, *in gorgeous turban and gilt trousers.*)

ISMAEL. This is the house at which I am going to conjure. Such is life! Ismael, whom no one recognises as the cruel

Bahadur Khan, the inciter of that famous Indian mutiny, which was suppressed two years ago by Mr. Eburne and Mr. Robert Romer in "A Sister's Penance," has come down to earning half-guineas by conjuring at fashionable entertainments. It is Allah's will. *[Exit into the house.*

MARY (*on ground*). Gurgle! Gurgle! Gurgle!

(*At this point all the Adelphi guests—who can stand a good deal, but not a conjurer—leave the house in a body, and walk home through the snow.*)

(*Enter, from house,* HAROLD *and* CHEPSTOW.)

HAROLD. Yes, Chepstow, I changed my mind about going into the Church, and I bought a commission in your regiment instead. We fought together in India, and here we are !

CHEPSTOW (*seeing* MARY *lying on the snow*). Hullo, here's a lark ! Here's a dying woman ! (*Chaffs her like an officer and a gentleman.*)

(*Enter, from house,* ISMAEL.)

ISMAEL (*sees* MARY). It is Mary Wage.

HAROLD. And you—you are Bahadur Khan ? Vengeance !

[Exit ISMAEL *very quickly. Tableau.*

ACT 5.—*The Village Church. Enter* MARY *and* ISMAEL.

MARY. No, Ismael, I can never love you. You murdered my husband, and you kidnapped my child. It would only be Christian to forgive you, and I do so with all my heart, but I do not think I could ever be truly happy with you. Where is my child ?

ISMAEL. Alas ! he is dead. Here is his grave.

MARY. Dead ! (*Goes mad again.*)

(*Enter* KEZIAH, *with* ROGUEY-POGUEY.)

KEZIAH. Not so. The arsenic turned out to be nothing but Epsom salts. He forged the child's burial certificate, having first insured his life.

MARY. My boy ! (*Becomes as sane as an Adelphi heroine can be.*)

ISMAEL. Ha ! Foiled ! But I will be avenged ! (*Seizes child and presents pistol at its head.*)

(*Enter* HAROLD *and* CHEPSTOW *with a company of ridiculous soldiers, armed to the teeth with penny canes.*)

HAROLD. There is your prisoner, the cruel Bahadur Khan. (*They seize him. Tableau.*)

Curtain.

OURSELVES. This piece is not worthy of Mr. Robertson. As the leading dramatist of the day he has a valuable reputation to sustain, and he should be careful how he risks it by producing pieces that his own good sense and great experience must tell him could never succeed. The story is at once ordinary and impossible. It offers little opportunity to the actors engaged in it. The scenery is contemptible.

Unluckily Robertson, who was always keenly sensitive to adverse criticism, was already in failing health, and it is to be feared that the mistake made in the Adelphi production told heavily upon him. He continued to work as hard and to talk as brilliantly as ever ; but, although he would admit nothing, his family and friends, noticing his worn looks, were getting seriously anxious concerning him. In due course came the inevitable medical examination and the terrible verdict—" Disease of the heart."

At this time he was busily engaged on " M.P.," the comedy that was to follow " School " at the Prince of Wales's, and it is wonderful to reflect how, while he was undergoing intense bodily suffering—

and no doubt ever anxiously thinking of the dear ones
who might at almost any time be deprived of his
loved companionship and supporting pen—he contrived to map out his natural yet absorbing plot, to
limn his delicate characters, to depict his pretty love
scenes, to be at once satirical, kindly, humorous,
fanciful, and homely, and again win success on the
simple, yet not easily followed, lines that he had
originated. Deaf to all remonstrances, he continued
to write, and to write in his best vein. He was, however, far too ill to leave his house, so that he was
unable to go to the theatre, and, according to his
wont, superintend the rehearsals. The end of the
play was actually dictated by him from his sick-bed.
Mr. and Mrs. Bancroft used to go up to Haverstock
Hill and show him, act by act, what they hoped to do
with his work, he being a little better in the finer
weather, and able to reach his drawing-room.

" School " was withdrawn after three hundred and
eighty-one performances, and " M.P. " was, with
brilliant success, produced on April 23, 1870.

On the fateful first night the poor author was
unable to leave his bedroom, and his anxiety was
intense. Between each act the Bancrofts despatched
rapid messengers with the good news of favourable
reception ; and immediately after the final fall of the
curtain he had the assurance of another well-won

victory. This success, there is no reason to doubt, prolonged his life at least by months, and rekindled for awhile the flicker of hope that was left in him. Indeed, he became temporarily so much better that, after the new play had been running for a few weeks, he was able to go to the theatre and see it, expressing, to the delight of the loyal company, his great pleasure at the manner in which it was performed.

We have said that Robertson was sensitive—and who is not?—to adverse criticism; but the sting of this was but momentary, and when it had passed away he would be the first to acknowledge the justice of well-merited censure. But of malevolent criticism —of which, in common with all men who come rapidly to the front, he received from writers of the baser sort his full share—he had an almost morbid horror. This fact may be illustrated by the following anecdote : On the day following the production of "M.P.," an old friend came in accordance with a thoughtfully-made promise to read the invalid the newspaper criticisms on his play. With manifest delight he listened to the appreciative notices of his work, written by the best critics, in the leading London papers, when suddenly he asked in a tone of voice that denoted apprehension :

" What does ―― say ?"

Now, his friend had brought the paper in which this

so-called " critic " had written his miscalled " notice,"
but it was so monstrously and cruelly adverse that he
had secreted it in his pocket, intending to leave without reading it.

" Do you wish to hear what he says ?" he asked.

" Yes," replied Robertson, with an anxious look on
his worn face.

His friend then produced the paper and read a most
unnecessary and unjustifiable onslaught on the piece
and its author.   Before finishing he paused, and,
glancing at Robertson, saw his head droop, and, as he
turned to find a handkerchief, a single drop of blood
fall upon the newspaper that lay on his knees.   All
the pleasure that he had derived from the encomiums
of those who were qualified to judge and impartially
review his work was wiped away by this one malicious
attack.   His friend, who describes this sick-room
scene as being at once painful and dramatic, was
asked in later days to help this " critic " in an hour
of need.

" No," he said, buttoning up his pockets. " Robertson was dying, and the man knew it.   I cannot forget
that drop of blood !"

Memorable performances in the first production of
"M.P." were the Dunscombe Dunscombe of Mr.
Hare ; the Chudleigh Dunscombe of Mr. Coghlan ;
the Talbot Piers of Mr. Bancroft ; the Isaac Skoome

of Mr. Addison (this was an admirably written part);
the Ruth Deybrooke of Miss Carlotta Addison; and
the Cecilia Dunscombe of Mrs. Bancroft.

This admirable actress has expressed her great
liking for this cleverly-conceived character.

"Cecilia Dunscombe," she says, "was a part I liked
immensely, and I always felt sorry not to have had
a chance of playing her again. She was written as a
type of a 'girl of the period,' who, if not carefully
handled, might on the stage become offensive. There
are many temptations in a part of this calibre to
enlarge upon the eccentricities of a 'good fellow' sort
of woman. I was careful to preserve all the points
the author intended when he wrote the play; but I
worked to make the audience like her, by giving an
amusing, but at the same time feminine, rendering of
her character.

"When poor 'Tom,' who was then fading fast,
saw 'M.P.,' he said to me: 'I must write more parts
for you, Marie; it does me good, for I can see you as
I put the words on paper!' He never wrote another.
I have an affection for Cecilia Dunscombe, and one
reason may be that this was the last part I ever
created for the author, although he would often,
during his sad illness, speak hopefully of the three
plays he had made up his mind to write for us to
succeed one another, which were to be called in turn

' Faith,' ' Hope,' and ' Charity '— such good parts for you, Marie,' he would say. It made me wretched indeed to hear him talk in that way when I knew how fatal was his malady."

A very interesting, and in every respect artistic and successful, revival of " M.P." was given at Toole's Theatre in July, 1883, under the management and direction of the author's son, Mr. T. W. Robertson the younger. In arranging with Mr. Toole for the first revival of " M.P.," his avowed object was to produce it in the theatre most in size like that wherein it originally saw light, so that, together with the best available talent to create the characters employed, it might have the author's intentions rightly carried out. That this was well and loyally done was amply shown on the first night of the revival, when the comedy, beautifully put upon the stage, went without a hitch from beginning to end, and provoked the constant laughter and applause of those present. On this occasion Mr. A. Beaumont was the Dunscombe Dunscombe ; Mr. E. D. Ward, Chudleigh Dunscombe ; Mr. F. H. Macklin, Talbot Piers ; Mr. J. F. Young, Isaac Skoome ; Mr. A. Chevalier, Mr. Mulhowther ; and Miss Gerard, Ruth Deybrook. Contenting himself with the cares of stage-management, Mr. T. W. Robertson did not figure in the cast, but his wife (Miss Cora Stuart) made a charming Cecilia Dunscombe ; and when, later on in the season, " Ours " took the place of " M.P.," he proved by his excellent performance of the difficult character of Hugh Chalcot how well he understood his father's intentions, and how admirably he could play his parts. Could Robertson have been among the audience that gave cordial greeting to his son, and constantly applauded his successful and highly-finished performance, he would not have regretted the fact that, in spite of parental warning, " Tommy " had, in the usual Robertsonian way, " drifted." His daughter, Miss Maud Robertson, was also a member of the company.

In the early autumn of 1870 Sothern wrote to his most intimate friend : " I am about to produce another comedy, ' Birth,' by Tom Robertson. I've much faith in it — a pretty plot, and my part peculiar and original." This he produced at the New Theatre Royal, Bristol, on October 5, 1870, and both there and in Birmingham and the other provincial towns in which he played it, his audiences heartily endorsed his privately-expressed opinion ; but although after the first performance he telegraphed to his friend " ' Birth ' a genuine hit !" he in his usual way suffered from want of confidence, and abandoned a piece in which he would have probably achieved a lasting success.

It was a thousand pities, and if Robertson could only have been there to superintend the rehearsals and encourage the nervous actor, all might have been well; but (though he struggled to Bristol for the first performance) in his then condition of health that was out of the question — and a good thing was given up.

"Birth" is a bright, witty, and sympathetic play, with a mad motive embodied in Sothern's character of Jack Randal. The author had written a serious play, in which he cynically and deliberately placed a character to hold his plot and characters up to ridicule. It was, on the face of it, a hazardous thing to do, but dramatic surprises were looked for in Sothern's productions, and those who saw "Birth" will remember how effective in his hands the whole thing was. Mr. Wyndham has succeeded as David Garrick. Why should he not try his hand at Jack Randal?

Sothern's letters to Robertson concerning this far too hastily condemned play are characteristic and worth quoting. It should be noted that he was on tour at the time, and it had been decided between author and actor that the piece should be well tried in the country before the latter's return to town.

In Sothern's first letter, which was written at Leicester, he says:

"Dear Tom,

"I've received the comedy, and like it greatly. Newcombe (of Plymouth) has no scene-painter. What say you to Bristol? A scene-painter, a far better company, and a much shorter trip for you. Produce it on October 5 at Bristol, eh? It would be such a —— hash at Plymouth! Send me the books as soon as you can, as I cannot begin to study until you have made the alterations you name. If I might suggest, I would say, give me a few more of your telling lines through others' conversation. If you can, don't let me, whilst I'm on the stage, be much of a listener.

"Yours ever,

"E. A. Sothern."

The second letter runs as follows:

"Books arrived all right. I'm sure you'll be glad to know that the more I read 'Birth,' the more sure do I feel of its being a success, and I like the part greatly. I wish I'd more time in which to study the piece. Bounding about from town to town, constant callers, rehearsals, etc., leave me so little alone. I do wish we could have given it more time; but my belief is you won't require to alter one line, and by playing it constantly in the provinces before I get to

London, all will be so clear and sure. I'm such a beastly nervous first-night actor."

Notwithstanding Sothern's nervousness, the first performances of " Birth " were received with enthusiasm, and he wrote :

" I sent you a telegram last night as soon as ' Birth ' was over. It went singularly well. I don't know why, but it's a fact, and I feel it every night, that the end of Act II. requires altering. The audience don't like ' Take my life, but spare my comedy,' when my friend Paul is supposed to be dead on the floor. Query : End the act seriously ? How are you now ? Better, I trust."

The next letter clearly shows that, although he felt one or two alterations were necessary, Sothern had still undiminished faith in the London prospects of the piece :

" I played ' Birth ' Friday and Saturday," he says, " and the end of Act II. is still the weak point, and both houses showed they thought so. Try and think out another ending. How would it be for the curtain to fall on Paul being shot ? I don't send you the press criticisms ; they'd only annoy you, as they do me. Will you see Buckstone, cast the piece, and commence rehearsals ? Give each act a week, first having the people perfect in their words. Coe will mark your MS. carefully ; and I shall leave open a clear week for my rehearsals, so as to have all as clear and sharp as possible. The third act should be nearly all set behind your second act: very easy, and saves so much time."

From Glasgow he wrote:

" The company is, with one or two exceptions, extra weak, and the enormous theatre awful for sound and sight. Calls after every act, but nothing like Bristol enthusiasm. I attribute it solely to these causes. What have we done to deserve TWO notices in the *Herald?* We shall see how it goes in Edinburgh, Liverpool, Birmingham, etc. The *Herald* notice has ruined to-night's house. The piece only played one hour and thirty-five minutes last night. That will show you how cold was the audience. It is the very d—dest theatre for cold, sound, and sight I ever played in."

And then, a few days later:

" I send you the criticisms of the Edinburgh papers. The Scotch press have evidently made up their minds they *won't* have ' Birth ' at any price. *That's* clear! However, there's no use worrying about it. Their infernal notices will play the devil with these last nights, but that is *all* they can do."

But this is followed by:

" Just been to box-office, and in spite of the slaughter booking is considerably better than ever !"

Then Robertson consented to make certain alterations, and Sothern wrote :

" Your resolve is sensible and plucky. I feel convinced the piece will go a season in London. The
volunteers at present are too often on the stage.
Once I am on the scene, I should be but little of a
listener. Those lines of mine in Act I. go off like
rockets, and are dead certainties, and the more I get
of that class the more brilliantly my part goes. I'm
an awfully bad long-speech actor, but give me good
lines or rapid asides, and I give the author the full
benefit of every word. I don't insure this on the first
night, for on that occasion my value is about thirty
shillings a week. I must know I have ' got ' the
audience ; and you understand, I am sure, what I
mean. I shall play the piece in Liverpool, as it is,
and if it runs I shall call for fresh rehearsals when I
get your alterations, and wind up with it in its new
form."

In Liverpool there was some adverse criticism, and
in reply to a reminder from Robertson that the
character of Jack Randal had been designed for the
London boards, and should not be too hastily condemned, because he did not at once find himself at
home with provincial playgoers, Sothern wrote :

" I note all you say about a London audience, and
quite agree with you. In my remarks I have been

very slightly led by the criticisms ; but when you find (before the notices appear) the audiences as they pass out, in each town, commenting on various scenes in almost the same words as in the last town, it's a pretty safe guide. At all events, I felt it but fair to you to give you the opinions of each audience as they reached me through outside friends purposely placed to catch the said opinions as the people passed out after the performance."

From Dublin, on Christmas Day, 1870, he wrote :

" We produced ' Birth ' last night. The first Christmas Eve performance *ever* tried in Dublin ! £135 ! The piece was infinitely better played than it has yet been. As usual, a genuine call after Act I., and then gradual lack of interest whenever I was off the stage. The fate of the piece here (where they'd never even heard of it before it was announced in the Dublin papers) has worried me more than all the other towns put together. I shall play it two nights in Belfast ; but I'm sorry to say I begin to feel its London success is hoping against hope. The feeling last night was universally against it. I had friends in every part of the house listening to the remarks of the audience as they passed out, and the said friends told me the condemnation was universal. Now, this has set me thinking seriously as to the safety of trying ' Birth ' in London. Quite understand me, Tom, that

I am quite ready to risk it if you are—the question is, whether it is not a dangerous experiment? I'm awfully cut up about it, for I like the part so much that I've shut my eyes and ears against all advice—against all criticisms. The press here, I fear, will, as usual, be very severe. If so, there's no use my worrying you with the notices. The case stands thus: Shall I announce my reappearance at the Haymarket in 'Birth' or not? A failure would do us both harm—and I now fear that failure is a certainty. Simply let me know *your* wish, and on that I'll act."

Of course, Robertson knew that with Sothern in this despondent state of mind about the piece its chances would be heavily discounted, and so he told him to give it up, and had to console himself with the impulsively expressed wish written, in characteristic fashion, on the back of an envelope:

"Don't worry until you are better; and when you are, write me another piece, and after that another. Ever yours, E. A. S."

It is rather a sad little story. The nervous and highly-wrought actor on his provincial tour—the sick and anxious author in his London home—and the probably too hasty critics who more or less (Sothern always had the more rather than the less in his super-sensitive mind) condemned the play that had come to them unstamped with the hall-mark of Metropolitan success.

There is no doubt that in his nervous anxiety about this play Sothern made mistakes, and unfortunately Robertson could not be at hand to strengthen and encourage him. Is it likely that men of such experience could have been entirely wrong in their first estimation of the play and its principal character? Is it not likely that with Sothern acting in a terrible state of nervousness and doubt, and supported by the provincial stock companies of those days, both were misunderstood by audiences and critics? As for the latter, it is highly probable that, had they for one moment thought that what they said would permanently kill the piece, they would have written either less or more. They saw a curiously-conceived play very nervously handled, and as a matter of course they pointed out faults. Sothern should not have accepted their verdict as a final one, and assuredly he was unwise in placing friends in all parts of the theatre to catch the carelessly-expressed opinions of thoughtless outgoing audiences. "What do you think of the new play?" asks Miss Smith of Mr. Jones as they meet in the *foyer*. "Well, to tell you the truth, I've been awfully bored," says Mr. Jones, who generally says the same thing each time he leaves the theatre, but who is a pretty constant

playgoer for all that ; and of this Sothern's friend
makes a careful note. How surprised Mr. Jones would
have been—nay, to do him justice, how sorry—had
he known that his stock phrase would help to stop
the production of " Birth " at the Haymarket, and, as
a matter of consequence, to keep it off the stage for
all time ! But the mischief was done, and Robertson,
who at the time sorely needed the tonic of success,
bore disappointment with a patient shrug. With the
author's son as Jack Randal, " Birth " was in later
years successfully performed at Dundee.

But the trouble told upon him, and day by day his
illness increased. It was in November, and while a
rehearsal of " Ours " (which was about to be reproduced at the Prince of Wales's) was in progress, that
Mrs. Bancroft says :

" On one cold Saturday morning—a typical London
day, when a cold white fog had penetrated into the
theatre—while we were going through the first act,
the hall-keeper came to us with a frightened look
upon his face, and announced that ' Mr. Robertson
was at the stage-door.'

" We were terror-stricken, knowing him to be in
an unfit state to leave the house, even in fine
weather. He further sent a message that he dreaded
the stairs which led to the stage (there were only
four up and, I think, six down, poor fellow !), and

that he would like to drive round to the door then used as the royal entrance, and, if it might be opened, to get to us that way.　Of course, all this was done at once; and in a piteous plight Robertson came for the last time amongst us.　Many of the company then spoke their last word to him, although it proved not to be his actual final visit to the little theatre he loved so much, and always called 'his home.'　He stayed for half an hour in dreadful suffering, and tortured by a cough which told what he endured. In an agony of pain caused by a violent paroxysm, he stooped down and knocked with a hollow sound upon the stage, saying, in a voice made terribly painful by its tone of sad reproach, to imaginary phantoms: 'Oh, don't be in such a hurry!'　We shuddered at the words, and, when he recovered, with difficulty persuaded him to return home; for he persisted in the thought that the mere sight of the familiar stage of itself would do him good, and hoped yet to come again.　The little band that formed our company then grouped together (there was no more work that day), and the talk was only of the visit, which none then present will have forgotten."

This revival of "Ours" took place on Saturday, November 26, 1870, with Mrs. Bancroft as Mary Netley, Miss Fanny Josephs as Blanche Haye, Miss Le Thière as Lady Shendryn, Mr. Hare as Prince

Perovsky, Mr. Addison as Colonel Sir Alexander Shendryn, Mr. W. Herbert as Captain Samprey, Mr. Coghlan as Angus Macalister, Mr. Bancroft as Hugh Chalcot, and Mr. Charles Collette as Sergeant Jones.

Against all advice, Robertson insisted on being present, occupying the box that had long been recognised as his, and making his final appearance on the scene of his greatest and repeated triumphs. It is pleasant to think that he was abundantly satisfied—a fact that is amply proved by the following letter, which on the next day he wrote to Mrs. Bancroft:

"6, Eton Road, N.W.,
"*November* 27, 1870.

"MY DEAR MARIE,

"'Ours' was acted so excellently last night that, as I may not see you for the next few days, I write to express the great gratification it gave me to see that the 'light troupe' had distinguished themselves more than ever.

"You know that I am not given to flattery, and that my standard of taste for comedy is somewhat high. I was really *charmed*; and I was very ill the whole night in discomfort and annoyance. The remark of everyone I heard was, 'What wonderfully good acting!' And I was pleased to find Boucicault descanting on it to a chosen few. He said that not only was the general acting of the piece equally admirable, but that he had never—including Paris—seen such refinement and effect combined as in the performance of the second act. He said, too, that the actors who had played in the piece before, acted better than ever. I mention this, because the same thing struck me. Bancroft was most excellent; and I have never seen him succeed in sinking his own identity so much as in the last act. For the first time in my life I felt grateful to the folks on the stage side of the foot-lights, and I am not given to that sort of gratitude.

"It was terribly late last night. If the revival should draw, and it should be worth while, could not the first and third acts be relieved of some ten minutes' talk? Cut wherever you like. *I* shan't wince; for I don't care about either the first or last acts. If they had been less perfectly acted they would have missed fire, and deservedly.

"Yours very sincerely,

"T. W. ROBERTSON."

In December, his illness became so pronounced that, acting on the advice of his doctor, Dr. George Bird, he consented (the weather in London being wintry and unsettled, and altogether opposed to his prospects of recovery) to winter in Torquay. Accordingly, on the 29th instant, he left town, taking with him a valet, named Hayland, who had been especially recommended as a sick man's attendant; but when he arrived in Devonshire, he found to his disappointment that the weather was as bad as that which he had left behind him, the cold being intense and the snow hardly ceasing to fall. In earlier days Robertson had been very successfully treated by Dr. Bird; and in a moment of high spirits he dashed off and sent to him the following:

"EPITAPH ON A MAN LIKELY TO LIVE.

> "Physicians four
>   Long time I bore,
>   To ease me all was vain;
>   At last I heard
>   Of Doctor Bird,
>   Who freed me from my pain."

Alas! his disease had now assumed a form that baffled the cleverest of physicians.

Unluckily his wife, whose long anxiety had resulted in illness, and whose devotion to him was a subject on which he fondly lingered, was unable to travel with him; and how he spent these lonely days, apart from those he loved so well, will be gathered by the following extracts (at once pathetic, humorous, and affectionate) from his letters to her:

"Royal Hotel, Torquay,
"*December* 30, 1870.

" Here I am !   The Imperial was full, and wouldn't
have me, so I came here.   It is very comfortable, but
we have a wretched day.   The hour is now 12.30 ;
the snow has been falling since eight, and will continue to fall the whole day, so I cannot stir out.
Still, I am better.   The air here is lighter.   I seem
to breathe more freely.   I passed the night pretty
well.   Hayland was very attentive, and he and I get
on very well.   In your reply to this, let me know
how you are ; and Maud, and Tommy, and the Baby.
It seems years since I left London.   Of course I have
no news.   Has the Baby expressed any opinion as to
my absence ?   Did you give the two children the
half-crowns I promised them?   *Hayland is going
to have his hair cut.*   I am very hungry.   Torquay
is in Devonshire.   I think I shall be very dreary
to-morrow.   God bless you all !"

"*January* 1, 1871.

" My first letter this year is addressed to you.   I
have not been so well since this morning ; it is now
3 p.m.   I think I am going through the process of
acclimatization.   The weather is warmer but a little
foggy, but nothing like London fogs.   *Hayland has
had his hair cut.*   I am of opinion that Torquay will

do me a great deal of good—*in time.* The climate is wonderful, notwithstanding the filthy weather. At the present moment it is thawing.

" You cannot conceive the desolation of my life here. I see no one—have spoken to no one. It seems to me that I am in a lighthouse—and alone !

" 4.30.—I have just returned from a drive in an open carriage. The air was delightful, though cold. The drive has done me a little good. A beautiful place this, reminding me of Ventnor. I am very sorry to hear about those infernal waterpipes again. Please send me the *Era*, when you get it to-morrow. *Hayland has had his hair cut!* In the morning I shall go to look after lodgings. What with Baby and Maud and Annie and the waterpipes, you cannot miss me as much as I miss you. I don't know what the devil I shall do next week. The solitude is awful. My only recreation is to have my back rubbed, and that palls after the second dozen passes. Kiss my darling baby for me, and my dear Maud, and Tommy when you see him. I don't know that I have anything more to tell you, *except that Hayland has had his hair cut.* This hotel is a good one. I am well served and waited on ; but I fear that it is dear. In a day or so I hope to get into lodgings, and then we can arrange about your coming. I am sure it would do anybody good, for the climate here is not of the same cruelty as in London. This—the last three days—is the first winter they have had yet. So now, my darling, good-bye. God bless you all !

" P.S.—*Did I mention to you that Hayland has had his*—— Oh yes, I did."

" *January* 2, 1871.

" The weather has changed. It is mild and raining, so that I cannot get out again to-day! I want you to go to a Morning Performance of a Pantomime, taking with you Tommy and Maud. *You must pay for your seats.* If I were you, I would go to the box office, Drury Lane, and take them. The children ought to see a pantomime once at Christmas. I find that our income last year (1870) was £3,760, not counting about £200 due on the year. This is about £500 less than the year before (1869) ; so that last year's profits were :

" £313 6s. 8d. *monthly.*

" £72 6s. 2d. *weekly.*

" £10 6s. 7d. *daily.*

" May we do as well this year ! I hope you and all my darlings are well. Eh, but it is dreary here without you ! I don't think I have any more to tell you or inquire after. *Hayland has had his*—— But, no ! I believe I mentioned that in my last. By the way, Hayland looks after me very well—is attentive, and zealous. Tell me the Baby's first joke, and her last but one. God bless you! You must come to me soon.—Yours so drearily, T. W. R."

"*January* 4, 1871.

"Hayland says that 'he thinks I am better than when I came down here.' I do not agree with him; but still I tell you what he says. Kiss my darlings for me. It will indeed be a bright day — fogs, notwithstanding—when I see your face and theirs again."

"*January* 5, 1871.

"I am much better to-day. The air and day have been heavenly, and I have had a drive out. I was very 'queer' yesterday, but am a different man now. If to-morrow is fine, I will begin house-hunting in earnest; up to the present I have been too ill. I had a good sleep last night, which has set me up to-day; until last night I have had very little rest since I saw you. Excuse these few lines. I am tired and weary, as I shall always be till I see you and my darlings again."

There are other letters written in the same strain; some hopeful in tone, and some despondent, but all expressing intense weariness; and after about a fortnight's stay in Torquay, which really did him more harm than good, he determined to return to London.

"Never," says his son, "will his home-coming be forgotten by those who were present. How altered he was! His kind face bore the traces of mental worry and want of rest, though the eyes sparkled as of yore. He could hardly walk up the steps to the front door, so difficult was his breathing, having to stay on each step for awhile, at the same time doing his utmost to pass it all off with jokes at ' Tommy's ' expense. There were some dozen steps to mount, and it was fully fifteen minutes ere he entered the house for the last time. A curious incident happened on this eventful evening—ominous in a superstitious sense, and the last of a succession of coincidences. It is a well-known fact that, on the first nights of ' Society,' ' Ours,' and ' Caste,' a dog, on each occasion, followed Robertson home, and nothing would induce him to turn them away. When the brougham stopped at the house it was pointed out that a dog had followed it from the station. Robertson took it as a happy omen, and directed that it should be taken in and fed; but nothing would induce it to enter the house, and it stayed in the front garden howling and leaving the food that had been placed for it there untouched."

Almost immediately after his return to London, "War" was produced at the St. James's Theatre. It was the last play he ever wrote; and he awaited its production with feverish impatience, knowing that it had neither the benefit of his care at rehearsals nor the style of stage-management that his pieces demanded. No one who was present at the first performance, on January 16, 1871, will ever forget the disgraceful scene at the theatre. Produced at the time when, in connection with the Franco-Prussian war, party feeling ran high, the subject was undoubtedly a dangerous one; and the unfortunate attempts of a M. Nertann, a French actor of large proportions, dressed in a tight-fitting uniform, to command the respect of his audience, together with the long waits between the acts and the general want of sympathy with the author, is better imagined than described. Against Robertson's wishes, too, the management had announced it as a comedy, when in reality it was a drama; and this was the cause of severe and audible comments at the fall of the curtain. Mr. A. W. Young, Mr. Lionel Brough, and Miss Fanny Brough did their best in the face of a hostile audience to carry their author to success; but their efforts were unavailing, and the poor play was, in the rough and much-to-be-deplored English fashion, hastily condemned.

Concerning this lamentable performance, Sothern wrote to Robertson :

"I saw 'War' on the first night. Having stupidly neglected to obtain seats in time, I went into the gallery, and couldn't get out again, or I would, for it was sickeningly hot and beastly. They foolishly gave out the report that every seat was gone ; and afterwards I, and lots of others, found out there was plenty of room in the dress-circle. The first act was charming, and all looked like a great success. The gallery was full of well-dressed people, and the universal feeling was, 'It's a go!' The religious tone of the second act obviously annoyed a great many ; and they talked so loudly near me that I could not follow the story except by the action. Between ourselves I thought, with two or three exceptions, the piece was d——d badly acted ; for the third act, *naturally* played, ought to have been very pretty and effective."

A little later on, critical *Mr. Punch* said : " Mr. Robertson's 'War,' at the St. James's, was a failure on the *first night*. We italicise the 'first night,' and wish to draw attention to the fact. A first night's audience is an exceptional audience, which expression might mean an audience fond of taking exception. Its verdict ought never to be accepted as final, nor in the present state of things dramatic ought professional critics to pronounce upon the merits of a piece until its third or fourth representation. Generally speaking, in spite of all the rehearsals, the author himself only sees his play, *as a whole*, on its first night. Admitted that this is not as it should be, yet so it is. We, in our own patented form, and holding the first night's representation to be *the* one on which no fair opinion can be formed, generally wait until the piece has reached its fourth night, and then, being probably at its best, it is a fair matter for criticism. We venture to say that if the public could have seen 'War' for the *first* time on its *fourth* night, it would not have been condemned.

"The first act would have passed muster as a specimen of one of Mr. Robertson's Prince of Wales's pieces, without the Prince of Wales's company; the second act should have been called a tableau, and M. Henri Nertann ought not to have been allowed to go mad. In the third act all the young ladies, excepting, of course, the heroine, might have been advantageously omitted, and then the excellent rendering of a capital situation by Messrs. Young and Brough, and the well-contrived denouement, would have brought down the curtain on a real, though not perhaps a great, success. The piece should have been in two acts and one tableau.

"The public, on the first night, was led to expect

some strong exhibition of partizanship apropos of
the present state of affairs on the Continent ; not
only from the title of the piece and the announcement that Mr. O'Connor, the scenic artist, had been
to Sedan for the express purpose of illustrating the
second act, but also from the injudicious selection
of French and German national airs by way of
overture—a 'happy thought' of the conductor's,
which went far, we are convinced, to help the failure
of the piece."

As far as the poor sick author was concerned, all
the mischief was done on that terrible first night.
He had arranged to have an account of the reception
of the piece sent to him after each act; but, antici-
pating disaster, and fearing that if things did not go
well he would not be told the whole truth, he gave
particular instructions that his young son should be
one of the party occupying the box set aside for his
representatives. The next morning—and during the
daily visits that at this time the boy paid to his father,
Robertson insisting that he should come home every
day from the neighbouring boarding-school for the
purpose of seeing him—he easily drew from his artless lips a graphic account of the scene of massacre.

After hearing it all, he lay back on his pillow and
said with a sigh : " Ah, Tommy, my boy, they wouldn't
have been so hard if they could see me now. I shan't

trouble them again."   And then, with a look of mingled sorrow and affection, he took the boy's hand in his, and was silent for a few moments, whilst tears trickled down the faces of both.

On Wednesday, February 1, Mr. and Mrs. Bancroft saw him for the last time.   They found him propped up in a big arm-chair, breathing with difficulty.   He talked to them for some little time, dwelling, among other subjects, on the new play he had conceived for them, and saying that earlier in the day he had jotted down some more notes about it.   " All this," says Mrs. Bancroft, " we knew could not be ; and when we went away we both felt we should never touch his hand again."

By the way, it is in connection with this sad interview that Mrs. Bancroft tells the following curious story.

" During Robertson's absence in Frankfort," she says, " when he left England to be married, I had a strange dream about him, which I related to a mutual friend, who some time afterwards imprudently repeated it to him.   My dream was this : I saw them being married, and when he was placing the ring upon his bride's finger I could see that it was lined with black.   Then I thought, when he left the church, two children came up to Mrs. Robertson with wreaths of immortelles in their hands.   I quite forgot all about this dream as time went on ; but poor Tom, it seemed, did not. On this day, when we were leaving him, and we saw too plainly that the sad end was near, he drew me towards him, and said quietly : ' Do you remember your dream about me, Marie ? The ring is getting black, and the wreaths of immortelles are made.' "

It was now, indeed, painfully apparent that no hope of his recovery could be entertained. He frequently spoke of coming death to his son ; and when, on the morning of the day that saw his earthly sojourn close, the lad paid him his usual visit, he said—and these parting words have ever been treasured : " Good-bye, my boy, and God bless you ! Come and see me to-morrow. If I don't speak to you, don't be frightened, and don't forget to kiss your father."

At half-past five o'clock on the same evening (it was that of February 3), and whilst sitting in his high-backed chair, he peacefully passed away.

On the same evening " War " was played for the last time.

CHAPTER VI.

Six short years of success had been vouchsafed to
Robertson—six short years, in the course of which he
had done so much to reform and elevate the English
stage—and there he lay in his wreath-covered coffin,
surrounded by the friends who loved him so well, and
who with bated breath spoke of his brilliant powers
as a conversationalist, the rich unction and appreciation with which he told a story, and the so-called
cynicism which was, after all, only a pretty affectation.
Everyone used to see through that. No one with
such a beaming and good-natured face, which was
ever running over with smiles, no one with such a
generous disposition or such an affectionate heart,
could be a cynic in the true sense of the word. He
made no enemies. He was as much beloved in private
life as he was appreciated by the public. No one
envied him the success for which he had struggled
with untiring energy ; everyone mourned his all too

early death. The winter of his life had been a long and cold one, and he died when the happy summer-time had only just begun. Such were the thoughts and words of those who assembled to follow Robertson to his grave, and which were embodied in a charming tribute to his memory, from the pen of one who knew and loved him well, that subsequently appeared in a London newspaper.

It was noticed that in a corner of the room where the coffin lay there remained two toys, Punch and Judy puppets, with which he had whiled away the hours amusing his baby-daughter Rosy. There they were, limp and lifeless, as if they had died in sympathy with him who had so often enlivened those present with his kindly, gentle nature and overflowing humour. Often had that room rung with the joyous shouts of the baby at the antics of Punch and Judy worked by the deft hands of Robertson, just as grown men and women had applauded the ever-ready, ever-wholesome jests of his characters on the stage.

He was buried, in the presence of a huge concourse of people, at Abney Park Cemetery on February 9, in the tomb containing the remains of his first wife ; and probably never around an open grave were more of manly tears shed than around that of Robertson, whose death at the early age of forty-two seemed almost cruel.

The chief mourners were his young son ; his brother, Edward Robertson ; his father-in-law, J. Feist ; his brother-in-law, W. H. Kendal ; Tom Hood, Tom Archer, Dion Boucicault, S. B. Bancroft, John Hare, Andrew Halliday, Edward Draper, E. C. Barnes, and Dr. Bird. On the evening of his funeral the Prince of Wales's Theatre was closed.

All the obituary notices which appeared in the newspapers and periodicals contained sincere and heartfelt expressions of sorrow at the early death of Robertson ; and Tom Hood, one of his dearest and best friends, thus wrote of him in the joking weekly of which he was the editor, and to which so many kindred spirits were attached. Truly was the paper christened *Fun*, when one thinks of the nature of its contributors !

" It is a very painful task to add another beloved name to the already too large obituary which records the losses this paper and those connected with it have sustained. Mr. Robertson was for a long time—until, indeed, his well-deserved success as a dramatist left him no time to devote to periodical literature—a regular contributor to these columns. The fame of his comedies has eclipsed to some extent the reputation he won by the clever magazine-work in which he was at first engaged. But the founder of our modern school of comedy can afford to let the minor renown pass; his claims on the love and gratitude of the public require no augmentation.

"When we consider how poor and trite our language is, we scarcely dare to try and put words to the grief which we, his friends, feel at the death of one we all loved and were so proud of. We had watched his courageous struggle in the old days, had rejoiced in his triumphs, and were aware of the undeveloped powers which, had he been spared a few years longer, would have won him a yet higher position as a dramatist; and we have known the long and severe suffering from which he has been released. He goes to his grave regretted by the public at large, but loved and lamented by his private friends with a depth and intensity it would be idle to attempt to utter."

Robertson left behind him many suggestions for new plays. By Mr. and Mrs. Bancroft mention has been made that he had an idea for a comedy to follow "M.P." entitled "Faith," the plot of which was to run on the lines of the immortal story of "The Vicar of Wakefield"; but no details of this intention could be discovered amongst his manuscripts.

Two outlines for plays designed for the Prince of Wales's Theatre—the one entitled "Passions," and the other headed "Political Comedy"—were found in his desk. In the forecast of "Passions, a Brigand

Comedy," it was designed that Hare should play the Prince (*Pride*) ; Coghlan, the Artist (*Ambition*) ; Bancroft, the Brigand Chief (*Gain*) ; Clarke, a Saturday Reviewer ; and the character Paquita (*Love*) was evidently designed for Mrs. Bancroft. Throughout the sketch there runs a satirical vein, and the Saturday Reviewer is shown as anxious to produce a newspaper to be called *The Sunday Skunk*, containing " all this week's envy, hatred, malice, and uncharitableness."

The notes for the " Political Comedy " are contained on five pages of manuscript, the most prominent character being a philosophical member of Parliament, who is made to say :

" I am an earnest man. I feel deeply on every subject !"

To the horror of his strong-minded wife he makes a speech against female suffrage ; and, when taken to task by her, the following dialogue ensues :

HE. I have saved my country. I stand upon my feelings as a member of this House.

SHE. Wait till I get you home !

HE. Madam ! near to this is Westminster Hall. In Westminster Hall is the Divorce Court.

SHE. Divorce—for what ?

HE. For cruelty and non-desertion.

In the contemplated dialogue there is also an amusing episode between a father—a severe Radical—and an inquiring daughter :

DAUGHTER. Are all men equal ? .
RADICAL. Yes.
DAUGHTER. One as good as another?
RADICAL. Yes.
DAUGHTER. John, the coachman, as good as you ?
RADICAL. Yes.
DAUGHTER. *Then why don't you drive him ?*

That this sketch was intended for the basis of a comedy for the Prince of Wales's Theatre is indicated by the fact that in it Mrs. Bancroft and Miss Carlotta Addison, who at the time that it was written were playing in "M.P.," are familiarly spoken of as "Marie" and "Lottie."

In the little pocket-book that he carried there are several suggestions for titles of plays, such as "The Period" (which is curiously like Mr. Pinero's "The Times"), "Choice," and "Perhaps." To the last-named is appended the note, "Query, for Sothern ?"

In works that have been published since Robertson's untimely death, mention of his name and writings has, of course, been often made, and from one or two of these we may, perhaps, before we conclude, be allowed to quote. To begin with, the delightful "Reminiscences of Mr. and Mrs. Bancroft," to which we are already so greatly indebted :

" Some peculiarities, referring especially to his stage-life, of so successful and distinguished a writer as Robertson proved to be, may be worth recording.

He always sat in the same box on all first nights of his comedies at the Prince of Wales's Theatre, and during their progress rarely looked at the stage, but watched the audience, glancing continually and rapidly from one part of the theatre to another, to gather the different effects the same point or speech might produce on various people, being, of course, familiar from rehearsal with the actor's treatment ; while between the acts he would often push his way into parts of the theatre where he would not be recognised, and listen to all the opinions he could overhear.   He also made a point of having someone, entirely removed from theatrical life, in each part of the theatre, whom he would see on the following day and hold long conversations with, carefully comparing the impression and the remarks he drew from these different witnesses, generally, he said, with valuable results."

In his most interesting autobiography, Mr. Joseph Jefferson speaks of Robertson as follows :

" Among the many new friends I made in London none was more delightful to meet than Tom Robertson. During my engagement at the Adelphi he was writing his comedies for the Prince of Wales's Theatre, then under the management of that vivacious actress and industrious little manager, Marie Wilton. Robertson's plays were nearly all successful, and deservedly so, too, for they contained original characters, bright and witty dialogue, and were entirely free from the French coarseness that had characterized so many of their predecessors. All honour to the memory of Tom Robertson, who was at least among the pioneers in working the reformation ; and to his successors, too, who, following in his wake, gave to the public musical extravaganzas more humorous and melodious than the Parisian burlesques, without one tinge of their impertinent vulgarity ; proving incontestably that wit and harmony in comic opera need not depend for their effects upon sensual music and licentious libretto.

"Tom Robertson was of all the men I have ever talked with the most entertaining. His descriptions of people, performances, and incidents that had passed before him during the early portion of his life were exceedingly brilliant. Events that would have been commonplace, when described in an ordinary way, were so coloured and illumined by his vivid imagination that they became intensely interesting.

"I lived at No. 5, Hanover Street, Hanover Square, and Tom usually dined with me once a week. He was perfectly familiar with dramatic literature, and discoursed delightfully upon the plays of the past.

"Goldsmith was his favourite author, whom he considered the very finest and purest writer of English comedy that had lived during the last century. And though I did not quite agree with him in this idea, he said much that strengthened his argument, pointing out the ingenious construction of his plots, the unstrained wit of his dialogue, and the natural conduct of his characters."

Robertson's admiration for the dramatist is probably summed up in the words written by Goldsmith in the preface to his comedy of " The Good-Natured Man," and which exactly embody in thought, feeling and sentiment his own views with regard to the stage : " The term genteel comedy was then unknown amongst us, and little more was desired by an audience than nature and humour, in whatever walks of life they were most conspicuous."

Mr. Jefferson also relates the following pathetic anecdote :

" Artemus Ward died not many months after his London début, attended to the last by Tom Robertson. A strong attachment had sprung up between them, and the devotion of his new-found English friend was touching in the extreme, and characteristic of Robertson's noble nature. Just before Ward's death, Robertson poured out some medicine in a glass and offered it to his friend. Ward said : ' My dear Tom, I can't take that dreadful stuff !'

" ' Come, come,' said Robertson, urging him to swallow the nauseous drug ; ' there's a dear fellow !

Do now, for my sake ; you know I would do anything for you.'

" 'Would you ?' said Ward, feebly stretching out his hand to grasp his friend's, perhaps for the last time.

" 'I would indeed !' said Robertson.

" 'Then you take it,' said Ward. The humorist passed away but a few hours afterwards."

In his "Reminiscences," Serjeant Ballantyne, speaking of the days when he used to haunt the once famous Evans's Supper Rooms, and of his meetings there with Thackeray, Dickens, Albert Smith, Douglas Jerrold, Shirley Brooks, and other literary lions, says : "A very constant guest was Robertson, the creator of a style of drama which, with the assistance of Mrs. Bancroft's talent, had filled with splendid audiences a theatre which for years before had wooed in vain the patronage of the public. Poor Robertson died only too early, almost before he could witness the triumphs of his sister, Mrs. Kendal, one of the most fascinating actresses of the present day."

Of her brother, Mrs. Kendal has said :

" I often hear his work spoken of as *The Bread-and-Butter School.* Bread-and-butter ! but what good bread-and-butter ! How fine the flour ! How carefully kneaded, and always served hot from the bakehouse ! Then the butter ! How fresh and sweet, what an excellent colour; what delicate, pretty pats, with just enough salt to give it a rich, delicious flavour! And then, again, how well the butter was spread over the bread—just enough, no more! And this bread, like all good home-made loaves, was all the better for the keeping. Everybody must eat bread-and-butter; then how necessary it is that these commodities should be wholesome and pure! We Robertsons never speak of Tom without calling him 'Napoleon,' for his *Bread-and-Butter School* was the *coup d'état* to many things. Sometimes I fancy people mean to be rude, and speak slightingly of his work when they call it 'bread-and-butter'; but at every tea-party I take my children to, I say, 'Begin with your uncle's fare *first*; you shall have some fairy poetical drama, called 'cake,' afterwards."

More than once in these pages mention has been made of the attachment that existed between Robertson and Dion Boucicault; and that the friendship was a true one will be shown by the following letter addressed to Mrs. Robertson, at Frankfort, some months after her husband's death, and when a little baby boy, destined never to see its father's loving eyes and bright smile, had been born. Boucicault, it should be mentioned, had been asked to act as the child's godfather:

"326, Regent Street, *June* 14, 1871.

"MY DEAR MRS. ROBERTSON,

"I beg you to tell the friend who represents me at the christening how much obliged I feel, but I must tell you privately how sorry I am that I am not there in person.

"We look forward with much pleasure to the time when you will arrive here; and now that I know it will be some time in August, I can look for a suitable lodging for you to begin with. You must not begin reckoning expenses as you do. Your health is the most important of all considerations—and that should be restored completely without regard to cost. All will go well. Compose your mind, and recover your spirits. Take great care of yourself, and kiss the little one for me.

"I have made him a little present on the occasion of his christening. You know I am rather practical than romantic. Well, amongst my property I have picked out a small investment which is worth £130, and brings in £15 a year. I have given him this, instead of a silver cup or a gold toy. It will be the nest-egg of his fortune."

But the best and the most lasting tribute to Robertson's memory, and the one of which he would assuredly have been most proud, is that built, not hastily, but year by year, and with unswerving loyalty, by his eldest son, the " Tommy " who has more than once been mentioned in these pages, and who, as we have seen, drifted stagewards.

The son's unbounded and almost unique devotion to, and admiration of, his father dated from the days of his boyhood. He was when Robertson died a mere lad, but Mrs. Bancroft says : " Shortly after this (*i.e.*, Robertson's death) his two children (by his first marriage) spent the day with us, and as we were walking round the garden, 'Tommy,' who was a small boy then, seemed to love to dwell upon the sad subject of his father's death, and the little fellow was very pathetic in his boyish remarks. All at once he said, 'A few days before father died I knew he was going to leave us.' 'How could you know it ?' we asked. 'Because he looked so handsome. I have heard that people get such a beautiful look upon their faces when they are going to die.' "

From that day to this the son's earnest desire to shed lustre on his father's name, to keep his memory green, and to popularize his works, has never for one moment flagged or failed. In this connection he seems to have taken to heart the counsel of Tom Hood, who very soon after his father's death wrote to him in words so tender and so graceful that no excuse is offered for quoting them here :

" I hope you are a good, steady boy, and attend to your lessons. You are getting nearer and nearer the time when you will have to think of beginning life for yourself, and that is a serious thing, as I can tell you from my experience, for a boy without a father, however kind his guardians may be. I suppose you have hardly begun to think what you would like to be ?

" You will, I know, be sorry to hear—but, my dear boy, you must be prepared to find this is a world where one often has to say ' good-bye ' for a long time to those who are dear to us—that your uncle Shafto has lately died in Australia. I am very grieved you should have this loss coming so soon after your great loss. But be a good boy, and try to grow up to be a gentleman, and, whatever you do, ask yourself if it is anything you should be ashamed of your father's knowing ; and if you do this, in God's good time you will meet all you loved hereafter."

As we have seen, Robertson's son chose to be an actor, and those who have had an opportunity of watching his career know that his greatest aim has been to give worthy representations of his father's best plays. For a long time he travelled with the comedies in the provinces, visiting and re-visiting the principal towns in England, Scotland and Ireland, and under his direction the " Caste Company " became quite a nursery for the London stage. In it graduated such excellent artists as George Alexander, the late E. D. Ward, Herbert Waring, J. H. Darnley, Edward Sass and Cora Stuart. In the case of this accomplished lady, who subsequently became the wife of the young actor-manager, a remarkable instance may be noted of an operatic singer becoming, in a good school, a refined and charming comedienne. Mr. Robertson distinguished himself as Hugh Chalcot, Sam Gerridge, and in other important parts. Under his superintendence, and prefaced by a memoir from his pen to which the present work is greatly indebted, the plays were some two years ago published in volume form, and the manuscripts have, in handsome bindings, been most carefully preserved.

It is not the purpose of this book to enter into any detailed description or criticism of Robertson's works ; they are constantly being acted, they can at any time be read, and we can all judge for ourselves. And yet we cannot conclude without trying the ring of some of his delightful lines. For example :

LOVE.

"Lovers are so d—d selfish ; they never think of anybody but themselves."—*Caste*.

"Love is like red-currant wine—at the first taste sweet, but afterwards shuddery."—*Caste*.

"When people love there's no such thing as money."—*Caste*.

"Love can laugh at the customary usages of society."—*David Garrick*.

"Love is a passion, and a feeling unworthy of the enlightenment of the nineteenth century. Love, too, doesn't pay; but it is an infirmity to which the best of us, even bankers and stock-brokers, are subject. We must pass through it. It is as alluring to the grown-up man as milk and pastry to the child; it is the whooping-cough of the heart, and, while the fit is on, it strains us terribly."—*Dreams*.

"But earthly love is perishable, and is worn away by time as snow melts before the sun."—*Dreams*.

"Love is a species of lunacy of which marriage is the strait-waistcoat."—*School*.

"Love is an awful swindler, always drawing upon hope, who never honours his drafts; a sort of whining beggar, continually moved on by the maternal police. But 'tis a weakness to which the wisest of us are subject—a kind of manly measles which this flesh is heir to, particularly when it is heir to nothing else."—*Society*.

"No woman can love a man as a wife can love her husband."—*Dreams*.

WOMAN.

"A sister is a sort of sweetheart who doesn't require attention; a kind of housekeeper you can't fall in love with; an agreeable spinster you can't marry. In short, a sister is as nice as—well, as somebody else's wife, without being so dangerous."—*Birth*.

"No mission is more holy than that of a wife—a mother."—*Dreams*.

"Women always forgive men when they are in the wrong."—*M.P.*

"Oh, woman, woman! divine, but dangerous!"—*The Nightingale*.

"Better battle than a discontented woman."—*Ours*.

"Woman considered from the point of view of reason is inferior to man."—*Progress*.

" Women are fondest of their sweethearts when they quarrel with them."—*Progress.*

" Seeing a lot of pretty girls accidentally makes one feel like going to church when you're not used to it."—*School.*

MARRIAGE.

" Marriage is one of those blessings that cannot be avoided."—*Ours.*

" Best to marry in your own rank of life."—*Caste.*

" How unhappy the woman must be who despises her husband !"— *David Garrick.*

" What pride to have a husband who can ride a horse or drive a coach a little better than his groom !"—*David Garrick.*

" After all, marriage commercially considered only illustrates the eternal law of supply and demand."—*Dreams.*

" What a pity it is that courtship should end in matrimony ! It would be better if matrimony ended in courtship."—*M.P.*

" People always quarrel when they're married—or single."—*Ours.*

" It is only after they are married that men begin to understand the purity of women, or their tempers."—*Ours.*

" If people didn't marry there would be no evening parties."—*Ours.*

" What was man intended for but to marry ?"—*School.*

" Marriage means a union mutually advantageous. It is a civil contract, like a partnership."—*Society.*

LIFE.

" People should stick to their own class. Life's a railway journey; mankind's a passenger—first class, second class, third class. Any person found riding in a superior class to that for which he has taken his ticket will be removed at the first station stopped at, according to the by-laws of the company."—*Caste.*

" After all, life is like soda-water. Childhood, effervescence, corked down and wired ; manhood, some sparkle, more vapidity ; old age, empty bottle, cart it away with the rubbish."—*M.P.*

"This life is a matter of bargain."—*Society.*

YOUTH.

"Oh, divine youth! Divine power to love, and still diviner power to inspire it!"—*The Nightingale.*

"Youth and age are only accidents. If one is good, and true, and tender, what does it matter in what year one was born?"—*Progress.*

"Youth soon fades away, but age lasts for ever."—*Progress.*

"It is so ridiculous, the fuss they make in praise of youth. Why, everybody had it once, and nobody can keep it long."—*Progress.*

HONOUR.

"A thousand Sepoys slain in battle cannot redeem the honour of a man who has betrayed the confidence of a trusting girl."—*Caste.*

"A man of real honour will spare the woman who has confessed her love for him, as he would give quarter to an enemy he had disarmed."—*Caste.*

ACTING.

"What money can compensate an actor for the loss of his art, the loss of fame, and all the brilliant excitements of his life?"—*David Garrick.*

"Regular actors may be all very well in their way ; but the amateur actor is an inflated simpleton, who only desires to exhibit himself for the gratification of his own petty vanity."—*M.P.*

"To be an actor requires thought, sympathy, and sentiment." —*M.P.*

"Acting is considered one of the learned professions nowadays."—*M.P.*

PROGRESS.

" 'Tis the train that is master of the hour. As it moves it shrieks out to the dull ear of prejudice, 'Make room for me, and those who dare oppose my progress shall be crushed.' Its tail of smoke is like the plume of a field-marshal, and the rattle and motion of its wheels are as the throb and pulsation of the progress of the whole world."—*Progress.*

" As to manners, progress has indeed altered them. Everyone is too much occupied to think, to feel, to love, or to improve. Progress does not permit sleep or sentiment, accomplishment or leisure."—*Progress.*

CASTE.

" Caste is a good thing if it isn't carried too far. It shuts the door upon the vulgar and pretentious, but it should open the door very wide to exceptional merit. Let brains break through its barriers, and what brains can break through, love may leap over."—*Caste.*

NATURE AND ART.

"O Nature! O Art! You should be twin-sisters, one the exact counterpart of the other ; and you are hardly tenth cousins, and have no mutual resemblance."—*The Nightingale.*

MONEY.

" Marriage is a mistake ; but ready money is real enjoyment— at least, people think so who haven't got it."—*Ours.*

" Pity the poor ! Pity the rich ! For they are bankrupts in friendship and beggars in love."—*Ours.*

" The man who don't want money should be put into an album and kept there."—*School.*

" The rich man is to be envied. He can load her he loves with proofs of his affection. He can face her father and ask him for her hand. He can roll her in his carriage to a palace, and say : ' This is your home, and I am your servant.' "—*Ours.*

GLORY.

"Glory to a nation is as honour to a man; without glory a nation is valueless, and without honour a man is beneath contempt."—*War.*

APHORISMS.

"Oh, alcohol! alcohol! What a foe thou art to the perpendicular!"—*Birth.*

"A man cannot help his ancestors."—*Birth.*

"One glass of bitter makes the whole world kin."—*Birth.*

"Poverty is a dreadful thing to a man who has once been well off."—*Caste.*

"The morals is a disease, like the measles; it attacks the young and innocent."—*Caste.*

"We may be fond of many things without having them."—*Caste.*

"When people talk unpleasantly they always say, 'Listen to reason.'"—*Caste.*

"It is easier to fight a furious man than to forego the conquest of a love-sick girl."—*Caste.*

"Nobody's a mistake—he don't exist. Nobody's nobody! Everybody's somebody."—*Caste.*

"An honest man is the noblest work under the sun."—*M.P.*

"Swells and their money are soon parted."—*M.P.*

"Speech is the index and the mirror of the soul."—*The Nightingale.*

"Boys never remain good after they get into knickerbockers."—*The Nightingale.*

"Oh, contentment! In what strange out-of-the-way holes you do hide yourself!"—*Ours.*

"Parentage is a mere accident."—*Progress.*

"Goodness and amiability must command affection and esteem."—*School.*

"It's a great comfort having no intellect."—*School.*

" There are men—and individuals !"—*School.*

" Capital commands the world. The capitalist commands capital—therefore the capitalist commands the world."—*Society.*

" The human heart is large enough to contain any amount of happiness."—*War.*

" Oh, these fathers ! What misfortunes they are to men of genius !"—*Progress.*

That Robertson was sensitive under adverse criticism, and strongly resented unfair, malicious, and ignorant opinions passed upon his works, we have already seen ; but that he attached great importance to the judgments of the stage censors of his day is amply proved by his own carefully-kept book of newspaper notices, in which good and bad—some so bad that his heart must have ached to read them—stand side by side. In spite of these the plays have lived, the best actors in them have made for themselves famous names, and the critics who from the first recognised and pointed out their value have learnt that at an important epoch they promoted the best interests of the stage.

One of those who wrote of his death, said :

" At a time when his powers were at their maturity, and his prospects were at the brightest, the brilliant writer, the witty conversationalist, the stanch friend, and the affectionate husband, has been snatched away from our midst. There can be no question, brief though has been the career of the dramatist, that he has exercised a strong influence over our dramatic literature, and has left an enduring mark upon the stage. In his graphic pictures of existing society, in his pleasant cynicism, his poetical love passages, and in the chivalrous sentiments vindicating the honour of modern knighthood, he has shown that the theatre can do more than reproduce worn-out types, and that something better than oft-echoed platitudes may be heard within its walls. In the fresh track that he took already may be found the footsteps of followers; but it must not be forgotten that he was the first to venture out of the beaten path. By the clearance he effected of the old conventionalities which had overspread the stage, he has let in an amount of light and air which has since enabled the playgoing public to breathe a much purer atmosphere; and if for no greater service than this, the claims of the departed dramatist to a grateful remembrance will not be lightly estimated."

It is in the highest degree satisfactory to know that, though more than twenty years (and in the world theatrical twenty years mean a very long time) have elapsed since these words were penned, the fact that they emphasize is universally recognised to-day, and that Robertson's comedies still hold the stage.

But when we think of his shortened life, grief takes the place of satisfaction; and, indeed, these pages cannot be brought to more fitting conclusion than by quotation of the words that, with sympathetic pen, he wrote concerning his dead friend, Artemus Ward :

"Few tasks are more difficult or delicate than to write on the subject of the works or character of a departed friend. The pen falters as the familiar face looks out of the paper. The mind is diverted from the thought of death as the memory recalls some happy epigram. It seems so strange that the hand that traced the jokes should be cold—that the tongue that trolled out the good things should be silent—that the jokes and the good things should remain, and the man who made them should be gone for ever."

INDEX

THE END.

BILLING AND SONS, PRINTERS, GUILDFORD.

J. D. & Co.